SUSAN HUMMEl

BY

MARTIN SOWERY

M. P. Sowery

The words 'based on a true story' are now subject to such variation of meaning as to require some explanation. Here, the key events related are true insofar as history and narrative coherence will allow, though the contemporary accounts of supposed eye witnesses show as much variation as the sworn evidence presented in any modern court of law. Some incidents I have made up to illustrate those events and the characters I have imagined for the participants are fictional. After completing the first draft of this book (inspired by the classic writing of Emerson Hough and my subsequent researches) I became aware of a non-fiction treatment of my subject's life by Kathleen P. Chamberlain entitled 'In the Shadow of Billy the Kid'. I deliberately avoided reading that work until my own was completed, therefore any historical inaccuracies and false assumptions I have relied on can in no way be blamed on Ms. Chamberlain. It is surprising we don't yet have more literary versions of the remarkable Susan. The principal male actors in this drama have been extensively mythologised, while she has faded to the margins of history. Any saga that endures must have its protagonists reinvented for the times in which the story is re-told. Consequently, I hope that the few liberties I have taken regarding the life and times of Susan Hummer might be judged pardonable by what few readers this novel may attract.

copyright in this work of fiction is claimed by the author 2016

Chapter One - Beginnings

My name is Susan Elizabeth Hummer. If you're old enough, you may remember reading about me in the newspapers long ago, although it may be my fame has already worn down to being no more than one of those names which seem vaguely familiar for

reasons you can't recall. Whatever legend anyone thinks they leave behind is only hard sand at best, scattered by the wind eventually, however high it once seemed to be piled. In my home state, my name still crops up in the tales older folk tell one another. The tale-tellers, journalists and history writers get it all wrong of course - maybe the writers more than anyone else. Up to now, what I've read

about my own story feels so distant and unfamiliar, I've come to believe either some other must have lived my life, or else my own memories are obscured or recoloured in imagination.

It was my nephew who suggested I should set down my thoughts and impressions, to put the record straight; though as I commence the attempt to aggregate my neglected remembrances, increasingly I doubt that such a miracle as a straight record of anything has ever existed. Who was likely to be interested, I objected? - for my nephew had already listened patiently to a sufficiency of my disconnected rambling that I should hardly address more of the same to him. That's important, because of course, every story is told to someone, and who it is told to affects how the tale unfolds. In the end though, it wasn't hard to decide who I should be explaining myself to, though that individual shall remain nameless and will certainly never read these pages.

How to begin was my next problem. Strange enough, when I started to think about what story I should tell, two clear images presented themselves, unbidden. The first was a young girl, maybe eight years old or less, lightly descending the staircase of a small house that is otherwise only a vague picture in my mind. It's not even light yet, and the air is cold - perhaps it's even Christmas time, but the girl is barefoot. She's wearing just a natural cream coloured gown of rough, thick cotton that is decorated with small red and blue embroidered design. Her parents are already downstairs, although it's early (for I know it is some time when poor Mama was still alive) and the girl is smiling in anticipation, though of what I can't recall.

This is such an early memory and one I'm sure has appeared in my dreams often, so that I'm no longer sure if the original moment was real or only ever a dream. Sincerely, I wish it to be a true memory, because I know the little girl in this picture is happy, in an uncomplicated way I can seldom recall feeling as later memories crowd in. The second mental image that surprised me was the face of poor Matt Slater.

It happened that one day on my ranch that we found a mother and calf trapped in a mud hole far away from Three Rivers. From the look of things, the young one had strayed into the ooze and then the mother got stuck whilst urging the calf to break free. It was a serious situation - tough enough to drag a human out of mud that's sucking them down, let alone the dead weight of a steer. We had some ropes around the mother, which was not in so deep, and we reckoned if we could extract her then we'd use what strength we

had left with on the youngster that was so badly mired. We'd scarcely begun the task and already the boys and myself had a good coating of that heavy crud that dries on you so quick but never

seems to flake off. We paused to notice a rider from Anderson's gang galloping up. He was there to tell me they had a boy caught with a running iron heating over a fire and a steer tethered for working on, right nearby. I left some instructions for the boys at the mud hole, and followed the messenger back to where Anderson was working.

    Anderson himself was a small man with tiny, angry features. I never felt at ease in his company, to be plain. It's doubtful I'd have kept him on, save he was good at the work. His nature was one of those that chafed most bitter at taking orders from a woman, although I tried to make it a rule to blame no man for that, provided he could ride and rope and do his part without shirking. At least, I would generally choose not to notice the attitude in any new man. I found once they understood I knew the business as well as any of them, either the problem would go away or the man would move on. Anderson was a little different to the others though. Maybe he was just clever enough to know he had a good place and hide his feelings, and that only made whatever resentment was burning him up flame longer and hotter. He was a good foreman, but I never ceased to fear he needed watching.

    Back at the mud hole, I'd wondered if my foreman might been making too much of the situation he thought he'd discovered, but the truth of it was clear as we rode up. There was a small fire burning with an iron stuck in it that the boys had left alone, and one of my own herd tied close with a rope halter round its neck. Someone drew the iron from the fire, with a cloth wrapped round the handle for protection, and showed it to me without a word. I'd already seen there was no brand at the business end of the thing, just a heated point of metal. Two of Anderson's men were standing with a dejected seeming figure between them, watchful even though their captive didn't look to have the spirit to make a run for it.

He wasn't much more than a boy, Matthew Slater. Nineteen years old, if what he told me was right. He was what you call slack-jawed, which is to say his mouth tended to hang open so you'd see what teeth he had were crooked and the gums too prominent. He was dressed in old clothes that would have fit someone larger and he had a manner of constantly swallowing, as if to gulp down some courage - it made that apple shape thing in his throat bob up and down excessively. As I climbed off my horse keeping my eyes fixed on his, it is no exaggeration to say he stared back with terror in his face.

Anderson gestured at the evidence and shrugged - nothing needed to be said. On the open range, the only reason a man needs a running iron in his saddle bag - one that carries no rancher's brand - is to use the heated point to redraw the existing mark on any cattle he may find, changing the original design to resemble his own or his sponsor's brand, and by this transferring ownership of the beast to whomsoever holds the revised fierra. I could see that my foreman was eager for my instructions - his eyes showed he regarded the situation as a kind of test I might pass or fail. I'd no wish to feel his expression upon me in this moment, so I spoke to the two guarding Matthew Slater, pointing out a tree that stood some little distance from our party.

"You give me a minute, then bring him to me over yonder," I bid them. "Mr Anderson, have the boys put out these embers and make ready for us to move on quickly when we're done here. We've some trapped livestock to assist." To be fair to him, he nodded and made no comment. "These two to bring a rope with them," I added.

There wasn't much shade under the tree, but the short stroll gave me a moment to think. I tried to brush some of the dried mud from my jacket and trousers, without much success. The two hands brought Slater across to me presently. They had glum expressions and it was clear they'd rather be working cattle. By now Slater himself was shaking uncontrollably. He kept gazing up at the boughs of the tree when his stare was not rooted on the dust at his feet..

"Tell me who put you to this work," I demanded. He gave me a name - one of my neighbours in the vicinity of White Oaks. I was not entirely surprised.

"To be truthful ma'am," he added without looking up, "he didn't so much put me to it, as let it be known that if there was good steers to be bought cheap he wasn't a man as would ask questions where they'd be from. Then he remarked you'd some fine cattle on your land and more than you could easily tend."

His words had the ring of truth about them, though they didn't help young Matt.

"Have you anything else you need to be confessing?" I asked him. He panicked then.

"I never set foot on your property up to now and never did any such thing as this before," he wailed. "I told my cousin Frank I was coming here and why. If you touch me it will be known about, for I shall be missed."

"Good," I told him, for there's not much point making an example of someone if nobody else gets to hear of it.

Things were different back then. Of course we had no choice but to hang him. One of the boys slung the rope over a tall enough bough and I put the rope around his neck myself - it wasn't something I could leave to another. Matthew Slater was whimpering all the while and I suppose he hoped to the end, even after he made water in his pants, that we were only proceeding to scare him and at some point the charade would be halted. I left the hauling up to the boys. It didn't take long. I asked them to be sure to dig the grave deep, not to hide the crime, for we'd committed none, but because no-one deserves to have his bones dug up by the coyotes, of which we'd plenty on our range.

It would be easy and probably true to say that young Slater would never have made anything of his life and if he had not been hung that day, he'd likely reach the same fate at some later juncture. I heard comments in that vein about others like him, too often for my taste. I still see his face, in my dreams or awake, not often, but vivid when it comes. For a long time after that day, I could not bear to have my foreman Mr. Anderson in my sight, and I was glad he moved on after the season ended. This was wrong of me, because the action I despised was my own, not Anderson's. It would surely have been within my power to choose not to hang Matthew Slater, if only I should also have been prepared to see the enterprise I had founded and worked for fail by my reason of my own mis-guided mercy. Let him live and I should have had a hundred Matt Slater's to contend with before the year was out.

Even so, I can't forget Anderson's freckled face, his hair like straw or his narrowed insolent eyes daring me to do what needed to be done. I remember too the features of those rough cowboys who had to pull on the rope that raised Matthew Slater by the neck - them not able to meet my eyes and me willing myself to look stern and composed in order to show I had the strength for the three of us to accomplish this thing.

Nowadays when there's talk of the electric chair, or the gas chamber, I'm compelled to allow I'm against such things. There's many worse people than Matt Slater, and the things some of them have done, it's foolish to pretend they deserve to live. Still I say, keep them in jail forever - we have that option now and we can better afford it than the cost to ourselves of becoming accessories to killing. If you think differently that's fair enough, provided you can truly say you'd be the one to fit the noose around that poor boy's neck or hold the rope as his feet set to twitching and kicking.

It's been such a long time. There's no rhyme or reason why such melancholy reflections should preface this chronicle, unless it be a reminder that most of the principal events of my long life occurred in a different time, when the world was not the one we live in now. In truth, I ought to start over - to begin at the beginning.

Chapter Two - Late Summer 1873

My name is Susan Elizabeth Hummer. After I was married, I was first Susan McSween and later Susan Barber. My first husband died and I divorced the second. My mother was Anna Maria Spangler-Stauffer. I left home when I was young. After my mother died, my father remarried and I could not stay in the family home. Before that we lived in Gettysburg, Pennsylvania and then Eureka, Kansas. I can trace ancestors on my mother's side through many generations of German nobility, before Anna Maria's grandparents came to America in 1731. Myself, I was born on 30th December 1845, a time which seems so far away to me now that sometimes I cannot believe I was alive in that age.

In fact, it was a Spangler who was cupbearer to the Chancellor of Frederick Barbarossa himself - they were with him when the Emperor was mysteriously drowned in the river Saleph on the Third Crusade. All this happened in the year 1190, and still the legend tells that when the ravens cease flying around the Kyffhauser mountain, the Emperor will return. It is difficult to explain the significance of such legends to the people I live among now, in the absurd and sometimes beautiful country which has become my home. They imagine, for example that someone described as a cupbearer must have held an insignificant, trivial position, useless for me to explain this was only the title of an office of power and responsibility. It means nothing to them if I say that Frederick was Holy Roman Emperor for more than thirty years. If they know anything of Rome at all, they only picture a man in a toga ordering Christians be fed to the lions.

Even my old friend Chisum was not much better. He liked to point out that his own father had founded a city at Paris. It was not so easy for a proud young German girl to discover tactful words to inform him that Paris, Texas was little more than a collection of huts compared to Paris, France and that even the real Paris paled in comparison to the glory of Rome. Poor John - he was possessed of sufficient self-regard that the trail of his of conversation invariably turned and found its way back to his own person. Some people called him a baron and he didn't object much, though he remained happily ignorant of what it meant to be a true aristocrat. For him, a man's true value was measured in head of cattle and what his word was worth. He did like to hear my half-remembered stories about the medieval knights of the Teutonic Order, but with him everything was practical. He'd ask me about the armour and calculate its probable weight. He had quarter horses, he said, that were strong beasts, good for working cattle, but they'd be no use in the business of medieval cavalry . A knight in full armour, he'd insist, would need a horse more like the sort they now used to pull loaded carts around San Francisco. They'd be big enough he'd allow, but not much of a gallop to them.

I'm a practical woman in my turn, even if it seems I've been fated to spin tales all my life, usually without having them understood. Everyone in this country tells stories - it must be the way they make sense of themselves and their world. They seem like orphans who have mislaid their actual past, using the stories they tell one another to create a shared meaning for their lives, since no future can be built without some kind of past, even if it be an imagined one (here my old friend Juan Patron would caution me that memory is always a work of imagination).

To this day, every occurrence in our state that is vaguely notable assumes legendary proportions by the end of a week, and within a fortnight each storyteller has their own version to offer you, contradicting the other accounts. What so many stories intend to signify is hard to say. When I was a little girl in my typical German family, every tale had a moral at the end, or at least a few words to make sense of what we'd heard, but after I came to New Mexico, stories ended with just a nod or a shake of the head - a shrug at most, followed by a moment for reflection. It was as if everybody should find their own meaning in a narrative, which perhaps they should.

I never minded John Chisum's demystifying of my tales from the old days with his mechanical speculations - it was a consequence both of his own complacent self-satisfaction and his humble determination to remain grounded in our everyday world. Women understand that men are like little boys - they still want every story to be about them, and Chisum, tended to lose interest quickly in whatever couldn't be grazed or herded. In any case, as I said, I'm a practical woman - the notion that you quietly take things apart to figure how they work and what they might be useful for is everywhere here, and why should it not apply to stories also - something I've learned living in this country. You could say it is part of my cultural inheritance too. I tell the few friends I have left that German is the language of engineers, enabling thought to be expressed with precision rather than in the way that sounds sweetest to the ear. In reality, perhaps this is no more than affectation, because the truth is I hardly remember any language other than American these days. When I speak it's as an American, and if I hear German at all it's because I'm re-reading a treasured text or listening to certain old music that still speaks to my heart.

If I'm asked to explain the Holy Roman Empire today, I can't forget the joke that it wasn't holy or Roman or an Empire, although I know the witticism means no more to my listener than the fact of the Empire itself. Nevertheless, I'm proud of my ancestry and it means at least I am privileged among my neighbours, since I have a past that is not entirely lost. Roots give a fixed point to look out at the world, which some of my fellow Americans sense even if they could not explain.

I still remember the journey from Eureka, Kansas to Lincoln, not long after Alexander and I were married. That would have been in 1873. The wedding was August 23. I was twenty-seven years old and young for my years, more concerned over the impossibility of finding a maidservant who would not be too slatternly or insubordinate to be tolerated than I was about the hardships of travelling. In some senses I had yet to leave Pennsylvania. However, it was clear to the young girl I was then that collars needed to be washed and starched and linen pressed, even if it should be necessary to do the work myself, else we'd be no better than the low born people who dressed themselves in whatever they'd dropped to the floor when they crawled into bed the night before.

Picture a small, trim-waisted girl with dark features and skin that quickly turned brown under the Western sky, even when mostly within the shade of the covered wagon. I was the opposite of the fair, big-boned Saxon woman people envisaged when they were expecting to meet Fraulein Hummer (I still had to remind myself that I was now Frau McSween). I favoured high collars and kept my black hair subdued under bonnets that were severe in style. My young self was too constantly aware of the need to stand up straight, and constantly dismayed when the mirror disclosed heavy lips that were more Austrian than German, and might even be described as sensual. I was proud of my dark eyes that I imagined as windows to the animation of an alert spirit, though I knew my face to be otherwise plain. In a word, I was prim. I had a proper awareness of my deficiencies but was not without some confidence in my just merits.

At that time, some people tended to regard my character as strict, and I will own the young girl I was had a tendency to frown more than seems necessary to me now. Perhaps even Alexander's family had reservations, fearing I might be too harsh tempered for their delicate boy. In defence of the young girl I was, I might admit that she was very conscious of being embarked on a perilous adventure, heading for an unknown land with uncertain prospects. The frown hid anxiety, as well as a determination to maintain the standards we had set ourselves in every particular, for in this way we would surely prevail over the difficulties we would face.

Alexander was a good man in his way, though how many good men require to be carefully managed? That he was clever, no one doubted. He'd qualified as a presbyterian minister before switching professions, and then he sailed through law school at the University of St. Louis. After he graduated, we headed west. Maybe it is not indelicate to suggest that a man whose first choice of career was as a minister of God might be somewhat lacking in the worldliness needed to make his way in a young country that rewarded ambition, but did not stand on ceremony. I remember I had ambition for both of us, even if I wasn't entirely sure yet of the goal to which it should be directed. Mostly I envisaged the place we would have in society, with home comforts and the quiet and respectful companionship of our peers. Alexander talked about the West as if he were going for a missionary. The frontier was opened by rough, hard men of enterprise, he'd say, but it would be civilised and made to prosper by the rule of law, for it was only through law that enterprise might be justly rewarded and transgression punished. How little either of us knew about the world back then.

My own family was left far behind, except insofar as no-one really escapes her origins. Americans described us as German Baptists, which meant only that in common with the American Baptists we had rejected the pagan idolatry of Papism. In fact we were Lutherans, with a strict view of family life that one hundred years away from Thuringia had served only to reinforce, in the same way as I later discovered that many 'English' customs still observed in America had long ago died out entirely in the British Isles. The quaint habits of an old country are always most cherished by those who travel furthest from it.

My education was on the same lines as was given to Sebastian Bach one hundred years before me, and not very different to what Luther himself (who was a pupil and chorister in Eisenbach, at the same school as Bach) would have received one hundred years before that. We had many pictures on the school room wall, providing visual clues to what we needed to remember, so that if we could recall the picture, even many years later, it would call to mind the learning that the picture represented. I can still imagine details of the famous picture of Buno's Dragon with historical scenes drawn inside and about the form of the beast. Even now I use mental images I've seen or invented in the past to remind me of whatever I've come to associate with them. It was good training for thought. The other important part of our schooling was music. Art and music were never mere decoration to us, they were to be used. Music was to lead us to God. Luther said the job of music was DIe Noten machen den Text lebendig - to make the words of his gospel come to life. For myself, I'm no longer certain that God is listening to the music, but I remain grateful to him for inspiring Bach to bring it into being.

People make the mistake of thinking Lutherans austere. The truth is that mine was a loving home where affection was openly displayed and there was great passion, not just for art and music but for life in general. Luther did not deny emotion, he only insisted that it could be turned to good or ill, so that every day of our existence was a struggle between God and Satan. For this reason, every German father as patriarch of his family held a special authority. As some kings have claimed a divine right to rule, so it was with our fathers, whose duty it was to guide and correct us. Correction included beating, for wives as well as children, when we gave way to Satan. Punishment was never administered in the heat of the moment, but in the calm that followed - I do not recall my father ever seeming angry when I was beaten, and somehow for me that always made the experience worse.

It was never in my nature to submit, and submission rather than the pain it caused was the intended consequence of our correction. My eyes would sting with tears of anger not shame. I don't recall I was ever beaten except when there was no alternative according to our custom, for I believe my father was himself repelled by the duty. Later on, when widowed, he remarried a woman who was more traditional in her views than my mother, and insisted he had been very lax in my upbringing, it very quickly became obvious to me that I should need to leave home as soon as possible. I had a sister, but we were not so close that separation would pain either inconsolably. She was young or docile enough to accommodate herself to our new regime, but I was conscious of something in my own spirit that was not prepared to bend.

Not long after we were married, Alexander, then a newly qualified lawyer, drew my attention to a reported case in which the Federal court of our United States was called upon to determine the legality of a former resident of Saxony habitually beating his wife with a horse whip. Alexander was scandalised to read that the court declined to intervene in what it regarded as a purely domestic matter. I can say I never regretted abandoning my Lutheran community, even when I was far enough away to acquire a perspective on the good that was in it. These days, I am inclined to believe that there are those in any society who will abuse whatever authority is delegated to them, whether the issue be domestic or civic.

But in those early times I am describing, I did not give much thought to my home, or to Kansas society or even to Martin Luther himself. We were headed into the unknown and I was eager to discover it (although I also believed we had some true intimation of what we should find). An author less celebrated than he deserves has offered us these words, "turn the white man loose in a land free of restraint and he simply reverts to the ways of the Teutonic and Gothic Forests. The civilised empire of the West has grown in spite of this, because of that other strange germ, the love of law." Alexander would have nodded his approbation to these words, if he'd had occasion to read them. We anticipated that fortitude similar to that which is needed to convert the heathen would be required of us, but neither of us had any notion of understanding the man without restraint. We had not yet known the lethal tooth and claw of his feral nature, which is far more dangerous than that of the savage who has yet to encounter civilisation.

The Teutonic Forests of medieval legend were dense with old gods, darkness and savagery, but Lincoln, New Mexico was a country of the plains. I'd had some anxiety that we might come to find a dry and useless land, but as we neared the county, I saw nothing like the deserts of my imagination. There was still plenty of running water, though in August the watercourses that would swell to mighty rivers later in the year were still but dried up beds with little streams meandering through their base. The land had pretty Spanish names, especially the rivers. There was the Bonito and the Ruidoso flowing off to the Hondo and then the Pecos River. Further on there was the mighty Rio Grande. We were headed for Lincoln which had an English name, but was part of Dona Ana county.

We saw good pasture too, although not prime grassland - it would never support a dairy herd of good Fresian cows. The grasses of the plain extended beyond the limit of our vision, so much that you could start to believe the tales of thousands of beef cattle roaming freely across the land. The air was so fresh, I told myself I felt more alive just standing in that landscape.

Our wagons were well marshalled by men who justified the confidence their quiet, efficient ways inspired. We and our belongings made good progress to arrive at the hamlet of Placita del Rio Bonito (recently renamed Lincoln, in honour of the fallen President but perhaps not yet worthy of designation even as a town) before summer's end.

My friends in the East had thrilled themselves by trying to frighten me with tales of what we might find. 'The Desert of the West', some still called the frontier - a place where there was nothing good to be found, only wastelands and the dregs of humanity that had fled civilised society. For years, politicians and right-thinking people had argued it was irresponsible to expend human and other capital in a futile attempt to tame the wilderness, when there was a nation still needing to be built in the East. That hadn't stopped many of them heading off to California in the forties when gold was discovered. Now a new source of riches was the Long Trail, opened up to deliver beef from the immense herds that covered the limitless plain to the packing and transit yards serving the ever growing and ever hungry centres of population of our continent. Alexander regarded the fever for gold as vulgar and destructive. On the plains, he reasoned, it took work and skill, not good luck to make a fortune. There was a chance to build something new, maybe even something better than what the East, which still mimicked the moribund cultures of Europe could offer. Yes he was an idealist, but then so were Chisum and the others in their own ways (they would have been horrified to discover it). When he became enthusiastic, Alexander could preach about spreading the benefits of agriculture and commerce as if it were the word of God. But everything depended on having law that citizens could rely on, he'd warn - else it would just remain man against man.

Those same Eastern friends of mine read all the lurid accounts that the newspaper correspondents and popular authors wired back to a society hungry for the excitement of the contemporary printed word, no less gripped by these despatches because they themselves had no intention to visit the source of the factitious narrative. The most obviously contrived details were believed, as though the intermediation of the wireless telegraph conferred authenticity as well as alacrity. There was a passion for news, real or imagined, about the country, about its savage indigenous peoples, its heroes and its villains. Above all there were the stories of the outlaws, regarding which Alexander would snort and say that the fables were clearly invented, but a murderer or a thief was never more than a common criminal, however wildly his daring or the numbers of his victims were exaggerated. I believed with Alexander that the path of real courage lay in another direction - and if he had resolved to pit his own fortitude against the perils of the new frontier, then I was similarly determined to engage fully in the struggle.

As for the ferocious natives, Alexander noted that the local Apache were confined to a reservation, where neglect (and it was strongly rumoured, abuse of contracts issued to business by the Federal Government for their subsistence) had reduced the Indians to a pitiful condition. Corrupt practices such as this were precisely what the law was needed to address. With these and other similarly uplifting topics of discourse to ease the weary miles of travel, we arrived at Lincoln in a state of near euphoria, notwithstanding the vicissitudes of the journey, sustained by our shared illusion of a future as prominent members of a society we should help to build with our own hands. The very next evening we were due to dine at the house of Major L .G. Murphy of L. G. Murphy and Co., who was to be Alexander's employer.

***

"Major Murphy is not quite all that I had imagined him to be," Alexander admitted to me after our first visit.

Our host had, to be frank, become intoxicated. The odour that came off him when we were introduced suggested to me that not only had the Major been drinking before our arrival, but that his drinking was habitual. I neglected to add this observation to Alexander's own comment as it might have seemed indelicate and in any case my husband required the opposite of discouragement in that moment. I subsequently had occasion to observe that during his all-too frequent lapses from sobriety, the Major became loud and more than usually dogmatic, with a tendency to blame the British

Empire in general and the parliament of England in particular for all the evils of the world. He also developed a taste for recounting episodes of his military career that were inappropriate to be shared with polite company, though I should admit that when sober, he could be most charming if he chose so to be. Initially I judged that, since he was my husband's employer, certain weaknesses had to be indulged if not overlooked, for the moment at least. I recall that I answered Alexander's comment on that first night by observing that the Major had been in the territory since the time of the first settlers. No doubt hard dealings were the basis of his rough manners.

    It turned out that Murphy had a partner named Fritz, a fellow countryman of mine as might be guessed, who had garnered such wealth in his time out west that he'd decided to return to his ancestral home in Europe, leaving Murphy sole custodian of the business. The Major declared to us that it wouldn't take long in this place for any man with some degree of education and an enterprising spirit to make himself rich. Perhaps in time McSween would become a partner to replace Fritz. Murphy did everything but openly brag that there was a fortune to be made from Indian contracts and dealings in land. In the case of the former, the Federal Government paid contractors handsomely to supply the reservations, but there were few if any checks to establish that the quality and value of supplies matched what was paid for, and if the red men complained they were apt to be disbelieved, being savages and therefore mendacious by nature. In respect of land, Murphy opined that the possible avenues for enrichment were many and various, but claimed it was a particular source of gratification to him that so many Easterners heading out to the frontier looked for land to farm or ranch, and when it came to title they very earnestly required a deed be handed over. Without actually admitting that invalid deeds might be drawn to serve his purposes, the Major joked that it was touching to see what degree of comfort a tenderfoot might obtain from a piece of paper.

    I remarked to Alexander that the drunken condition of his employer and even his coarse manner of speech should be a lesser cause for dismay than the apparent dishonesty of which he boasted. In mitigation, we agreed that in drink a man may frequently make himself out to be worse than he actually was, although the why of that sometime truth is difficult to fathom. We should reserve judgement as to the character of Major Murphy until circumstance should demonstrate it more fully.

"Meanwhile," I said, "we may take heart from what we heard to confirm that this territory is indeed a land of opportunity, yet unformed as we have imagined. A man might do great things in such a place without stooping to methods commended to him by the likes of Major Murphy."

The next day, Alexander began his employment while I supervised the unpacking of the few possessions we had brought to the apartment we should rent as a temporary home. Most valued among them were my family jewels and a small piano, which had thankfully weathered the journey in good condition, with barely a string needing tuning. I have never pretended musical virtuosity, but at the end of his day a husband may take comfort from soothing music that a wife ought to have sufficient accomplishment to provide, or so my thinking ran in those days. I admit my practice that afternoon was immoderately extended and somewhat selfishly directed on some particular sheet music of favourite German composers who have long provided me with comfort that is almost spiritual in nature. Alexander took strength from his personal relationship with God. I often felt the same confidence that fundamental and unchanging truths existed when hearing my own poor renderings of these favourite scores and imagining them as they were intended to be played.

Most days in the next few weeks I would catch sight of Alexander coming along the street from work in the late afternoon. The road was busy and choked with dust, but I would pick him out easily in the crowd. He was always neatly dressed in a decent suit and hat of a man of business, but more than that, he was differentiated from the crowd by his erect carriage (I used to marvel that, when he felt a need to assert himself professionally, he would somehow draw himself up even more straight-backed than before, till you thought the bones must lock). Along with the business suit, there'd be a rolled umbrella under one arm and a case full of papers in the other.

Alexander had plenty of work from the first day and there was much for him to learn about the reality of practice and local custom. He was kept busy, which was what his nature required. As for me, in that early time the arrival of a woman from the East was unusual, or to be accurate I should qualify, the arrival of such a woman who was with a husband and who might be presented in polite society was a novelty. There were invitations to afternoon tea and other quaint local entertainments. It took a rather depressingly short time for me to get to know everyone in town who regarded themselves as decent. Everyone without exception treated me with such exaggerated courtesy that I first thought they might be making fun, or else they mistook me for someone more important than I actually was, say a princess or a countess at least. I soon came to realise that the fixed postures, the too fine handling of a teacup and saucer, the stilted dialogue and rather suffocating politeness were what passed for good manners in Lincoln County society. It was as if the people here were imitating some model of refinement that had long passed into memory in York County Pennsylvania, if it had ever truly existed there or anywhere else.

Sometimes, though he'd be careful to hide it, I was aware that Alexander was finding the work a strain. It wasn't the heaviness of the workload or its difficulty, but the assumptions he laboured against that held him down. He'd complain his clients became impatient when he was taking statements of their cases. They felt that when they'd paid him and told him their objectives, it was up to him to come up with a story that would support their claim. "You're the lawyer," they'd say. "You tell it as it ought to be." He spent hours trying to explain that the attorney's job was to advise his client on the law according to the circumstance of the case and then to put the client's argument in the best way the client could have done it if he'd been a lawyer himself. In that way everybody was equal before the law - it wasn't the attorney's job to make up stories. "They look at me as if I'd just been talking Hebrew or Greek" he said.

The relationship with Murphy was not easy. When he needed to see the Major outside of work, Alexander generally contrived that I should accompany him, with the unspoken understanding between us that the presence of a lady might inhibit Murphy's discussion of the sordid schemes in which he was engaged and with which he seemed determined Alexander should become implicated - or at least he should behave less like an outrageous drunk before the end of the evening. In this way I came to know Lawrence G. Murphy as well or better than I should like, though I must admit that if his speech and manner were in any way inhibited in my presence, then he must have surely been a wicked son of a bitch when unfettered by polite restraint.

I must admit that Murphy's establishment was impressive in its way, as much for the considerable proportion of the town's space that it occupied as for its general appearance. The Major chose to live in the place in which he conducted business, in the manner of the urban populations of antiquity. The ancillary buildings included a stables that conclusively demonstrated Lincoln was not a one horse town, and a store with rooms above that doubled as a prison when need should arise, for our settlement did not yet possess a jailhouse. The dwelling house had been constructed with more attention to comfort than style, seeming to have been extended in stages. Nevertheless, there was a sense of proportion demonstrated in its rough construction and even some features that could be termed decorative, for example the broad staircase that flew up from Murphy's entrance hall, and the balcony with painted wooden rail from which the autocrat could survey the comings and goings of his town. The house stood out in Lincoln by virtue of being the only building on main street seemingly erected by some person who had at least a vague awareness of the existence of a science of architecture.

It was during an evening social at the house of Murphy that I first made the acquaintance of John P. Wilson, a corpulent, sponging sorry individual who had a paucity of wit to match his absence of integrity. Wilson was the local Justice of the Peace and therefore a supposed pillar of our community, which was indeed resting on shaky foundations if such be the case, as subsequent events would confirm. It would be partial of me to describe Wilson as a crony of Murphy's, more accurate to say that he sought to be a crony of any person of influence or possessed of sufficient means to cross his palm with silver. Indeed Wilson made a virtue of his biddability. He also made a point of taking Alexander aside and talking to him quietly whilst I provided the sociable cover for their discussion. There was some case going on that Wilson felt my husband was making needlessly difficult.

"You don't have to make every issue a matter of high principle," Wilson had to look up to speak to Alexander. He had a lazy eye and his chins jiggled as he spoke. "You're a natural orator Alex and people respect that. A man might go far with the gift of speech that has the power to move. But son the Lincoln courthouse is not the Forum of Rome. You don't need to be poring over those books of statutes and old cases to quote at us - your client's don't expect that of you. Here we get along fine with common sense and neighbourliness."

When Wilson drank whiskey, his face reddened. Though he was fat, I remember him as a small man in every way. Alexander was holding a glass of soda water.

"The law is the same in every place, large or small, or else it is nothing," my husband replied. HIs health had never been good, and he was not physically strong, but there was strength in Alexander's spirit. Wilson stretched to clap him on the shoulder.

"Great goodness but you are a spring of purest rectitude arising in the muddy brook of our sordid town," Wilson exclaimed. "I don't mean to discourage you son. I'm merely pointing out that in New Mexico we live alongside our fellow man in more of what you might call the natural condition."

"Have you read Hobbes, I mean Thomas Hobbes?" Alexander enquired. Wilson shook his head, continuing to smile his fatuous grin all the while.

"Mr. Hobbes treats of the lot of mankind in its natural condition and concludes of such a life that it is nasty, brutish and short, No better than the desperate struggle of all against all that we see in the animal kingdom."

Wilson shook his head in mock wonderment. "And how does Senor Hobbes propose we address that conundrum," he asked, "given that it's human nature he takes such a dim view of?"

"Men must agree to submit to authority, of which the rule of law is a fundamental part," Alexander answered readily. "Society is Leviathan, a great and awful beast, like a huge whale. Sometimes we may sense it's oppression, but we cannot fight it, since only by accepting Leviathan can we be truly free."

"You men from the East are obsessed with whales," Wilson smirked. "Here we are a long way from Nantucket. On the plains, I guess that many a man feels free inside his own skin, but I will maintain my argument for the natural condition. Are you catching any of this Lawrence?"

Murphy himself had just lurched into our immediate proximity. Our host was bearing an opened bottle of whiskey in one hand and a glass in the other, though it was but early in the evening. He poured a generous measure into Wilson's near empty glass and offered to top up Alexander's soda water with the spirit, which my husband wordlessly declined.

"I'll not offer yourself any, Mrs. McSween, for I know that would only cause offence."

"I've taken no pledge, if that's what you're guessing Major, but I confess I have no taste for the strong liquors."

"I do prefer good Spanish wine and French brandy myself," Murphy nodded, "but until it arrives, I shall make do with the whiskey and be glad."

Wilson summarised the previous conversation and requested that Murphy deliver his own view of the matter. I anticipated some attempt at humour that would likely be in questionable taste. Murphy paused, as if to collect his thoughts, before he spoke

"Society will have its pound of flesh," he said, "and men cannot live well without authority. It is true that we must delegate some part of the internal fire that animates us to society, but I hold that the man who delegates all," he paused and looked hard into the face of my husband, who met his glare calmly, "has naught but water left in his veins. Without that retained spark of flame, if we lose the undelegated personal right to choose what we call good or bad, we are no longer worthy to be called men."

"Enlighten us sir if you will," Alexander asked with more than natural politeness. "In what does this undelegated right consist?"

Murphy appeared to be greatly annoyed and struggling to contain his anger. "Why lad, in the will. It is my will that determines my fortune, not the hand of providence or some imagined kindly mutuality. My will and the reach of my arm, which my determination has greatly extended."

I sensed a risk of confrontation and intervened to move the conversation to a less fraught path.

"I suppose Major, that your views on the world are formed to a great degree by your time in the military. I have understood that action may change a man fundamentally."

"I'm hardly the man to pronounce upon that, Mrs. McSween," Murphy replied. "I did my time in the service, but apart from slaying a few Indians I saw but little of war - a circumstance that I do not regret, since there's no profit to be made from it unless you're in the munitions trade."

"It's a curious thing for an officer of rank to deny the need for rule and order," Alexander observed. "This town now bears the name of a great legislator, whose legacy we should strive to be worthy of."

"Oh, men must be commanded,"Murphy replied negligently. "That's something quite different. As for politics and law, you're from Kansas, you've seen what can happen. When the federal legislature voted to admit the state, granting it self-determination in the matter of whether slavery was permitted, the abolitionists and secessionists flooded in from all parts and began a bloody battle that persisted for years even before the civil strife of which Mr. Lincoln was in large part the cause and which caused many a poor boy's life to be unnaturally brutish and short."

I was rather shocked by this comment. "Were you in favour of slavery, Major?"

"I'm not for or against any human institution," the old man laughed, "though I deplore the hypocrisy of those who'd justify it on the basis of natural superiority of one race over another, when there's no more than brute force involved. A Nigger's no worse than a Mexican or an Apache for me, though in Lincoln County we've few of the former but more than enough Mexicans and Indians. "

"Most of our Spanish speaking community trace their ancestry to Old Spain, not Mexico," my husband observed.

"They've fine manners indeed," Murphy agreed, "But it's men like you and I that are needed to make the country. I have hopes you'll rise to it McSween. You're a fine lawyer, but you've the heart of a Celt in you somewhere, else I'd not have hired you. We're not like those bloodless English that have oppressed our own race these centuries past, whose yoke is now thrown off. This is a land of boundless opportunity. Will you not reach out your hand to grasp it?"

We were standing in a little alcove. Alexander set his untouched glass of soda on the window ledge and when he spoke again it was more like the clear and sonorous voice that he'd employ in a courtroom.

"In the first place sir," he began, "I'm neither English nor an Irishman, but an American. We fought a civil war to unite this nation and it dishonours the fallen not to acknowledge that."

"Only the living worry about honour," Murphy muttered.

"And one thing I'll not do sir," Alexander declared, "is set myself above my fellow man and in doing so abrogate the rule of law that makes us better than the cattle that make this county rich."

Murphy's laugh had a bitter ring. I'd never been more proud of my husband. At the same time I contrived, somehow, that we should leave the place then, before further words were spoken that might not be unsaid.

***

Despite what may be conjectured, in the time that followed my husband and his employer were able to co-exist without enmity springing up between them. The local people might shake their heads and say that an honest lawyer was a thing to behold, rarer than a five legged steer, nevertheless Alexander quickly won the respect of the little community. The poor ranchers found disputes might be resolved by inviting McSween to comment on the rights and wrongs of facts set squarely before him, without need to invoke the expensive and ultimately frustrating mechanisms of the local court, where Justice Wilson's rulings might be bought and sold more dearly. Most of our neighbours only wanted to make certainty in their dealings and smooth out the rough edges that history and custom set up between them.

The Major was too canny not to see that the prestige and even the business of L. G. Murphy and Co. benefitted from the industry of my husband and the trust which the town placed reposed in him, even if he affected bemusement at the lengths to which Alexander was prepared to go to ensure that he'd be able to give a true opinion of a case. For reasons I did not understand, Murphy himself went to great lengths to curry the favour of the holders of the many small ranches in the vicinity, even to the event of sponsoring their projects, thus it pleased him that Alexander had their trust.

In regard to the administration of justice, I might comment that Justice Wilson was understood by all concerned, including his own person, to be a non-entity. His stamp was required for making matters official, and as a last resort he'd be called upon to rule upon certain intractable disputes that could not await or did not merit the consideration of the County Judge, but for most practical matters the rubber stamp in Wilson's office was regarded as being of more utility than the Justice himself.

In so far as the policing of public law and civil order was not a question of self-governance for the inhabitants of Lincoln (it was never an unruly settlement, at that time) authority resided in the person of Sheriff Brady, though it might be considered surprising that such a small town had bethought itself to swear in and maintain a full-time officer of the law. In fact, it should go without saying that Brady was the creature of L. G. Murphy and Co. though I knew him first as an amiable personage, very much devoted to the quiet life.

As Alexander developed his practice, we quickly took the opportunity to open a general store. I fully agreed with my husband's conviction that we should not disdain commerce or regard it as incompatible with his professional status, and as well as moving into larger premises (the apartment was seeming more and more cramped as time passed) the enterprise gave me a useful purpose. I can say that before long it contributed to our domestic increase in equal proportion with Alexander's legal fees, which did not always provide a regular income. If I ever reflected that in Pennsylvania my taking up the life of a shopkeeper might be regarded with some horror and even a cause for exclusion from my social circle, it was only to be thankful that here I was free of such stifling concerns. Major Murphy showed no sign of resentment that Alexander was adding another string to his bow, as he put it. He said that any man worthy of the name should look to branch out on his own account where there was so much opportunity for all.

Sometimes I remembered the near confrontation between the Major and my husband. It was troubling for many reasons, and it shamed me to admit only to myself that in regard to the purely intellectual issues in dispute I held some convictions that were closer to the ramblings of the tipsy ex-Irishman than pure philosophy of Alexander. Perhaps it was my German ancestry - not just medieval chivalry but the more distant memory of the forest. I loved the forests of New Mexico. They reminded me of the great German forests that I had never seen and knew only from stories, in the trees where the Roman legions entered and were swallowed up, where hardy savages prayed to the Nordic gods and the spirits of the trees themselves and lived lives of simple and harsh nobility. Can such things be passed down through generations who have never known the place of their origin - perhaps in dreams? At any rate, the rule of law that Alexander loved to talk about seemed insufficient for me in itself. Something of what Murphy had said about the will and what he called the undelegated personal right stayed in my mind as life began to show itself to me, though without any notion that my life might ever be different from the one Alexander and I had planned.

I knew that my husband was a good man. There was a moral certainty to his dealings that was reassuring to one such as myself who'd thrown over the supposed certainties of her own domestic world and was unsure where that left her. Perhaps there was even something of the patriarch in Alexander, though we had it clearly understood between us that in all matters we should regard ourselves as equals. HIs view of life was not so different from my Lutheran teaching - he regarded each day as a test.

I treasured a memory from our first walking out together. Alexander was very correct and proper as we walked alongside a creek in some wooded place. A dog had got itself into the creek and was trapped in the muddy bed. It set up an anguished wail that was distressing to the ear, for the creature was likely to drown. Other passers by were ignoring the scene. It would have been otherwise if the beast had been a horse, for there was a creature of value, but a dog was worth little and easily replaced in regard to such employment as it might discharge. Alexander excused himself and put aside his coat. He took up a heavy bough and waded into the muddy flow. At length with the aid of the improvised staff he was able to free the animal sufficiently for it to crawl along the branch and out of the mire that was sucking it down, whence it duly sprang upon the bank, shook itself vigorously and ran off without looking backward at us.

At first I was a little cross with Alexander as he struggled from the river, apologising for the condition of his breeches and shoes, which I suppose were ruined. HIs health was delicate and a soaking such as this even in clement weather was a more risky undertaking than it would have been for a more robust individual. He explained that he'd had no choice. The regard we have for dumb animals, he told me, is the clearest indication of the regard we have for others generally. We must make use of beasts and their produce, but that necessity did not excuse cruelty or neglect of them. He seemed to have worked out in advance all of the moral problems of existence, in order that when life should confront him with an actual dilemma, he'd not be paralysed by doubt as to his honourable course. I believe that was the afternoon when I determined we should be married.

Murphy was clearly a different kind of man. What I most feared was that my husband's moral inflexibility might come upon an equally immovable obstacle, in the form of the Major's stubborn determination to have his way in all things. I resolved I must attempt to divert any course of events that might occasion such a calamitous collision. But then came our first dealings with Herr Fritz and his family, although even before that, I made my first visit to Bosque Grande.

***

I have never been what you would call pretty. The highest compliment a man might accord my appearance would be to say that I had handsome features, which is several steps down from pretty, but perhaps less fatuous. I can't recall that I ever minded. As a child they said I was strong-willed, which I suppose is how any little girl that doesn't smile meekly and do as she's told is labelled.

Nevertheless, I always took care over my appearance, as any woman wishing to be considered a lady had to do in those days. I have an old photograph of myself and there I am - short, naturally curly hair, jet black then, in a tightly laced sombre gown with the neck open and a length of crimpled silk around my throat. I took perhaps an excessive delight in my bonnets, which were not easy to obtain. It's a shame all my other photographs were lost in the fire later on.

I don't recall what I was wearing for our visit to Bosque Grande that first time, but I do remember that I worried over my appearance more than was usual for me. The ranch was home to the great man of Dona Ana County, of the whole state in fact if it had been a state at that time. I was still under thirty years old and a young girl in some ways. When I was told that John Chisum had eighty thousand head of cattle, I tried to imagine all the herd penned in fields around the ranch - it was beyond imagination - we might spend days getting to the house.

In fact as I learned, the cattle roamed freely on open range, mingling with the stock of other ranchers. No rancher knew for sure where his cattle were at any given time, only that they bore his brand - the fierra of ownership that marked his property until it should be supplanted by the brand of venta, meaning sale. When Alexander explained this to me, I protested that surely such an arrangement would lead to many disputes about ownership, for example of calves. Surely the courts would be overwhelmed with so much litigation.

"They tend to resolve such matters by custom and practice rather than legal process," my husband's smile was rather apologetic. "For example, a rider carrying a running brand in his saddlebag on the open range is apt to be lynched if he's apprehended where there is a tree handy."

He told me that a running brand was a branding iron that was like a poker, without a design at the end where a blacksmith normally crafted the owner's mark. A thief could heat this in a fire then use it to add to the design of the original brand to create a counterfeit. I asked him how much a cow was worth.

"About ten dollars."

"And for this they will risk a hanging?"

Alexander pointed out there were a lot of cows on the open range.

And so I found nothing like eighty thousand head of cattle awaiting my gaze at Bosque Grande, but there were still an awful lot of cows. The ranch itself was as impressive as a single storey building could be to my eye (in those days I still had an ideal of home I should one day own that would resemble the mansion of an old Southern plantation) but Bosque Grande seemed vast and comfortable, rather like its owner as I was to discover.

Chisum was waiting and himself came forward to shake hands with us as we stepped from our carriage. He was a large, friendly man who looked like he'd taken some hard blows from life at times without being bowed down by the experience. There was little ceremony, and soon we were ensconced in a parlour of the ranch where a girl brought coffee for the three of us, pouring it into cups from a steaming pot that she held with a cloth. There was sugar but no milk - every cow was for beef.

The great man said that he was sorry he'd not welcomed us the territory earlier, but he was invariably busy, as we would appreciate. He made a point of telling us he'd heard that Alexander McSween was a man who was good as his word, saying this as if there were no higher compliment he could offer anyone.

"Mr. Chisum," I asked him, "is it true that your cow-herds will sometimes hang a man who they find trying to steal a cow, without benefit of a trial?"

He admitted that it was so. Sometimes that job had to be done, though it was not a thing a decent man would brag about after.

"Sir, you have to stop it. You have the power. It cannot be right to resort to murder over an animal that is worth ten dollars."

He didn't get angry. Perhaps he found me amusing, especially if he noticed Alexander carefully looking at his shoes. He just smiled that slow, genial smile I later on came to know well, and explained that I should understand what life was like for a cowboy. They spent their lives on the range or on the trail, with just a few male companions and nothing to do from waking to sleeping but care for animals that were too dumb to find grass for themselves and just kept finding new ways to get lost or killed. They'd spend weeks or months on the Old Trail ('the Chishum Trail, some are calling it now, you may have heard' - such trophies mattered to him) and by the time the drive was over, they could think of nothing to do but blow their little pay in the course of a few days and sign on for the next drive. The cattle and his horse were what such a man truly cared for - if I saw the risks they'd run to save a single steer for pay that was scarcely more than board, then I'd not doubt it. When such men came upon rustlers seeking to exploit their hard labour and care, it was not surprising that tempers ran high.

"And besides," he concluded, "think that you could be a thousand miles from the nearest jailhouse. What are you to do with your scoundrel - extract his solemn promise that he'll not repeat the offence, when he knows it's unlikely you'll see him again on the long road? Do you think that would really do it."

That was the John Chisum I first got to know - proud and self-satisfied in his way, but eager for stories about everything in the wide world. He'd hear out even the most outrageous liar before letting the man know (not by calling him out but with just some dismissive shift in his manner) that he didn't think the tale was worth much. I suppose on his many trails he'd had time to listen to many stories, reliable and otherwise, as well as to learn that doubting a man's word to his face, at least if he was a decent worker, offered some risk and no gain. Later on I suppose the trail finally got washed out of his soul and he was weighed down by the heavy load that rich men always bear. After that he could be short with people, or so they say. He was never less than charming to me.

Chisum told us that before we left there were a few things he wanted to say, given he'd heard that McSween was a man who was honest and wanted to do right. The first was, we'd hear stories to the effect that when he drove his great herds up north, the cattle of the other ranchers would get carried along on the drive and he wasn't particular if in the end he sold cattle that rightly belonged to other ranchers as well as his own. It couldn't be helped, he said, that sometimes where you drove your herd others would join, but that was never his intent, and whenever they could the boys would cut out the other brands from the 'long-i' and 'jiinglebob' steers and send them off back home. If not, he'd see that the neighbour got value for his animal. The small man was apt to be resentful of the large man, but that was not to say, he asserted, that the large man was always trying to do down the small. He'd no reason to stoop to larceny.

"What's a few more to me either way," he asked "when I've got more than eighty thousand of my own longhorn to worry about?"

Second, he knew that some of the smaller ranchers stole from him. "I'm not speaking of a cow or two maybe if the winter's been hard or her brand looks so old as to be doubtful," he said. He could understand that where there was ambiguity a man might resolve it in his own favour. That was human nature and maybe his own men would do the same. But there was wholesale thieving going on. He could stand it and it wasn't in his interest to start a war, but he'd not be made a fool of indefinitely - it wasn't ranchers who were behind it, he claimed.

Who then, McSween asked him? Chisum told us first that he wasn't a man for name-calling. He preferred to consider himself above such low practices. On the other hand he did not like to see an honest man mixed up in a bad business. He suggested that if Alexander thought about who was making friends with all the local ranchers, lending them money on easy terms and getting them all stirred up about the supposed depredations of the Bosque Grande operation, maybe if he thought too about who had the profitable contract to supply beef to Fort Stanton where the army had a lot of hungry men and didn't much care where the animals came from, then perhaps he'd also understand why cattle that disappeared from Chisum's herd almost never turned up anywhere else, with brands altered or otherwise.

I looked at my husband blankly.

"He means that Murphy is behind the stealing," Alexander explained.

I was thrown into confusion. I knew Major Murphy to be uncouth when drunk and unprincipled in his business dealings, but to hear that my husband's employer was also suspected of being a thief launched me into a moment of crisis.

"Mr. Chisum," I protested, "these are serious allegations to make. How can we know that we should trust you over Alexander's own employer?"

My husband started to rise as if to apologise for my presumption, but the rancher waved him be calm.

"It's a fair question," he allowed. He called the maid. "Maria, get me my box."

The girl duly arrived a few minutes later bearing a closed cylinder, made of tin, that was sealed and locked. It had attachments for a leather strap that would allow it to be carried over the shoulder. Chisum broke the seal and unlocked the container. From it he drew a sheaf of papers of varying sizes, some of them badly weathered by time and use, and these he presented to Alexander.

"My powers of attorney," he declared. "For your professional scrutiny."

As Alexander read the papers, Chisum explained to me that to grant a power of attorney to someone was to delegate authority for them to deal with your property as if it were their own.

"I don't leave Bosque Grande without this cylinder under my coat," he said. "It's travelled the extent of this country with me. In there you find the names of just about any rancher of any account for hundreds of miles around. Every one of them has their property roaming across this open range. These papers express their confidence that I'll care for such property as if it were mine and in the end bring home a fair price for it."

Alexander nodded and carefully began to put the papers back in place.

"You mightcn't accord much more esteem to these gentlemen you never met than to myself," Chisum continued. "But should you choose to regard all as self-interested ruffians, at least consider that they have discovered that self-interest directs them to repose their trust in me."

I'm grateful to Mr. Chisum that he didn't dismiss my comments as those of a silly, innocent girl. That was never his way - he was a gentleman in his own fashion. Those in any way acquainted with me will appreciate that I came in time to a less forgiving view regarding the treatment of those involved in thieving of livestock, but I never found reason to alter the favourable impression that our host made on me that day.

***

      The time when Lieutenant Scholland and his wife came to visit, not long after our excursion to Bosque Grande, was a somewhat bizarre experience in comparison. I was still green enough to be nervous about hosting even a small dinner party, our first in the town I believe, and I probably fussed around nervously, making preparation for the evening more difficult for Alexander than it already was. Scholland was a serving officer, stationed at Fort Stanton. He was the brother in-law of Colonel Emil Fritz (retired) who in turn had been the partner of Major Murphy until he decided to cash in his wealth and return to Germany. Now Murphy was reputed to have other partners, but he still held assets on behalf of his former associate, which was why Fritz had made indirect contact with Alexander as the attorney responsible for the company's affairs.

      The evening was something of a disaster. It was clear from the outset that Scholland and his wife detested one another. The lieutenant was also glad of the opportunity to practice his German, although Alexander spoke not a word of the language and of the three supposed Germans present not one had actually visited Europe. The evening proceeded in confusion as a subject would be taken up in one language and continued in another. There were frequent uncomfortable pauses in the progress of trains of thought that departed in one linguistic mode and arrived or failed to arrive in others. My own German was not perfect - Scholland's was barely comprehensible.

      Scholland was a spare man of medium height - not gaunt like Alexander but with the same erect posture and nervous energy. HIs movements were small and very neat, like a bird to my mind, although I suspect he saw military precision in the mirror. He was very much the professional soldier - pressed uniform (was he obliged to wear it for social visits, I wondered?) dark hair and beard clipped short, boots polished to a shine - so much that one wondered if such a man could possibly have been engaged in an actual conflict. Like myself, he was one of those dark-skinned Germans, with a full mouth and eyes that were uncomfortably intense.

The Schollands made a very odd couple, as the wife was rather his opposite. She was a big-bosomed, heavy-boned lady, about the same height as the Lieutenant, but she seemed always to be sitting or leaning, as if standing were too much trouble. To avoid being cruel, I'll say that she dressed negligently. The most enthusiasm she showed all evening was when I brought out the meat course. Generally, she'd sit back in her chair as if to move further away from her spouse, watching rather than listening to his discourse with a more or less disbelieving expression and an occasional roll of the eyes. Every so often she'd respond to a comment by making a 'Pfftt' sound through pursed lips and fluttering the stubby fingers of her upraised hand in a gesture that had no meaning to me. On later reflection I considered it probable that they had not started out their marriage in such opposition. It was more that their mutual antipathy drove them in contrary directions, as seems to be the common progression between unwilling partners, so that the officer became more of a martinet as his spouse grew more slovenly.

Schollard gave me to understand that he heartily approved of his brother in-law's decision to return to Germany. Did I not agree that all true Germans should feel blessed to stand in the Homeland in this glorious moment in history? I had to ask him what he meant, though as I suspected he was referring to German unification and the recent victories over France. The French were no good at fighting he said, though they always managed to win the peace. I suggested that if that were true it would imply that the French were the cleverer nation. Schollard dismissed this suggestion as if the very word clever disgusted him. He was similarly unimpressed by my speculation that wars which were resolved with the humiliation of one party were apt to give rise to further wars. "Let them come" he snarled dismissively, from his seat in my parlour in Lincoln County, New Mexico.

I confessed that it was difficult for me to imagine Germany as one country. For me the Homeland had always been an idea and a language rather than a state. I remembered what I'd been told about the many dukes and princes, archdukes and kings, each with their own fiefdom that might be no bigger than a city. Out here where the plains stretched out wider than Europe itself, the notion that home was a place on a much smaller scale was comforting. Might it not be better for each place to keep its own character, like the Italians who had a common heritage even though they would surely never be a single country? The Lieutenant considered my attitude unpatriotic. He started to talk about Prussia and the victories of General Blucher. I will admit that by this stage I had fairly risen to the bait and I told him that it was certain that if Germany was to be organised as an army camp then the Prussians were the best people to be in charge, but my own Homeland was the one of Bach more than Blucher. As a hostess, the evening was not my finest hour.

Since the purpose of the evening was supposedly social, there was no excuse to call proceedings to order so that we might get to discuss business. It was only after we set to wash the dishes following the departure of our guests, with great relief on my part at least, that Alexander informed me of the real purpose of the visit.

"Frau Scholland wants a divorce," he explained.

Of course, hearing this I had to review the evening in a new light, though it is odd to record now that at the time I had a very imperfect understanding of what it meant to be granted a divorce. I had never heard of anyone who had actually been divorced, other than kings and princes in history, and I assumed that it would only be possible in cases of depraved behaviour or extreme cruelty. As we dried and put away the plates, Alexander explained his theoretical understanding of the law (it was certain that no one in Lincoln had yet invoked the dubious procedure - in fact some of our neighbours who were coupled as yet enjoyed matrimonial contracts of questionable legality). I began to pity the Schollands, who were clearly making each other more unhappy day by day, as if all the qualities of relationship that a marriage contract should engender between parties had faded between them, leaving only the capacity to cause misery.

It was not even easy, given the protocol of the day, for the unhappy woman to meet my husband in the absence of her own, hence this stratagem of a social meeting. Further instructions would be delivered through an intermediary, Alexander explained. He apologised for subjecting me to the evening, which had turned out worse than he'd expected.

The divorce would not be straightforward. Besides the difficulty of obtaining instructions from his client, Alexander had to contend with the undeveloped jurisprudence of the country. No one he consulted knew of any procedure by which a marriage could be deconsecrated, or who might have legal authority to pronounce such a decree. If I had known that divorcing couples could not cohabit, and that this would lead to the odious Frau Scholland residing under our roof for a brief but uncomfortable period, I might have tried to persuade Alexander to decline the case, even without knowing the fatal implications that the Fritz estate would ultimately hold for us. Alexander told me there was a further complication, which I came to hope might work to our advantage.

"Emil Fritz is a sick man. He's gone back to Germany to die," Alexander confided. "He married his sister off to Scholland years ago, seeing the Lieutenant as the only eligible bachelor with his roots in the old country, but neither Emil or his sister is happy at the notion of the Lieutenant as Fritz's heir."

Again I felt sympathy for the officer. He was considerably younger than his bride and would have married with some expectations. Fritz was happy enough to see his sister married off, until it looked like making his brother in-law rich. On the other hand, the mental impression I unwillingly formed of Lieutenant Scholland retired from the service and adopting the posture of a man of wealth and power was an image unedifying in the extreme.

"Murphy has managed all Fritz's affairs since he's been gone," Alexander continued. "Fritz took cash, but there are other assets. Now he doesn't trust Murphy and wants to instruct me, but that sets up a conflict of interest with my employer."

I thought this over, and remarked that there would be no conflict if Alexander were no longer employed by Murphy, but set up on his own account under the style of McSween and Co., Attorneys at Law. We'd discussed it often enough, as the only workable solution to our current situation - engaged to the service of a man we knew to be lacking in ethics and suspected of criminality. McSween was unusually timid on this score, less in regard to his prospects as a practitioner on his own account, than for fear that Murphy might make it his business to crush the upstart. I was strongly in favour, not only since this was the next step in realising our dream, but also because I wanted to get my husband away from L.G. Murphy and Co. I could see that Alexander suffered in his current employ even if I made no enquiries as to the compromises of conscience required of him on a daily basis.

In the long term, I feared for Alexander's soul. A man who gives himself over to vice unwillingly is more damned than one who chooses villainy, since he is conscious of his damnation, and one who falls from a position of high principle falls further and lands harder. Following this logic, although I'm no puritan regarding alcohol, it's clear that the smell of whiskey on the breath of a righteous man is of more concern than an open bottle in the hand of a vagabond. Of late my husband had returned from work after meetings with clients on more than one occasion with that telltale scent of liquor on his breath, regarding which I kept my own counsel. But now I made it my business to persuade him that the moment was right to begin his independent practice.

Once persuaded, Alexander threw himself into the new project with his customary enthusiasm. In fact it could be said he fair revived in spirit. Sooner than I could have hoped, we were ready to open for business, the consulting rooms being in an area of the store newly set aside for the purpose. Once more I was surprised by the behaviour of the Major, for if he felt himself thwarted to any degree, he showed it not at all. He even came to visit and wish us well.

"Really it's time, Mrs. McSween," he said as he shook my hand. He'd not been drinking yet that day and he was more charming for it. "I've always said, your husband is a man of ability and suchlike cannot indefinitely be kept under another's wing. It does me no injury if the attorney of L.G. Murphy and Co. is known to be an independent man. That's just to move with the country as it grows, which all of us desire fervently. I hope and trust we shall always remain friends"

"As for Alex," he said, clapping my husband on the shoulder and offering a warm smile. "I'm sure he won't forget where he got his start. Honest affection and loyalty are more important than a sign over the door, as we both know. Nowhere more than at the frontier, where a man depends on such few friends as he can muster. I'm sure we understand each other."

"Thank you sir, and thank you for your kind wishes".

My husband's reply seemed genuinely affected by Murphy's generosity, though sometimes it was not easy even for me to separate the natural enthusiast from the politician in McSween. Whether or not the Major was sincere, I can say that the brief days these new conditions of our lives endured, were the happiest of my life.

***

In Lincoln and elsewhere in Dona Ana County, Spanish was as much spoken as English. Most people learned to speak whichever was not their native tongue through their everyday dealings with fellow citizens, recognising words that were incorporated in general parlance until they developed an alternative vocabulary that was sufficiently accurate to be broadly intelligible. As a woman, my opportunities for such organic learning were limited. Since I've never easily tolerated any form of exclusion and owing to the practical necessities of maintaining our family store, I felt the need of instruction in the matter of Spanish. In any case I'm one of those that if she does something, wants to do it right. Picking up fragments of expressions and half-understood phrases was not a mode of education suited to my taste.

After making enquiries, I was recommended to make the acquaintance of Senor Juan Patron, and in due course introductions were made. At the time when Juan consented to assist my study of Spanish I was not aware that he was a person of significance in the county, likely having better ways to spend his time than cajoling a not very quick student in the business of phonetics and grammar. It was only later, when I knew him as a friend dear to my heart, that I appreciated this early kindness.

Afternoons when I was able, I'd make my way to his house, which I can only describe as gracious, in the old Spanish style. The garden was inside the house, in a kind of courtyard, and we'd sit in the shade while the girl brought us coffee or some sort of tea that Don Juan preferred and he'd patiently explain not only Spanish but the history and customs of Spain. Sometimes I think my host was telling his stories of the old times as much for himself as for me. There was something dreamlike in the air in those days and I seemed to understand more easily than seemed natural, even when so many words and phrases were new to me.

Juan Patron was the senior figure in the local Spanish community, which still referred to our hamlet as La Placita. He had a wife and two small daughters, though I seldom saw trace of them and think perhaps they lived elsewhere some of the time. He was always dressed carefully in the Spanish mode, sombre and not showy as I'd been told was the style of rich Mexicans. In fact he was not pleased when I suggested that the town was largely Mexican.

"This place has never been part of Mexico," he told me. "The Spanish explorer who found it named it the new Mexico, probably more in hope than expectation, but there were no Aztec or other Indio here, apart from the Apache and their brothers - and little gold either. The old families here came direct from Spain. Afterwards of course it became part of the barter with the French and the new Federation of States, though the land remains the land whatever flag is planted on it."

He told me about Cortez and Pizarro, and Columbus who he called Admiral Colon. I once asked him if the decline of Spain and its Empire made him sad. He shrugged.

"Every kingdom has its time. For a while, God willed that it should be Spain which had the ships and the men of courage. It is a question of the longest arm also. The reach of a man with a sword is greater than that of the man who has only a stone dagger, especially when the swordsman is mounted on a horse. Then along come the men with six-gun revolvers and rifles, whose reach is much greater than the sword."

"You believe that we are in the age of the six-gun? Alexander and I hope that this is not the case."

Don Juan shook his head. His expressions and movements conveyed an impression of great melancholy, although it was hard to say whether I was mistaking the dignity of his manner for a sorrowful temperament.

"You are right of course. The reach of Colt or Sharps may exceed that of steel from Toledo, but the men who hold these weapons do not see far ahead of them and their time is passing also. The man who has the longest reach is always the one who holds gold, as it was in the past times. With gold in their hands, our vecino Snr. Murphy and his friends Dolan and Riley extend their arms all the way to Santa Fe and beyond, perhaps even to Washington."

I found such talk discouraging. "You speak of wealth as if it bought only influence and corrupt dealing. But Mr Chisum is richer than King Murphy, and yet he seems to be an honest man."

"That may be," Don Juan nodded, "but one honest man who will not buy influence is opposed by many dishonest who are in league. In any case, your friend Chisum cares for his herds and nothing else, and he makes the mistake of thinking himself untouchable by the corrupted."

The warm afternoon sun made each of us yawn in turn. Juan Patron's voice resumed, clear, grave and unhurried as the day.

"I understand your husband is a brave man in his way, and I hope he will be a successful one. In my own case, I am fortunate to occupy a space somewhat outside history. I may concern myself with the improvement of my garden, the education of daughters, and your own charming company. The conquistadores are dead. The men who followed them, with something more valuable than gold, namely a deed of appointment sealed at el Escorial have gone home fat and rich to build palaces for themselves in the north of Spain, where there is snow in the winter and you don't die from mosquito bites or dysentry. We are left behind with our yellow and red flag and our memories."

"Don't you think of going home - to Spain I mean."

Juan Patron smiled and leaned forward in his chair. "This is my home. I'm an American now, the same as you Frau McSween."

The afternoons conversing with Juan Patron were luxurious interludes. My life was becoming busier as I assumed more responsibility in the affairs of our commonwealth. Alexander's legal practice quickly occupied all his time The firm of McSween and Co. was successful from the off. Local people already knew Alexander to be an honest attorney, and Mr Chisum sent us lots of work. He declared that formalising the deeds to his holdings was overdue and he'd but been waiting for a man he could trust to do the job. The business of holding land, he said, was excessively complicated in comparison to ownership of a cow that only needed your mark burned into it to prove title. The newly arrived brought more business for us. Lincoln was growing every week. The wagons brought mostly decent people with long term settlement in mind.

We'd high hopes for our little community, confident it was becoming a sober and prosperous town we'd be proud to call home.

Chapter Three - 1876

For weeks, the territory had been anticipating the coming of the Englishman. The whispering started directly his agents visited us to make arrangements for his arrival. Supposedly he was a lord, or a baronet at least. He'd left his stately home and ancient family far behind for reasons none knew but many were prepared to invent (a disappointed love affair, a quarrel with an overbearing family, or found out in various kinds of criminal activity and fugitive being but three popular examples). He was coming, if not to seek his fortune (for it was generally agreed he stood in possession of substantial means already) then assuredly with the spirit of free enterprise as his spur, for his proxies ever wanted news of commercial opportunities. We invented fascinating histories for our supposed aristocrat. Nor did our small community want for theories regarding his immediate intentions. I was most amused to receive the intelligence, solemnly imparted, that the new Lord intended to build a stone castle, surrounded by a park to be stocked with imported livestock, from which he'd sally forth occasionally to hunt stag and wild pig. As to his prospects, the general consensus was that there were sufficient villains living amongst us (by which each speaker meant his neighbour, not himself) to guarantee that the newcomer would be swiftly relieved of his wealth, for riches are everywhere regarded as a great burden for a fool to bear, and thereafter he'd doubtless be sent packing.

For my own part, I cannot recall what I expected of the new arrival, though it is certain that I ought to have recognised the moment I laid eyes on John Tunstall that he was a man in the grip of general enthusiasm - after all my own husband was similarly afflicted. It was no surprise that so many stories had preceded our new neighbour's coming. With him it was evident from the most brief discourse that here was a man who'd listen to a hundred outlandish schemes and find some merit in each to recommend it to his attention. In a small settlement like ours, one man of true enthusiasms was danger enough, two together (for it was inevitable that such kindred spirits as Tunstall and my husband should either attract or repel) might be a terrible thing. Nevertheless, on that first day when his coach drew up in town and I, and every other citizen who was not required to be more usefully engaged, watched helpers begin to unload his trunk of belongings and accoutrements, my only reflection was that he appeared to be a man of charming and singular appearance.

    John Tunstall was not in fact a lord, nor did he pretend to be, though he had a lordly manner; by which I mean his behaviour displayed a bundle of qualities that are commonly associated, rightly or not, with the aristocratic caste. He was unfailingly polite and courteous in his dealings with all levels of our society, even Mexicans. As regards matters financial, he affected a nonchalant, you might even say negligent air, as though money were too vulgar a thing to be discussed. He'd the fine manners of a riverboat gambler, save that the gambler's assumes this character in an impersonation of naive liberality put on to draw the cupidity of his victim. Tunstall's openness was sincere. As to his naivety, although it was not so complete as some observers, licking their lips like hungry wolves as they observed him descend from the coach, might have hoped - well even so, I suppose I must allow he was naive in his way.

    I recall my impression of a large man, overdressed for the heat of the day in an outfit that was unfamiliar in style but expensive looking (it was a relief that he'd not affected the despised 'western-style' attire in which some of our more extravagant new arrivals had seen fit to comport themselves). When he descended and turned away from the coach, I saw he'd longish hair the colour of straw, a little sparse on top, the kind of pink complexion that the sun reddens but can not brown, and eyes that were an unusually pale blue. He was tall and he seemed filled-out - not fat but well-fed like a prosperous Eastern farmer; the opposite of Alexander in that regard. He looked around briefly, seemingly finding whatever he saw satisfactory to him, then he put on an English hat that seemed too small for his large head, gripped his valise under his arm, and proceeded toward his lodging, leaving the matter of his heavier luggage to those attending on him. I remained at a distance appropriate to those who have not been introduced and we exchanged not one word that first day.

It might be imagined that our townspeople, generally intolerant of pretension of any kind, would have discovered in Tunstall's somewhat superior air the grounds of resentment, but I do not remember this being the case. For myself, it could not be other than pleasing that our community had acquired one more individual, besides my husband and Juan Patron, who knew how to behave in society and with whom one might converse on subjects that were not utterly superfluous. I do not mean to infer by this that my other neighbours were intentionally rough or empty-headed. The Spanish ladies of the town displayed their native elegance, but we had little to say to one another. The few men I knew in town were prone to attempt gallantry, with unintentionally humorous results, or else confined their speech to trivialities under the misapprehension that the matters which actually consumed their daily attention, namely the business of cattle ranching and its associated trades, would be of no interest to a lawyer's wife. By contrast, John Tunstall was the kind of man who, when swept up by an idea or project, could not but assume that every other person of his acquaintance would find it equally fascinating. I conjecture that such persons may become wearisome in certain social milieus, but for a woman of some culture and intelligence ensconced in the county of Dona Ana, New Mexico, the flow of conversation that issued from Tunstall was as welcome as new water in a dry creek.

Of course, Mr Tunstall was quickly invited to dinner at our home. Beyond the social obligation of making welcome, McSween was now the thriving attorney of the territory and it would only be natural to hear the new man's intentions and offer some preliminary advice if it were needed. And in fact, Tunstall admitted that coming to the county, he'd had it in mind as a priority to make the acquaintance of McSween.

"My agents assure me that you are a man of business in whom one newly arrived in the territory might repose a degree of trust. To be plain sir, you have the reputation of being an honest man. I was also warned this description could not be applied with equal surety to some of our more entrepreneurially-minded neighbours."

"That last is certainly a fact sir, and shrewdly put," my husband admitted sadly.

Tunstall explained that he planned to buy a ranch. He already had a name for it - something Spanish in keeping with the territory - el Hacienda Feliz would be appropriate, he thought. He intended to ranch horses mainly, rather than cattle.

"The fact is, I know something of horses and very little about cows. Besides which, with due respect to all concerned, my enquiries about the place inform me that it is a capital offence here, punishable with summary judgement, to steal another man's horse, but to purloin one or more of a neighbour's cattle is regarded as a matter of but small moment. I'd rather not be the victim of thieves preying on my business."

McSween allowed that there was a regrettable tolerance of a degree of misappropriation of bovine livestock ongoing at the present time, even to the point that ranchers themselves shrugged and claimed that the thieving, or resolution of doubtful ownership as they preferred to put It, generally evened out. He advised Tunstall would likely hear such persons add that it was the movements of herds of the great men that swept their own poor stock away. 'And by this they mean Mr. Chisum, whom I believe notwithstanding to be an individual of full probity in that regard and in all others'. McSween further opined that the fictitious predations of Chisum were largely advanced as justification for the petty larcenies of his neighbours. The country would change in time, McSween claimed, though he agreed that a prudent newcomer might do well to husband but few steers and keep those near to his own place.

"The open range is not for all time," he declared. "We men of business know that property will make its claim as a precursor of a more civilised commonwealth."

"The country will be tamed in due course," Tunstall agreed. "For now it is the very fact of it's uncivilised condition that draws me here, or rather I should say the opportunities that such a state represents."

Now that the conversation had broadened to the general state of the country, Tunstall warmed to his theme and began to expound what might be termed his personal philosophy. He talked a great deal about what he called the 'material interest' by which he meant business, which he declared to be the primary engine of progress in our current century. HIs creed was mixed in with his own plans, which were somewhat lacking in organisation and coherence at that time, but it was clear for him that the material interest was the means by which humanity would be raised from its present condition into a new and happier age. What was needed was the scientific approach, plus capital. Without capital in the nature of both investment funding and the human capital of men of vision, nothing could be achieved. He believed himself a person not deficient in either vision or the funds needed to realise that vision. He'd an adventurous spirit, he told us, and besides the good fortune of being born wealthy carried with it responsibility. You couldn't leave money languishing in a vault, it needed employment. The only question was where it might be most usefully put to good purpose. It was clear that the proposed Feliz ranch would be little more than a preamble to his ambition.

As my husband was listening to this tangle of words his eyes began to shine with the same bright light as seemed to animate Tunstall's own. I'd seen the look before enough to know it. He'd dreams of his own to fuel our new friend's flights of imagination. There was so much that could be done and should be done, they agreed.

I stood to refill our coffee cups from the pot that was warming on the stove.

"It seems to me probable Mr. Tunstall," I ventured, "you don't as yet know so well as some of the men who've already made their subsistence in this locality what businesses might succeed here, or how they may be operated with most utility and hopes of success."

Tunstall admitted this was true, although he claimed he was a quick learner.

"The country is hard. We've seen that even a resolute man may fail in his venture," I continued. "Perhaps what creates progress is many men trying for their different dreams, like seed cast upon the earth. Some fall on the stony ground and some prosper. Alexander will tell you that we have some men of the latter kind here already, hardened by experience."

"They set their sights too low. They will take years to grow the country," McSween grumbled.

"They lack capital, which is essential, as Mr Tunstall has observed," I replied. "They can only invest in their business what little surplus they have been able to generate at the end of each year."

"Or else persuade Murphy to give them his backing," my husband muttered, " and then be beholden to King Murphy forever more."

"My point exactly, Alex," I concluded. "To realise the triumph of the material interest in Lincoln requires that its enterprises be furnished with capital, in the form of credit. In order to raise commerce in the county, it needs a bank. Might not a savings and loans business be your best first venture in Lincoln Mr. Tunstall?"

***

My old friend Mr Garrett has written of the Lincoln County Bank that it was set to be an institution that would bring prosperity to the territory, which was of a certainty the intention of its founders, for they were both men who viewed their own personal increase as incidental to the realisation of their grand dreams for the future.

The official opening of the bank was cause for local celebration, even among those locals who had only the vaguest notion of what purpose a bank might serve, but yet shared the conviction that any town pretending to amount to something beyond a collection of shacks should boast its own financial institution. Major Murphy attended and smiled throughout, though his comments betrayed that he viewed the proceedings and perhaps the venture as an amiable charade. Of late he was somewhat diminished, like a man suffering some ailment that won't give him peace, or one prematurely aged. Whatever it was made him peevish, but he'd set his irritability aside for the day of the grand opening at least. Later on, I'm sure he'd come to resent his reduced hold on the town due to the availability of credit extended to men who preferred to owe a fixed rate of interest to the bank rather than the uncertain cost of being in King Murphy's debt. It seemed to my own eyes that the Major loved influence even more than money, though perhaps the two were inseparable in his mind.

At our little ceremony, Wilson the justice made a fatuous speech and everyone cheered. In reality, the physical beginnings of the bank were less than impressive, its offices consisting of a set aside portion of the general store of McSween and Co. My husband and his new partner had occasion for some confidence however. A number of small ranchers who'd long had their desire set on making improvements to their respective estates had approached the bank to set terms for credit even before the official opening - a circumstance likely unknown to Major Murphy at that time which would not have improved his temper had he been aware of it.

Alexander and Tunstall had contracted to a partnership for the purposes of the bank only. The legal practice and store remained ours and Tunstall would have his Rio Feliz ranch and the other businesses he planned to develop - what Major Murphy called the deranged pipe dreams of the crazy Englishman (though I believe in fact opium was unknown to the county at that time). Tunstall himself claimed that he knew nothing of the day to day management of banking and he hadn't come to the New World to apprentice in the trade. He was happy to provide capital and leave my husband, with his reputation for honest dealing, his lawyer's eye and his knowledge of the local people, to administer loans and manage funding. In practice the bank took up an increasing part of my day, since Alexander's legal work frequently called him across the county as well as demanding so much of his own time.

I can state truly that to the best of my knowledge my husband had now ceased to resort to the strong liquors that provided occasional solace during his service under Murphy. His was a character that required a sense of purpose to avoid becoming becalmed and sinking into depression. In this period his energies were galvanised to positive effect, and though I saw even less of him in the home, I believe we were both happy. It mattered little that Mr McSween, the public speaker whose powers of oratory were famed across the county, was developing a habit of bringing his rhetorical forms and declamations into the domestic hearth, where to my ear they played sententious and hollow, as if the public man were overtaking the private. Men have their foibles, and taking themselves too seriously is not the least common of them.

At home, I could overlook the ripening fondness of my husband for hearing the sound of his own voice, while in our small community, this same quality was encouraged more than indulged. Rather as one will urge a caged bird to sing for entertainment, one who speaks well my be called upon to deliver a performance, though what he has to say may be considered as lightly as birdsong. The occasions for his perorations may be various, but it is clear that the orator succeeds to the extent that he moves his audience and arouses their emotions. Sadly, in the moment the natural speaker comes to apprehend that his gift has the power to recruit others to follow his direction, his character is apt to be changed by that perception, and thus onto the stock of the common man, the soul of the politician is grafted.

***

Over breakfast one morning, Alexander informed me that Emil Fritz was dead. His son Charlie had sent word he was coming West to administer the American part of the estate. Of course, Alexander had drafted an American will in regard to assets within the jurisdiction directly the unfortunate Scholland was legally banished from the marital home of his disenchanted spouse. I still felt sorry for Lieutenant Scholland, but not so much I'd want to see him again. The will provided the American assets should vest in Emil's sister.

Alexander gave me this information calmly, but his manner was unusually grim. Since we had not known Emil Fritz personally, grief was not a likely reason. McSween's demeanour puzzled me.

"There's some land and a few trivial investments," he told me. "The principal asset of value is a policy of insurance on the life of Emil that he took out for his sister's benefit in the sum of ten thousand dollars."

"I don't see a problem there," I replied. "If the policy is paid up, the ex-husband has no claim, and you can prove Emil is dead - his sister will be rich."

"Emil was partner with the Major remember. Murphy assumed the role of trusted friend. The policy is currently in the safe of his office, supposedly for safe-keeping."

"Then he must hand it over. The policy isn't his."

"I may be doing the Major a disservice Susan, but I have the impression he would have in mind to administer the policy himself and that maybe he'd come to think there'd be no need to pay a nickel to the grieving sister until he'd defrayed certain expenses, real or contrived, upon the estate. To a man like him, meekly handing over the paper is like turning ten thousand dollars from his own pocket over to Frau Scholland - or worse to me on her behalf."

I entertained no high opinion of the proprietor of Murphy and Co., but I did feel that my husband was overestimating the potential difficulties of the case. The next afternoon, Alexander secured a private interview at the offices of King Murphy. When he returned he was visibly agitated and red in the face.

"He heard out my description of the facts of the case," Alexander reported. "He didn't question anything. In fact he just sat behind that big desk, all hunched over but with his eyes fixed on me and a grin that got broader and broader. When I'd done he reached over and patted my hand that still lay on the blotter after making my point. He patted my hand as if we were old comrades or he was my wise uncle. His touch was cold as a dead man's Sue. Murphy's sick if you ask my opinion."

"What did he say to your petition?" I asked.

"'That is a most interesting tale', he told me, then he coughed some, 'but as we both know, I have the policy secure in my safe here'. I believe at that point he actually winked at me."

"He is a low person indeed."

"We talked some more in that vein, with him dropping broad hints and me declining to notice them. Finally he lost patience and came out with it direct. 'For God's sake man,' he told me, 'you're a man of business and an attorney registered at the State bar. Tell me how you propose we shall carve these monies up between us and let's discuss in earnest - then we can move to other business, of which we both have plenty requiring our attention'".

"My God, what did you say?"

Alexander was still so angry, even on giving his report, that he could not remember in detail what he had said to the Major. Likely it was the sort of response that makes the parties sworn enemies for life. I was shocked to hear of Murphy's larcenous proposal, but I was also dismayed that my husband had so far forgotten himself as to lose restraint, as was always likely to happen if his dignity or integrity were put in issue. I feared that such a reaction would only make the inevitable further negotiations in the case more difficult to resolve. Alexander claimed the worst of it was the old miser didn't really care about the money, even though it was a tidy sum. What he really wanted was to compel McSween to re-enter the circle of associates who did as King Murphy did, if only to demonstrate that for all his pretension, McSween was no better than the rest of them.

I calmed Alexander as best I could, though my own heart was pounding. He was expounding his intention to have Wilson issue a summons the very next day. I persuaded him finally that this would be futile, if only because the pliable Wilson would be issuing a summons for Murphy one hour after he issued for McSween. An intermediary was needed, but the lawyer should be the intermediary between contesting parties. What should you do when the lawyer was so incensed on his own account as to be incapable of mediation?

The next day there was talk circulating in the town that Murphy had been raging through the night, shouting that he'd see McSween in hell and break him in this world first before he was done, crying out that he'd been betrayed when betrayal was the one vice he could not stomach. Somehow the Englishman Tunstall became included in his threats and vitriol (giving credence to Tunstall's assertion that Murphy, who he'd barely met, hated him on principle with a passion that had more to do with the history of the Irish potato blight than any personal issue between them). I hoped that the rumours about Murphy's rage were exaggerated, and feared they were not. It was another two days before McSween and Co. formally wrote to Murphy and Co. requesting, in the interests of avoiding potentially costly litigation, the handover of the documents that were in custody of said Murphy on behalf of McSween's client the estate of Emil Fritz, deceased.

***

It was later that same week. I believe I was walking up main street, hurrying on some errand, when I heard a commotion and turned back to see what was occurring. We'd had fine weather and the street was more dusty than usual - a great cloud of it was thrown up, obscuring the view of whinnying horses and hurrying people. A gig or trap (local people sometimes referred to a buggy) had pulled up sharply before the surgery of the doctor(I should say medical practitioner, for our local surgeon did not pretend to have completed a formal course of professional training).

When I came upon the scene, they were trying to unload one of our citizens, a quiet rancher who'd lived among us for many years, from the carriage in which the rancher's neighbour had brought him. The poor man was clearly afflicted - calling out incoherently and screaming when he was moved. He could not be still and was twisting away in the spasms of his agony until someone called out they would need to restrain him.

At length the unfortunate was brought down and conveyed into the surgery. The doctor thanked the small crowd for their efforts and closed the door firmly against our further view of the scene. The man's cries continued to be audible in the street, but muffled thankfully. The crowd began to disperse. The neighbour who'd brought the victim into town, a rancher I knew tolerably well, remained on the street, as if unsure what to do next. He was still holding onto his neighbour's hat, gripping it with both hands as if it were the vessel in some religious service. We nodded to each other.

"His horse fell," he explained. "Came down on him and crushed him then kicked him in the guts as it rolled away dying. I'm guessing he's all ruptured up internally. Doctor can't do anything. He'll be dead by evening."

I was struck by the calm, flat tone in which he spoke. We could have been discussing the weather. The neighbour looked around him as if seeking something. Then he seemed struck by a thought that lifted a weight from his mind.

"Here," he said, offering me the hat which I took without thinking. "Nothing more to be done here. I'd best get back to the ranch. Work don't wait."

He raised his own headgear in a polite valediction and was quickly back on his cart and gathering up the reins. It was as though my acceptance of the hat transferred further obligation of neighbourliness to my hands.

Of course his prognosis was correct. There was nothing to be done and the injured rancher duly expired before nightfall, but something in the the detail of that small tragedy stayed with me. Reflecting on the curious incident, what shocked me was the degree of calm that the Samaritan displayed. If he'd rushed off, white-faced and heaving of stomach, after witnessing the horrifying injuries of the neighbour, even if he'd fled through embarrassment or awkwardness at not knowing what behaviour was expected of him, then it would have been more easy to understand his rapid flight. But it was more as if the incident was an unremarkable part of everyday life - that one need not even be surprised when the head of the family you'd been living next to for years was one moment trotting across his holding admiring the improvements he'd made and planning what he'd do in the coming season and the next roiled in mortal agony with his spirit confronting the void.

Alexander had warned me earlier that the people of our society viewed life and death with a fatalism he believed had something to do with the county being an old Spanish territory, but to see this for myself was a different thing. I knew the neighbour who gave me the hat was a good man, not overly callous or rough. He'd simply done what he could and from there he was accepting of what fate should decree, as with a cow that you gave up trying to pull out of a mudhole when it was clear the effort would be futile. There was always other work to be done.

Making my way back to the store, I must have been lost in reflections of this nature when I recognised a figure approaching me from the contrary directions somewhat late, else I might have found some pretext to alter my path. I should explain that the buildings of our main street were furnished with boardwalks that conjoined to form a continuous ambulatory passage. One could pass from north to south and back again without needing to step into the street below, which was a saving on footwear as well as an easing of the senses for those sensitive to the odours of the street. The boardwalk was shaded by the overhanging roofs of the various establishments that lined the street, but even in the shadows the bent form of Major Murphy, hobbling in my direction with the assistance of a walking cane, was unmistakeable.

I might still have turned on my heels and fled, or I could have suddenly crossed the street as if having made up my mind to head in a particular direction (I'd been frankly loitering up to that moment). If I did neither, our paths were sure to cross. I resolved that if the experience of confronting Murphy was likely to be unpleasant, the feeling I'd have if he could say he faced me down would be more disagreeable. I'd not give him the satisfaction. I walked on, willing that my footsteps should remain as unhurried and calm as before.

As we neared each other, I thought he was going to ignore me altogether. At the final moment before we crossed, with neither looking the other in the face, he muttered something that sounded like 'McSween'. the voice was almost a hiss, but he was not a well man. It might have been 'Good day Mrs. McSween' that he'd intended, so good manners dictated that I should stop and offer my own good day to his person.

Murphy was wasting away. When I looked into his face I could believe for the first time the rumours that his attorney Dolan was now running the business day to day - a worse man than King Murphy himself by all accounts.

"Your husband," he near spat at me. Then he seemed to lose strength and for a moment he leaned heavily on the wall of the building on which we were standing, a dependency not without risk, given the fragile construction of some buildings of the town.

"Major," I said to him. "You are unwell. Let me help you back to your place."

"Help me?" he rallied with visible exertion. "I'm past help. I'm eaten up from the inside. What's living to me now but a succession of pains, greater or lesser? And yet I want to keep on. What I tried to explain to your husband, but he couldn't understand, as a man with milk in his veins. It's a matter of will, Mrs. McSween. What separates us from the beasts. Not laws, but our undelegated right as free men to make our own destiny."

He began a fit of coughing but he was able to control it. I stood rooted to the spot, uncertain for the moment what held me there - whether it was fear of him, the horror of the situation, or the reflection that it was my duty to help the invalid if I could.

"When there's no more left of me than a sack of bones with breath in it, I'll still be more than a match for your McSween, the traitorous dog, for that reason if no other. My will is fixed and I'll not be thwarted by the likes of him - a man I made, who turns round and kicks me in the guts like an unruly pony. I mean to break your husband Mrs. McSween, and it's not for the money. What do I care for the money? It's that I can't abide his pious expression that tells me he thinks he's above the rest of us, or his betrayal, or his finangling with that oh-so Englishman Lord Tunstall. If he's a lord, I'm King, and a king gets first taste of whatever is in the kingdom that is sweet. Those who deny me my taste will feel my bite. What do you think of that Mrs. McSween?"

"I think and hope that if you were restored to a better condition in yourself, you'd understand that there is no reason for this feud between us. If my husband has done you injury, it's not with intention. His only care has been to do his duty by his client."

"His client," this time Murphy did actually spit, though he at least he took the trouble to limp a few steps and expectorate into the street. He turned his face away from me as if there was nothing more to be said on the subject. We said our good days politely enough considering what had been exchanged, and at that we parted.

***

John Tunstall was a moderately efficient marksman. He'd a brace of fine hand-tooled shotguns he'd purchased somewhere in Europe, which he used for hunting out game on his estate, 'for the pot' as he'd say. HIs dogs would scare up a rabbit or it might be a bird that would rise up flying ungainly and squarking while he tracked it's path calmly, and then bang, more times than not he'd bring it down cleanly dead. I imagine it's not an easy thing to bring down even a partridge that flies slow but crooked.

Juan Patron had advised me that the upper classes of England were uncommonly skilled in the matter of slaughtering small game. It had long been one of their principal occupations in the centuries since their passion for hunting had exterminated all the larger faunae of their island. Naturally I was aware that the shotgun was a weapon that my fellow New Mexicans regarded with disdain, offering neither the long range accuracy of the rifled barrel nor the handiness of the six shot revolving pistol.

I recall an occasion when I'd been too slow to avoid an invitation to share coffee with the odious Justice Wilson and one of his cronies (I tended to shun the judge's company, but of course living in what was effectively a village imposed certain social obligations that could not be ignored entirely). The Justice was an unlikely expert on matters of ordinance, since as far as I know he never fired a gun. Notwithstanding, he was able to expound at length on matters of calibre, preferred types of ammunition, the clear superiority of the Sharps rifle over other brands, and countless other aspects of the business that I was not even aware were controversial. Wilson held that possession of a shotgun was an affectation fit only for a man who had no eye to shoot. The soft slug from a .45 calibre revolver, exploding from a short barrel, would flatten as it flew, creating a spread that was not inferior to that of a twelve gauge cartridge at close quarters. It would make a hole near as big and with the extra weight of it you'd have as good a chance to kill or maim, plus you could carry the weapon on your hip, near at all times, and you'd still have four or five shots left if you failed at the first try.

"But why would you want to maim your quarry?" I'd naively asked. I'd understood that if you couldn't make a clean kill, a wounded animal was likely to flee and it might be more trouble than it was worth to pursue and finish off the unfortunate creature. Justice Wilson laughed and explained that one used the rifle for hunting creatures. The revolver was principally a means of resolving disputes between humans.

I'd not seen the matter in this light before, and it caused me to reconsider my opinion of those few of our neighbours who carried handguns. I was thinking about that conversation when I next visited Tunstall at the Feliz ranch, not only because I could hear the pop of a shotgun from the scrub behind the house as I sat in the parlour awaiting his return, but also for the reminder it offered of the manner in which the contention of man against man was apt to be resolved in our territory.

The purpose for my visit was partly social and partly business. Alexander had instructed me in the keeping of accounts and from time to time I would ride out with the ledgers to update our partner on the progress of the business of the bank. It was always refreshing to spend time with Tunstall. He seemed to breathe a different air to those of us in town who were affected by the daily skirmishes and petty affronts that punctuated the increasingly bitter rift between my husband and Murphy. Although John was conscious that Murphy had penned him in the opposing camp and hated the newcomer for being independently wealthy, and worse than that English, this intelligence did not seem to weigh heavily on Tunstall. In fact he was too busy with his own plans for future and ongoing projects to reciprocate Murphy's animosity, which must only have served to further inflame Murphy's hatred. For John Tunstall, falling out with people was simply a needless waste of time. Even so, I had come to seek his help regarding the ongoing dispute that seemed to me a fire that was fuelled by more than the administration of a disputed will; to the extent that we all risked becoming enveloped in its flame.

Tunstall had chosen a pleasant spot for his Rio Feliz ranch, which was aptly named. The horses were corralled near to the house, with space for their gallops, in contrast to the ranches I was accustomed to see where the livestock roamed at will. The stables were always clean and Tunstall maintained a domestic staff that was adequate to secure his comforts. He claimed that the pittance his Mexicans demanded in return for their work obliged him to employ so many of their number as he might find use for, so they should not be overburdened and at least some cash should begin to circulate in their economy. Despite what might be anticipated as the outcome of such a strategy, I saw no evidence that his Mexicans despised Tunstall - indeed they showed him more loyalty than others later would.

Tunstall apologised for keeping me waiting. His politeness and his negligence were ever at war with one another, as if he wished to be more attentive to others but his own consuming enthusiasms called his attentions away and made him absent minded. As a consequence, he was forever apologising. He said he regretted that matters urgently requiring his attention had held him back, though we both knew that he'd been unable to tear himself away from firing off his gun at some target. He suggested that, the day being so fine, we might take tea on the verandah.

We quickly closed the business of the ledgers, for Tunstall was no great enthusiast of numbers. I believe, had it not been my duty to ensure our partner was kept informed as to the progress of the bank, he'd scarcely ever have requested to peruse them on his own initiative. When this task was done, I told him I'd something on my mind for discussion. I said that in the town, the escalation of hostility between the rival houses of Murphy and McSween was becoming a dangerous matter. My own husband was too proud to seek a rapprochement with Murphy, and the latter would bow the knee to no man. It was hard to see where it might end, but clear neither side would profit from conflict. I explained where the matter stood in regard to the will and policy of life insurance. I said I regretted Tunstall himself was being mired in the contention, which had nothing to do with him.

"We can't always choose who will hate us," Tunstall laughed. If he was in any sense dismayed by the situation he concealed it well. "To the Major's Irish Patriot eyes, I'm double-damned first for being an Englishman and second for backing your husband. Our bank diminishes the influence that he wields in the county under the feudal system of patronage that keeps his ranchers subordinated. It's that he can't forgive. This squabble over a will is but the pretext - if it were not that it would be something else."

"It would be depressing to credit that," I suggested, "for then one must suppose there is no end to the dispute but for one side to be crushed."

Tunstall laughed again. "Murphy can't win. The feudal system is everywhere supplanted by the material interest directly it arises. Progress can be slowed but not halted. Science and commerce will deliver peace and prosperity even here."

I was doubtful. "They say that Murphy and Dolan are close with the politicians in Santa Fe. These men divert the flow of commerce for their personal benefit. Mr Chisum describes them as the parasitic growth on the flowering tree of our commonwealth. They must suck at every enterprise, cheating on contracts with the federal authority, dividing what was free land into packages of dubious legal tenure to sell at profit, till at length there'll be no more open range."

"Mrs McSween, do you believe it's conceivable you could have politics without corruption? Even the noble Gracians of the Roman republic were hacked to pieces by a hired mob when they tried to favour the many over the rich few. The progress I'm expounding derives its momentum from history, which is as inexorable as the tides that eventually wash away surplus promontories. Murphy and his venial associates will be swept away by the tide of progress like those useless headlands."

I hoped that he was right, but more than that I hoped we should all be alive to see it. I recalled that Juan Peron had not sounded so confident about the territory. When I asked the old patrician to explain for me the incident of the stricken rancher's hat - why a neighbour could be so unmoved by disaster affecting one who might be called his friend that he'd prefer to return to his cows than await the doctor's report - Juan had claimed there was a fatalism in the roots of the country that gripped the souls of all who remained there long enough.

"Many make the error of thinking this is a New World," he sighed. "In fact this territory is more ancient than the Europe that made the culture of our forebears, you and I. Europe has been fashioned by a few centuries of society, but what we find here is something that has been the same for maybe thousands of years."

Also there was death in the soil, he claimed, remarking that perhaps the Spanish had brought it with them from Castille. Juan Peron understood that times changed, but he saw little evidence for belief in progress, particularly he doubted the notion of progress when applied to the human spirit, which was everywhere twisted by gold - either the possession or desiring of it.

I did not attempt to relate the substance of this conversation to Tunstall. He was already fairly launched from his general disquisition on the nature of history onto a more specific review of his intended projects. He said that the agriculture of the region required a system of irrigation. Ours was a bountiful territory of mountains forests and rivers. It was a grave mistake to think only of the plains and desert. Did I know how few acres were currently under cultivation, or what miserable yields they produced? What was needed was a system, and first a dam to create a reservoir. The overlooked areas should be surveyed. Likely they'd also yield minerals, perhaps even precious metals though in his personal view every gold prospector who struck it rich set back progress in his own person and that of the ten or hundred others who'd follow in his wake with minds fixed only and always on digging up some of useless yellow nugget.

"Do you not approve of gold, John?"

"It makes pretty ornament, I suppose. More importantly, the bullion to which we attach a fixed and arbitrary value facilitates the exchange of goods that drives commerce -

without it we'd be reduced to barter. But the discovery of more merely reduces the value of the existing quantity. It does not increase the general wealth by one loaf of bread or a single cow, though it may enrich the finder. The conquistadores brought gold by the ton from Mexico back to Spain, and the result was to ruin their own country, for you'd eventually need a few ounces of gold to buy any small thing of utility, until it became useless to undertake honest work in Spain, since the wages you might earn would buy nothing. This is a phenomenon that the social scientists call inflation. Gold does not itself rust, but too much gold corrodes a civilisation."

No wonder our Spanish neighbours seemed so gloomy, I reflected. But then I had to return Tunstall's attention to the more pressing matters at hand. His own personal safety could be in issue, I warned him, if some of the dark mutterings and veiled threats had any substance.

"It's only talk," Tunstall assured me, "but if you're really worried, why don't you talk to Chisum?"

"Why him?"

"The real feud of Murphy and his Santa Fe Ring is with Chisum. Murphy is angered by McSween only because he sees his personal will being thwarted. Chisum is the big man of the territory and the Ring judges that he's not being bled for their enrichment as he should be. They can scarcely dent his self-sufficiency, only by stealing a few cattle and setting the small man up against him. They mean to grab lands for no consideration and sell it to others at a high price. Chisum and his herds, and a few others like him, stand in their way. The work that your husband does for Chisum, marking out parcels of land and regularising legal title, is more dangerous for him than administering an estate for the sister of Emil Fritz. Your husband is known to be an honest man, who'd be universally popular in the town. The small whisperings against him propose his guilt by association, as the Murphy faction give the ranchers to understand that McSween is the creature of Chisum who they ought to regard as their enemy."

I had not thought of things in that way before, but my conversation with Tunstall brought no improvement in my peace of mind. Before, I had imagined that our domestic happiness was at risk through a stupid quarrel that had potential to escalate fatally - and that was bad enough. Now it seemed to me that our true situation was more akin to being adrift in a small boat on a squally sea at the mercy of the waves that represented forces we could not see which tossed us one way and then another regardless of how we pretended to steer. Perhaps I would talk with John Chisum, but first I needed to make my husband alert to the risks of our little vessel foundering entirely on unseen rocks.

My anxiety must have communicated itself to him, for Tunstall moved to console me. "There, Mrs. McSween," he offered, "it is ever the lot of women to worry over their men. I'm sure Alexander knows what he's doing. We'll have a stroll on the property presently. That will serve to calm your nerves. My but this country is pretty - the waving grasses, the cottonwood trees, the view that seems to go on forever. I like to hear the way Chisum describes politicians. You see there's something in this landscape that urges even a hard-headed man like him to put some poetry in his expression. Out here you'll see things more long and broad than the narrow perspective of the town."

"You're a romantic materialist Mr Tunstall," I charged him. "Women worry about men only because the behaviour of men leaves them no option. Men don't require the inspiration of a fine prospect in view to prefer seeing their dreams over what's in front of their faces - this is the blessing and the curse of their nature, but women may not indulge themselves. I'll allow the cottonwood tree has a pretty appearance, but the wood is like paper and it's useless for all practical purposes. As for my husband knowing what he is about, I've met few individuals of either sex who truly knew what they were doing until they'd done it, at which moment the damage is generally already done."

Tunstall laughed loud at my outburst as if I'd told him a particularly good joke. He said I'd found him out entirely and claimed he felt pity for Murphy and any other adversary ranged against one such as myself. He had a delicate way with words and I fancy he viewed the world more clearly than he let on, though I'm not sure how far he truly saw. Despite his protestations about being ruled by science, he struck me as one of those who, when intelligence directed him to a line of thought that deviated from his conviction of how the world should be, preferred to remain in a state of ignorance rather than grant his perspicacity freedom to override his happiness.

▲▲▲

Naturally, McSween wouldn't give his attention to any word of compromise that I suggested. My husband could be as obdurate as Murphy in his different way. Worse, he'd now conceived he had a duty over and above his obligation to do the best for his client (my husband was adept at discovering duties that compelled him in directions which seemed inevitably to coincide with his prior emotional leanings - he would have made a fine preacher). He must speak, he declared, for that section of our community which was prepared to stand up to the bullying tyrant. The people were depending on him, he reckoned. A mule is more pliable than a speechmaker who is so much applauded that his powers of oratory persuade him he invariably speaks the truth.

"I wrote to the Governor again," he told me. "The town administration is a scandal. Wilson and Murphy don't keep any books of account whatsoever. Can you even imagine a municipality where there's no record of what's collected or paid out?'

In fact he'd pointed out this fact to me previously, and while I was first shocked at the revelation, I'd had time to think about it now. "Murphy doesn't hold any public office," I pointed out, "so it's difficult to see what the Governor could say, even if you could get him interested." In any case, I added, so far as incomings were concerned, the townspeople didn't pay any tax. If expenditure was unavoidable on repairs or improvements to the few common amenities, Murphy generally disbursed the funds from his own purse.

"He pays with what he's already stolen," McSween raged. "Public crumbs compared to the private banquet he keeps for himself."

"That may be so, but think about it from his side for a moment. I doubt that King Louis of France bothered himself with accounts. He thought that the country was his and he was the country. Don't you feel Murphy sees things the same way? He's the King, but he can be benevolent, so long as everyone accepts his rule. Then we come along and upset the balance."

"The man is a criminal."

"Undoubtedly, but he has his supporters. Not all of them are men he's bought and paid for."

But I found not one chink in my husband's armour that might open to persuade him Lawrence Murphy was a man with human motivations rather than the devil incarnate. With another kind of adverary you might reason, seek common ground, reach grudging understanding - but confronted by the devil you must cast aside him and all his works.

Alexander admitted he was making no progress in obtaining the original policy, which remained in Murphy's safe. Justice Wilson had allowed his application for an order that it be delivered up. A few hours later he'd granted interim relief on the application of Dolan, on behalf of Murphy that McSween be enjoined from all meddling with the estate of the ex-partner of Murphy and Co. Wilson was spineless - he'd grant any application and none would be enforced. Alexander said that now he'd secured a grant of probate for Fritz's will, he'd collected affidavits from independent sources attesting the existence of the policy and its broad terms. He intended to visit the offices of the insurance company that issued the policy. They would certainly have a secure copy of their own policy and the insurer was legally bound to make payment to him as executor of the estate. All this sounded promising, except that Alexander could expect to be gone for at least two weeks. I assured him that I was more than capable of managing our businesses in the interim, though we agreed a pretext was needed for his absence. The last thing I wanted while Alex was away would be for our oppressor to have notice that his own stratagems were on the brink of failure. Who could say to what desperate measures he might resort were he in possession of that information?

***

Over the years, Mr Chisum became a dear companion and I would visit the Bosque Grande ranch regularly. Chisum held many acres but he belonged to the country as much as it to him - his placid amiability was more in keeping with our landscape than the hot temper of my husband or the obscure enthusiasms of Mr. Tunstall. In this respect the cattle baron was like my friend Juan Patron, although there was no sense of weary resignation emanating from John Chisum. With Juan, it was as though the soil of the country had worked under his immaculately manicured fingernails and into his bones until fatalism was infused to the marrow. In Chisum's own person defeat was a concept unknown. He seemed well fed and satisfied with the comforts he'd earned, but still he radiated a sensation of power if only it might be roused - like some heavy old lion that prefers to doze in the sun, but if you should cause it to stir, watch for the claws. It was rumoured he'd a wife somewhere east, but preferred to remain at Bosque Grande where the lion could rest easy. I believe he had a woman at the ranch who was Mexican, or perhaps Indian. In any case, the arrangement was very discreet and none of my business.

Usually I'd visit my friend at the ranch, for its affairs kept him always busy, but I am thinking now of an occasion when the mountain came to Mohammed. In fact it would have been difficult for me to leave town just then, with the bank and store to run as well as making Alexander's excuses to those of his clients who'd not been advised of his sudden absence. Perhaps visiting our place in person was Chisum's way of advising the town that we were under his protection and should not be trifled with. Whatever the motivation, it eased my mind that he'd finally responded to my standing invite and I was very pleased to see him, even if it be only a brief social call.

I will own I was fascinated to observe the great man away from that ranch that I had almost come to think of as his castle and throne room. When we are accustomed always to encounter another in a particular environment, it is instructive to meet them elsewhere - our intuitions of what we believe to be their nature are tested. I had guessed that the potent (nay imperial) presence which Chisum carried about him in his own halls might be diminished in an more neutral location. This moment confirmed instead that the force of his personality was lodged within his ambulatory person.

On arrival at our place, Chisum despatched his attendants on errands that were unspecified to myself and came into the house alone. I took a cloth and lifted the coffee pot off the stove. Chisum sat at the kitchen table, a solid rough slab of furniture on which he placed his hat. After our initial greetings, for the moment he said nothing.

"It's pleasant," he commented finally. "Not a bad place you have."

"The bank office is across the hall for now, so we're a little cramped."

"The bank is a brave and useful enterprise," Chisum told me, "and likely to be an engine of future prosperity for the town. Do you take precautions against robbers?" He sipped his coffee, which was hot and bitter as required.

"We have a safe," I told him. "Should we do more?"

"A guard might be a tolerable worthwhile investment if you can find the right man," Chisum suggested, "during the hours you're open for business at least."

"I have the feeling that if the security of our funds were invested in the person of a custodian, our more unruly elements would take measure of that particular man to assess whether they felt they might get past him. One man like themselves, set against them you might say, could be viewed as presenting a challenge, and I've noted among us a predilection for taking up any challenge that is issued. Finally the thought occurred to me, it may be the power of what they can't see, the shapeless authority of an institution, would provide a more effective deterrent than a guard with a rifle."

Chisum laughed. "You could be right at that. You've certainly understood the natures of our citizens. All the same, a resolute character with a firearm handy should be useful to have around in case psychology fails."

"But then if there's a robbery, there'll be shooting as well. In any case I'm sure we may rely on Sheriff Brady to protect the peace without usurping the function law enforcement to our private venture."

"Don't talk to me of Brady," Chisum replied sternly. He did not elaborate the thought and I did not press.

My friend was comfortable with silence, but he must have sensed my own agitation growing with the passing moments as I tried in vain to discover a way to open the subject. that was on my mind

"Something's gnawing at you Susan. Best come right out and say it."

I told him everything - not just the facts of the Fritz case, but my own hopes and fears, even my doubts regarding my husband's character - that he was an honest man who might bring us honestly to ruin. I repeated Mr. Tunstall's observation that our petty quarrels were bound up in the greater issue between Murphy and Chisum himself. My words must have come out confused, spilling over where the bucket was most full, rather than following the dictates of logic or coherent narrative. When I'd finished, I felt more ashamed than relieved. Chisum heard it all with barely a movement. If I looked up, his eyes were ready to meet mine, more with an expression of waiting patiently to hear me out than to offer challenge or contradiction. His hat was on the table before him and his arms rested on the table top, the tips of his calloused fingers just barely meeting as if he were about to begin an act of prayer.

He could hear the crack in my voice, but he didn't rise from the table and offer the comfort of a human touch (which I should have found intolerable at that moment) instead he listened to my tale calmly and then sat for a minute after as if weighing the words seriously.

"Tunstall's right in one way," he began finally. "If there's to be an altercation, it will be about more than the proceeds of poor Fritz's assurance plan, though in that respect the rapaciousness of the Major should not be underestimated. Ten thousand dollars is still a lot of money. I'm interested to know what you'd have me do about this state of affairs."

"Mr Chisum, you are a power in this territory and I believe an honest man. You must know that dishonest men intend you ill. The Murphy faction stirs up the ranchers against you. Your assets are plundered. Your reach extends beyond these small men that plot against your estate. You may call allies to your side in a struggle - the federal government for example. You must know that if you do not break the power of these men, they will surely try to break yours."

Chisum sometimes had a certain smile that was equal parts warming and infuriating by its complacency. He showed me that smile now.

"Perhaps you mistake me Susan, you'd have me confront these men in their natural habitat. If I should take against the Santa Fe men and their allies in the field of politics, at which I'm thankful to proclaim myself a novice, I'm like to end as a fish flopping about in a dried up creek. Let me tell you what you are up against, if my intelligence is not faulty.

"First, Murphy himself. He's a schemer and a character without scruple. Of his military career I know nothing, but having achieved his discharge he took to commerce directly and his trading methods were such that he was expelled from Fort Stanton shortly afterwards, though the resourceful villain managed to secure and keep a profitable government contract for the supply of necessities to the reservation Indians, contributing to the ongoing misery of the Apache and Commanche peoples stationed hereabouts, due to his custom of skimming value from the government remittances for his own account. This circumstance alone should alert you he has friends in high places, for it's sure the bounty of his fraud is shared out among those who procured that such a profitable contract be issued to a notorious rogue such as neighbour Murphy.

"He maintains his relations with the quartermasters of Fort Stanton, who must feed many a hungry cavalryman and have little curiosity as to where the quantities of beef delivered may originate. I know very well Murphy has long kept close friendship with every brand blotcher, rustler and running iron freehand artist in the county. Well, if a man steals my beef to feed himself and his family, I'll hardly notice - the country is still quite empty thanks be to god. Even the men that take my brand and mangle it to resemble their own to incorporate the occasional wayward steer in their own herds would hardly matter, but that Murphy gives them an outlet, and so their industry multiplies. He has the contract to supply the army. When my steers vanish, there's little hope they'll be located, for within a few days they'll be steaks on the mess tables at Stanton. The result is you might say I'm suffering an epidemic of vanishing."

I felt excited and indignant at the same time.

"But this is exactly what I am trying to tell you Mr. Chisum. You must strike at these people, with resolution, for they certainly mean you ill."

"Hold on a moment," Chisum occupied himself momentarily with rustling among the contents of his pockets. I suppose he was unconsciously rummaging for his tobacco (as the natural accompaniment to an engaging discussion) before remembering at whose table he was sitting, for he gave up the activity suddenly. When he spoke again, there was some anger in his tone.

"First, I was telling you about Murphy, and what it boils down to is you must remember that for all his pride, Murphy is a coyote."

I suppose I looked quizzical at this.

"On the plains ma'am, we suffer depredations of wolves and coyotes, and perhaps the former take more than the latter, though it is the coyote that is most despised. The difference is, your grey wolf is a bold creature. He'll come at you if he must and he'll keep fighting even when he knows the game is up. The coyote by contrast is a coward that slinks after easy prey. He'll steal what the wolves have killed for preference, to save on risk and effort. With the coyote, there's no question of a fair fight, though he can be just as ferocious. He'll run then sneak back upon you when you're least prepared. Do you take my drift?"

"You think it beneath your dignity to take up arms against such a creature?"

"The fight is not fair ma'am. To put matters bluntly, it would be wrong of me to tell you that Murphy has the civic authority of the territory in his pocket. More accurate to say that he and our supposed rulers are engaged on a joint enterprise for their mutual benefit. For example, I am aware that your husband has written on several occasions to Governor Axtell denouncing the abuses of Murphy."

"How could you possibly know that? The correspondence was confidential."

"It doesn't matter that I know, but Murphy knows it too. You should advise your husband to send no more epistles in that direction. All he will gain is the unrelenting emnity of men who are advised that he has discovered their secrets, and perhaps Axtell is not the most senior of them."

"Alexander has written to the Federal Government too."

"Good luck with that. Maybe an adviser will enlighten President Hayes as to the geographic location of New Mexico by and by."

"Mr. Chisum, you talk as if our situation were hopeless. What do you mean to do?"

A faraway expression came over my friend's battered face. "Sometimes when you're on the plains, on the Long Trail I mean, driving the herd north, a storm will come and it may be so bad you can't tell the earth from the sky, let alone find the path. There's only one thing you can do that is not completely foolish - settle the cattle as best you can and wait it out. Storms don't last forever. That's what I should recommend in your own present circumstance, and as regards politics and graft, it's what I shall do too. I'm a simple man. I know cattle. If I attempt to wrestle down these coyote on their own ground I fear they'll make short work of me. You must realise Murphy is dying - the cancer will take him in months, maybe less. Dolan will take over - worse than his boss, but he lacks some quality of inspiration that Murphy possesses - for better or ill I can't say. With Dolan you may reach an accommodation, for his only interest is money.

"These men cannot hurt me grievously as they are, and if Murphy's ambition betrays him to the purchase of greater influence, he'll overreach and bankrupt himself and his enterprise before my interest is harmed. I know the extent of his treasure you see, better than he does himself. Imagine a steer basking in the sun of summer. The gnats bother it by buzzing in. The creature wafts its tail, seeking relief. The gnats are momentarily deterred - perhaps one or two of them perish - but the steer has enough sense to know that chasing after the gnats individually is folly. The great beast must endure the irritations of the season, knowing in fall the insects will perish."

I found his complacency painful. "Do you then mean to do nothing?" I demanded.

"Along the lines of what your husband would have me do? Petition Washington, file a suit for the dismissal of the governor, institute civil proceedings of misfeasance in the state courts, demand elections? Regarding those avenues, yes I'm going to do nothing. Regarding the men I can't see, I'm going to do nothing. But by god if I come across one of the creatures of those faceless men engaged in the theft of my livestock, that man will perish by lead shot or the rope. You may have heard of the difficulties we experienced a few years back - a progression of skirmishes that it pleases some extravagant people to refer to as the Pecos War?"

"I've heard of it of course."

"I won't pretend to you that everything was done under due legal process. Out here the trial by combat persists, and will remain the court of last resort until the day when something resembling an even-handed rule of law is introduced. That day will come, Susan, and your husband is working to make it come, but let him not overreach too soon and come to failure. Murphy is not the worst we could face. Meanwhile we must defend what Mr. Tunstall calls our material interest with stout hearts and severe judgement. In the end, the Pecos conflict was resolved by force of arms. I've set new men on my payroll whom I believe would be equal to the test if martial conditions should arise once more. I can spare some of them for your personal protection."

"You mean hired gunmen - vigilantes?"

"I prefer to call them regulators, for I want no more from them than they should compel what the statutes and regulations would require of our citizens if the writ of true law were enforced with an even hand in Dona Ana county."

"Alexander would never agree. Besides I cannot but imagine we should remain safe in town even if matters worsen."

"Then what about your friend Mr. Tunstall? His position is isolated and your enemy may strike against him to get at you."

"But why would anyone want to harm Mr. Tunstall, who has nothing to do with any of this? What could they hope to achieve?"

"Ma'am, they say some people will tear the wings off flies, even though you and I can not envisage what profit might be gained from such cruelty. Speak to Mr. Tunstall, Susan. Some of my people will be available to answer the call if you or he should need to make it."

Chapter Four -1877

When I received a wire from McSween advising me that the Fritz policy seemed without value, my Christian response should have been a feeling of sympathy for the disappointed Frau Scholland. I own that in fact my heart leapt on reading this intelligence, not from sorrow but only joy. Now my husband might honestly say he'd done his duty while the offending scrap of paper could remain forever gathering dust in Murphy's safe. There was nothing left to fight over.

News conveyed via the telegraph system is like the tweeting of a bird - the author has limited characters available and the message risks being so condensed as to be unintelligible. Nonetheless, I quickly understood that having travelled east, Alexander duly made himself known at the offices of the life assurance firm which he attended to present his client's case. There was little that could be argued against the force of evidence he had amassed in support of Frau Scholland's entitlement to the ten thousand dollar proceeds of her brother's policy.

Having delivered the claim, Alexander took his leave, no doubt with the satisfaction of knowing his job well done, and having arranged to return in a few day's time when the office should have made arrangements for the remittance of monies due. However, when he presented himself at the appointed hour of the day in question, he was dismayed to find the offices locked and a hastily penned sign on the door advising that the firm had ceased to trade.

My immediate response to the telegraph was to demand how soon I might expect his return. He wired that he intended to stay a few days more in order to discover whether anything might be retrieved from the situation. It would have pleased me to take the correspondence straight from the telegraph office to the establishment of Murphy and lay it on his desk for perusal. Of course that was not to be considered. Even so, I returned to the store with much lighter step than I had set out.

I'd gotten into the habit of avoiding the eyes of certain of our townspeople. There was an undercurrent - of feeling, of rumour, call it what you will - in the settlement that was ugly. People were divided as to whether they were for the Murphy or McSween faction. I had no apprehension that either of the rival camps would actually attempt anything against the other - it seems inherent in human nature to take sides, even or especially in regard to a contending in which one has no direct interest. For most of my neighbours, the struggle between the great man and the lawyer meant nothing more than a sporting contest - say an imminent boxing match where the presumed characters of the fighters were sufficiently contrasted to arouse heightened interest in the outcome. It's generally supposed that a prurient interest in the lives of others is due to idleness on the part of the observer. I can say that the people of out town were seldom idle - life made demands of them and most were industrious by nature. It was more that the monotony of their existence offered little day to day variation of their emotional state, to the point that they suffered a weakness for the actual or supposed dramatic narrative of surrogate heroes.

I had few illusions about the families I lived among. Murphy might have done well to offer the citizens a theatre for their amusement, in the manner of the old Roman emperors who are said to have purchased quiescence with bread and circuses. They considered themselves down-to-earth, no-nonsense folk, with practical concerns, but such people require exercise for their emotions like everybody else. Generations of my German Baptist family had imagined characters for themselves every bit as prosaic as the self-images of my current neighbours, and yet under the surface they could not live without their myths and legends - the sacred forest, the old gods and the mysteries of their race.

In a way, I was lucky. My family had lived in America for almost a century and a half, but the roots of our ancestry were preserved even in one like me who had revolted against her heritage by my early marriage and flight. I believed I knew who I was. My neighbours originated from every part of Europe and beyond, but the only way you'd know would be from their names and the slight inflections of their speech. With a few exceptions like Juan Patron and Murphy himself (whose patriotism for the old country of Ireland had surely increased with every step that carried him further from Dublin) the people seemed rootless. If they even knew from where their forbears had travelled to the New World, it meant but little to them. The result was that for the most part they but vaguely sensed a lack within themselves that was felt more keenly for being inexplicable. My neighbours did not yet know who they were. They had not carried with them any ongoing shared story, locked within so deep that it need not be spoken aloud to be understood. Their lives were starved of myth since the flame of the old world had flickered out within them. That hunger could only be sated by the creation of a new mythology. You might say they were in the process of constructing one as they went about their daily business.

I think it was for this reason that narrative was so avidly consumed at our frontier. Any notable event was transmitted by a network that depended on no telegraph but was not markedly slower in transmission, with the distinction that every tale would mutate in the telling, depending on where each storyteller found the most interest, so that we'd know seven different versions of the same incident within a month of its occurrence. It was not customary for our frontier poets to draw an overt moral conclusion to conclude their sagas - that would be regarded as overly sententious among such practical and grounded folk as we believed ourselves to be. Rather, the storyteller would be inclined to sink back in his chair, possibly showing his open palms with a mute expression as if to say 'Well, over to you. What do you make of that?'. The stories themselves were simple enough, but in the way they were told - in what was added or stressed, what was essential and what soon forgotten - one might gradually uncover the unspoken history of hearts seldom laid bare - hopes and fears, past regrettings and tentative speculations about what kind of men and women we actually were or might hope to become.

Alexander could persuade himself those citizens moved by his oratory cared in the same way as he did for justice, for the coming of civilisation, for the ending of corruption in our state. I could see that he was mistaken. It was true that one of his speeches would arouse strong feeling in the crowd of his listeners who would afterward agree that a powerful voice had been heard speaking truths that needed to be declared. Afterwards that same crowd would disperse and make its way to homes where each constituent part slept soundly in its own bed with a generally improved sense of well-being, not detained from slumber for one moment by any

reflection on the meaning of the orator's words. Alexander imagined himself at the head of a crusade that did not exist outside of his imagination. His auditors enjoyed his edifying speeches in the same way as they found satisfaction in a good dinner. No less than our friend Tunstall, my husband was in the grip of enthusiasm, and vulnerable as any man with his brain so inflamed to so far mistake his audience as to believe his own enthusiasm generally shared. All of this made Alexander a dangerous man, to himself and others.

  To conclude, this was the reason why I had begun to avoid people's eyes - not that I was afraid of any person in town, but I no longer cared to observe the expressions which conveyed only that a passerby was for McSween or for Murphy. I'd come to view the whole sorry dispute as no more than an entertainment for the town, notwithstanding the risk of it proving disastrous for the parties themselves

  Mr. Chisum had spoken to me about the Pecos War of recent memory. From Juan Patron I had the bare facts of what occurred. From others I obtained versions of the legend and heavily embroidered anecdotage of the time. It was not a war. It was a quarrel between ranchers as to which cattle rightly bore what mark that was settled with some firearms and bloodshed, naturally greatly exaggerated after the event. When the violence was exhausted, the parties resumed their lives with the machinery of law making but little effort to allocate responsibility for the homicides and associated criminality that had occurred. The lesson I took from this history, was that beneath the apparently still waters of our community, there was a capacity for anarchy and mayhem lying deep but waiting its chance to rise bubbling over the surface like a devouring Kraken. It was easy to imagine that monster possessing our spirits for a time, leaving no trace of itself after but only devastation in its wake.

As with the revelation of the purpose of hand-guns, the information I had regarding deeds in which some of my apparently civilised neighbours were reputed to be implicated caused me to re-evaluate my view of the community as a whole. Juan Patron, who was on the whole prone to an overly poetic mode of expression, claimed that there was blood soaked into the soil of our territory that made the air heavy in a way the living could feel. The weight of it was death. According to him, I might sense that same heavy atmosphere in the place of the corrida where the sticky blood of so many bullfights had drained into the sand so that even sound moved through the air more slowly there. He said that every now and then, the ancient heart of the land would begin to pump, compelling its human tenants to move to its inexorable beat, held in the seductive grip of death that required of them its tribute. I expected Mr. Chisum to smile when I related Juan's florid description. Instead he just shook his head.

"These Spanish certainly have a way with words, but he may have a point."

***

Alexander's return was delayed longer than I had hoped. The situation in town was not much improved, given that our persecutors remained unaware that the cause or pretext for dispute had come to term unviable. In fact, things were worse than before he left. Half-spoken insults or threats and occasionally actual hissing accompanied my perambulations in town, and of course these were retained in my mind more vividly than comments from the other half of the community that wished to shake my hand or inform me what a fine man my husband was. Bosque Grande was a distant refuge.

Increasingly, I sought respite at Tunstall's Feliz ranch when I was not detained by business, even though I was relatively safe (in a physical sense) in town and the Feliz was an isolated location. Often I rode out of town more slowly than I needed to, only to make the point to myself that I refused to be intimidated by all the foolishness. For the same reason I prohibited myself from turning to look the way I had come once I had quit the town limits - common prudence suggested it might be sensible to check I was not followed, but I was anxious that if I should turn once, I might never be done with looking back.

A welcome invariably awaited me at Feliz. Tunstall was the same as always - head filled with his diverse plans, seeming unconscious of any threat to his person or his prosperity. Having discovered what I could of the ways of the country in condition of feud, I had prevailed upon my friend to accept Mr. Chisum's offer for his protection, though I am sure that Tunstall went along with this in a spirit of humouring me rather than for any concern on his own account. Chisum sent a number of men - his regulators. Given the size of the deputation, I believe they may have been instructed to make the ranch a base for their operations on behalf of the Chisum enterprise as much as to protect the person of Tunstall. In hindsight I fear that I may have exposed Tunstall to further peril, rather than helping him as I intended, in that he would now be perceived as aligned squarely with the interests of Chisum's Jinglebob brand. Even at the time, when I first saw the condition of the ruffians who landed at the Feliz as its supposed guardians, I was not sure that I had done well.

None of the party made a singular impression upon me, though I came to know them better later. Taken as a group, it may suffice to say that the look of a cut-throat will not differ markedly between continents or according to the weapon of assassination he prefers. There were others, but the names I easily call to mind were one Sturlock, whom the others called 'Doc', Charlie Bowdre (a local boy from a respectable family) and William Bonney. It was the latter that I particularly noticed first, because he seemed not much more than a thin, half-grown boy. He drew attention by his boisterous good humour, always laughing at some childish thing and making fun of himself and the others in an innocent way. I assumed the men kept him around as a mascot or court jester and of course they all referred to him as 'Kid'.

The leader of the party, Dick Brewer was a stolid, dependable seeming man of the type that I thought would commend itself to Chisum. He seemed somewhat out of place among his fellows - he was older, slower in his movement. A man you'd want for steadiness rather than initiative or quick wits. Whether the others would follow his lead if it came to a crisis would be a difficult one to call.

Tunstall didn't mind the boys cavorting in his yard, boasting to each other and trying tricks with their horses, so long as it was understood they were not to fire off pistols that would scare up his own beasts. He said they were just boys - some had the reputation of being dangerous men, but his opinion was that in New Mexico, where facts were scarce and stories were many, dangerous men made their reputations with their mouths more than their deeds. Tunstall was more interested to tell me of his impatience regarding the return of McSween, whose services he required to assist with an extensive survey that would be a vital precursor to transforming the land. He enquired as to the workings of the bank and heard my report like a dutiful schoolboy. He told me there'd been no suspicious movements of strangers in the environs of his property so far as he was aware.

In my memory of that time, it's always mid-afternoon at the Feliz ranch, with the sun making the cottonwoods bright and the horizon stretching away forever. The smell of good horses, freshly brushed and combed - their quiet whinnying close, and further off the conversation of clear voices and occasional soft laughter. I should include the clinking of a tea service (there was always tea). It wasn't long before Tunstall had the boys mark out a croquet lawn.

He produced a set of mallets and hoops he'd brought from England and proceeded to teach them the game. Some of them became tolerably skilled at it, notwithstanding Tunstall's lament that the condition of what served for a lawn made a lottery of their aim. It made for an idyllic scene. Just sometimes you'd catch them arguing over a point of the game and have an impression that with men like these it wouldn't take much before even a trivial argument over a silly pastime might escalate with fatal consequences.

One day I overheard young Billy giving his opinion on his employer. At some point there must have been a dispute over wages, for the boy had conceived the notion that he'd been cheated (he seemed barely strong enough for useful work and I reflected that any remuneration he was paid would have been akin to charitable donation). In any case, Billy swore that Chisum was on the list of men he'd one day put in their graves by way of revenge. The notion of that young, underfed boy going against Mr. Chisum was somewhat pathetic, but I was sufficiently alarmed to mention the conversation to Tunstall, who'd been busy in the stables.

Tunstall laughed my concern away and advised me that his boys (as they'd quickly become in his mind) spoke of killing men for trifles in exactly the same way that unruly infants planned violent revenge in the playground. It wasn't pleasant to the ear, but nothing would come of it. He said that when the present uncertainties were resolved, he intended to find gainful employment for such of the boys as could be persuaded to accept it, and he entertained hopes that some could be brought to learn a trade and so become useful citizens. As ever, his reflections were focussed on some point just beyond that far off horizon of the present time.

Back in town one day I found myself in the company of the odious Wilson. Invariably he could be found in the same establishment, sipping coffee with one or other of his rancher friends and no doubt exchanging gossip, or local news as men prefer to call it when they talk between themselves. I never understood how Wilson got to be so fat when outside of his office all he did was drink coffee all day. I never observed him to eat, though I suppose he must have feasted regally in private. If he caught sight of me passing by, he would rush out to greet me, insisting that I should join his table briefly and showering me with what I suppose in his mind passed for gallantry. He was invariably polite and subtle in his insinuating, for example by passing on trifling revelations of doings in the Murphy camp, that he was on my side. I think he imagined he was inviting me into his confidence.

The advantage of Wilson's company over the society of my neighbours, was that I could look into his face without concern, knowing that I'd catch an open expression, solicitous of my welfare and with the best interests of the community at heart. Knowing also that he'd present exactly the same face to Dolan or such others of the Murphy clan as crossed his path, prior to disclosing any secrets I might confide to him, removed the tension of suspicion from our dealings. There was no question of my being able to trust Mr. Wilson, howsoever trifling might be the issue in concern.

By coincidence, the ongoing symposium between Wilson and his acquaintance that day was touching on the nature and career of the gunfighter (considered as an ideal or generic figure) although it was really no coincidence, since Wilson, the least martial character I knew, set himself up as an authority on matters pertaining to the Old West, as it was already known even in those early times. The reputed doings of lawless men were the justice's chief entertainment. I ordered a lemon tea and resigned myself to bearing so much of the tedious discourse as polite society dictated, though in fact I had lately developed some practical curiosity in the subject.

The conversation pursued a line of enquiry as to essential nature of an archetypal 'bad man'. I should clarify that these gentlemen did not intend to signify moral opprobrium in attaching the epithet 'bad'. Quite the reverse - the Justice and his acquaintance seemed in awe of the doings of these murderers. Their contempt was reserved for those aspirants to the title who posed for a while as bad men, without ever attaining the levels of depravity requisite to the status. The two were in agreement that the serial murderers of the current time were in every way markedly inferior to the killers of the past.

"What makes an efficient gunman?" I ventured, when there was a pause in the bloodthirsty dialogue.

"Mostly the qualities are natural," Wilson replied. "A cool nerve under pressure, which means the hands should be steady and the heartbeat slow. The eye of a hawk to catch the smallest movement even without looking directly. The speed of a snake so that he'll have the gun in his hand and be aiming without so much as thinking, though he'll not fire before he's fully trained on his target."

"And I suppose an absence of reluctance to kill a fellow human being," I muttered.

"That too," Wilson agreed, without catching my tone.

"Has there ever been such a thing as a gunfighter who might be considered an honest man?" I asked him.

"That would be Hickok", the rancher opined.

"Wild Bill," Wilson concurred. "Never was a truer gentleman. If it was ever to come to the trial, he'd give fair warning to his opposition, and think they'd come at him in twos and threes normally. He started as a buffalo hunter and after that he was in the war as a sniper for the Union and then in the matter of espionage within the Confederacy, by which employment he almost sacrificed his life on several occasions. Later on he was in the Indian Wars, somewhat against his will and I believe he essayed the lawman's role for a time. No one else emerged from so many scrapes or killed so many men unless it be in the Trojan Wars of antiquity, and yet the strange thing is that no information was ever laid against him, for every time he'd get into the way of a fight it was not of his choosing."

"Some of those fights he was in," the rancher considered, "the men he was up against had to face his reputation as well as him. They fired on the legend, that was bigger than the man, and hence they missed their shot. Even though Bill was shot through a few times but lived to tell the tale."

The story of this modern day Parsifal had aroused my interest. One such knight with a true heart would be worth more to our cause than the callow mercenaries in Chisum's pay.

"Is it known where I might contact Mr Hickok, were I of a mind?" I enquired.

"In Deadwood, at the cemetery," they laughed. "Shot in the back of the head over a game of cards by one Jack McCall who was duly apprehended at the scene and quickly tried and acquitted at the behest of his friends, before he fled to the next town where he was re-arrested and duly hanged for a murderer."

"HIckok tried retirement," they informed me. "A quiet life in the East, employed sometimes in a spectacle based on his exploits, but the theatrical life disgusted him and the West was calling him back to meet his fate. He left a wife back East and a crazy half-squaw near blind with pox and cheap whiskey who continues to mourn him at Deadwood."

Wilson's histories were succinct but not to the point that was of interest to me.

"Is there no such man living, close to the territory, who might be persuaded to champion a just cause?" I asked them, to be plain.

Wilson barely hesitated. "The man you mean is Patrick Garrett. He was a buffalo hunter like Hickok and Cody. Garrett's scared of no man and he's true to his word if he says he'll attempt something. But he's an adventurer ma'am, who scarcely worries if he has money or not. He's been urged to stand for sheriff at various settlements, but has so far declined to put himself forward for election, declaring if folk want him to do a job they can ask him, rather than invite him participate in some competition over who can brag their own merits loudest."

The rancher nodded his confirmation of this short summary. "How would I recognise Mr Garrett, if we should happen to meet," I asked. They howled at that one.

"If you saw Garrett, you'd know him," Wilson asserted. "For a start he stands six feet four, maybe more. There's no other round here so tall."

"When he was a poor cowboy," the rancher agreed, "he'd to sew an additional length onto each leg of his pants in order to cover his over-extensive limbs."

"You'd conjecture that such a man would present a big target and not survive long in the kind of life he's led," Wilson continued, "but Garrett has not been shot once. I hear he explains that he's slow and deliberate with a pistol, but quick to know when it's use is needed."

"With such a policy, you'd likely not miss," the rancher allowed, "but then your man is at the mercy of any that can get off a quick shot, whether it be accurate or just lucky."

"Like I said, Garrett has not been shot yet."

I left them to their various controversies on the most effective means of slaying one's neighbour. Patrick Garrett - Murphy, Dolan, Riley and Brady - were we to have no respite from these bellicose Irishmen? McSween himself was no better, save that he was on the side of virtue and wanted to play at being a soldier in a holy war. I put the notion of finding a holy knight behind me - clearly there was no modern Parsifal to be found, even if our current social organisation appeared to me more and more cast in the mould of the Dark Ages.

***

McSween held his battered valise aloft before he climbed down from the carriage. He thumped it with his free hand like a Greek warrior banging spear on shield. The horses were whinnying and neighing, impatient for their ration of oats and rest at their long journey's end.

My husband grabbed and hugged me in an unusual display of public affection. "I got the money," he whispered in my ear.

The story I heard later was that Alexander had made enquiries to discover the whereabouts of the principals of the insurance firm, who had not as he had feared left town. When confronted individually, they first denied responsibility. Later, having been persuaded both that McSween had understood their business sufficiently well to see them jailed for fraud and that he would make it his business to see them prosecuted, the partners collectively sued for peace, the condition of which McSween successfully contended should be full remittance of insurance monies due on the life cover issued to Emil Fritz (deceased).

It was his biggest success in the law to date, and entirely due to his own merits and determination. I congratulated him - all the months of hard work had finally borne fruit. Perhaps 1878 would be a good year for us after all.

"You must administer and close the estate before Murphy and Dolan hear news of this," I warned him.

If only it were so easy. It is said that a lie travels round the world in the time it takes the truth to put on its trousers, Similarly the process of disbursing an estate in accordance with law is painfully slow, while theft is the work of a moment. Worse, the process of administration is public. The house of Murphy knew of the recovery of the funds even before Mrs Scholland herself. And now there was cash in the balance, rather than the hope of it.

We soon received a summons, stamped by Justice Wilson, to deliver all funds held in the estate of Emil Fritz to the custody of L. K. Murphy on behalf of Murphy and Co. My husband cross-petitioned that Murphy be barred from meddling in the affairs of the estate unless and until he should deliver audited evidence that the firm of Murphy had any financial claim against the estate. Further petitions and cross-petitions ensued, like the ranging shots of two opposing warships about to come broadside to one another. Wilson sealed each petition and approved each application, however mutually contradictory they might be. Eventually even he could not evade responsibility to set a date for the hearing of the matter in the local court, though he suggested first that the matter should be referred direct to the state judicature (for which there was no precedent in the absence of a first instance hearing) and then that the decision in the case should be a matter for a civil jury, to which Alexander objected, not on the grounds that Murphy and Co would undoubtedly pack any such jury with citizens whose loyalty to Murphy was unquestioned, but on the technical basis that our legislative code delegated responsibility to the person of Justice Wilson. Privately he was convinced that Wilson could not but find for Murphy when push came to shove and his position in the town was at stake, but he was equally confident that the Justice would make such a hash of the proceedings that there would be ample grounds for appeal to the state tribunal.

A few days before the hearing, Alexander was accosted in the street by Andrew Boyle, one of the hired thugs whom Murphy and Co. had imported into the community to meet the supposed threat of the regulators. Given that Boyle had served in the British Army which Murphy so despised, it was a measure of how desperate matters had become on both sides that Murphy was prepared to engage such a man. Boyle was a drunkard, and he was in his cups when he shouted to my husband from across the street. When Alexander ignored him, Boyle continued his affront, bellowing obscenities and hurling clumps of mud, with which the street was liberally supplied, at the upstart lawyer, all the while exhorting his fellow citizens to join the assault. It was pleasing to note that not only did no other citizen join in the literal mud-slinging, but several public spirited individuals moved to stay Boyle's hand and detain him pending the tardy and reluctant arrival of Sheriff Brady. The incident was not significant in itself, but we could not be sure that Boyle was not put up to this outrage by order of his employer. If Murphy and Co. should begin to feel that the town was moving against them, who could say what their response might be?

Up to the last moment, there was some hope that we should be delivered by the cowardice of Wilson. The Justice had contrived to defer proceedings until a date which should rightly have been allotted to proceedings heard before the Circuit Judge who served the County. The Circuit Judge, rather than Wilson would hear the case. Unfortunately the president of the Circuit, Judge Warren Bristol sent word to Sheriff Brady that no cases would be heard that month. The Sheriff was instructed to see that the proceedings of the court were opened and adjourned. Alexander told me that such chicanery demonstrated clearly enough that the reach of Murphy and Co. extended into the judiciary of the state and probably beyond. Judge Bristol was either intimidated or had been bought. The Fritz case could not be postponed indefinitely, so Wilson could not avoid hearing It after all. On a more positive note, McSween opined that proceedings which were to have been reserved to the Circuit Judge and had not been delegated for the ruling of lesser officials could not lawfully be determined at local level, so there'd be grounds for appeal whatever finding Wilson managed to contrive.

"You're telling me that the entire process is a sham?" I asked him Alexander nodded grimly, remarking that it was no less serious for all that.

The small courthouse was not so packed as you might imagine. Our citizens had everyday business that could not be neglected. In any case it was not as if they were to hear the details of some grisly murder - the procedural wranglings of the civil court were by general consensus dull. The first matter of business was to open and adjourn sine die the proceedings reserved for the attention of Circuit Judge Bristol. Next Andrew Boyle was brought before the Justice to answer a charge of drunkeness. Boyle enjoyed having an audience and kept the sparse crowd entertained with his fatuous replies to questions and his mock seriousness. His friends in the public area stamped and cheered their approval. Wilson brought the matter to an early close before the courthouse should become out of hand entirely.

"Thirty days," he pronounced. Jeering and angry mutterings commenced in the public area. "Suspended," Wilson added.

Next was our case. Dolan, the attorney of Murphy and Co, had deigned to appear for the Applicant. For the Respondent, McSween raised the preliminary issue that the locus of the court to determine the current proceedings was not conceded for reasons which he would elaborate later and therefore anything he might say that day on behalf of the Respondent was without prejudice to his argument that this court had no competence to try the issue, by which he intended no slight upon the dignity of the honourable Justice.

I had suggested he would hardly get Wilson on his side by denying the man's authority, but Alexander explained that if he wanted to use the argument at a later date he needed to raise it now.

Wilson said he'd hear the case, although it was a matter of personal sadness to him that two such pillars of their community should come before him in contention. He suggested the parties might settle their differences like gentlemen and he was prepared to allow a recess for discussions to proceed.

"That won't be necessary Wilson," Dolan told him.

Dolan was assured and confident. He stated that the deceased and Lawrence Murphy had been partners and that Fritz had deposited the policy with Murphy as security for financial dealings between them in which Murphy had advanced funds. The details of transactions within the partnership were not available to him now but could be presented to the court at a later date. There was no formal assignment of the proceeds of the policy in existence, but why would Fritz have given the policy to Murphy to hold if it were not as security for financial dealings between them? Dolan stated that Murphy had no wish to deprive the sole named beneficiary of her enjoyment of the residue of the estate. His client merely wished to safeguard its own position by retaining the funds pending the issue of a final account. He was not in a position today to say what was owed, but the beneficiary would get a full account and payment of the residue, being in effect the ten thousand dollars due on the policy less the monies prior owed to Murphy and Co.

McSween argued that the court must go on evidence. There was no evidence that Emil Fritz left New Mexico owing one cent to L.K. Murphy or his business. Witnesses heard Fritz saying that the policy was for the benefit of his sister and with Murphy for safe keeping only. The house of Murphy was merely requesting the court to sanction in advance the larceny which it intended to practice upon the estate of its former partner.

Responding to my husband, Dolan asked the court to admit in evidence a paper which he handed to Wilson before it was passed on to McSween. He requested that Alexander identify it.

"Where did you get this?" Alexander demanded. "It's a private document."

"How it came into my possession is not important. Is this or is it not a true copy of a bill for professional services rendered and delivered by you to the beneficiary of the estate?"

"I'm obliged to render an account to the beneficiaries."

"We'll take that as a yes for now," said Dolan. "Can you enlighten us as to the items under the heading of disbursements?"

"They are my expenses in dealing with the estate. Costs I've already laid out from my own pocket."

"A not inconsiderable sum. And above that your own charges."

"Yes, all perfectly normal."

"And at the bottom, underneath the total assets which amount to ten thousand dollars plus some trifling matters, it says 'less our costs and disbursements' and then 'balance due to you'."

"The estate meets my charges. How else is Mrs. Scholland to pay?"

"And you are deducting your substantial costs and overheads in advance, yet you seek to deny my client that same certainty, knowing that there's nothing to stop the beneficiary removing all her assets from the jurisdiction and high-tailing to Germany, for example, directly she receives your client account cheque."

Dolan knew very well that comparison of McSween's fixed legal costs with Murphy's speculative claim was a false comparison - they were very different in law and in fact. Nevertheless he'd done some damage, not just with the attack but the revelation to McSween that his own office was not secure from Murphy's enquiries. Alexander was rattled, and in any case he knew that his best hope on this day had been to show that Murphy's claim was so much without foundation or merit that the adjudicator would have no alternative but to reject it. Now when the court rose he told me that he feared we should lose. The afternoon session proceeded without drama. After the advocates wrapped up their cases, Justice Wilson announced that he was minded to adjourn the matter that day pending his further deliberation. This was unexpected - Alexander told me that it was near unknown for interim applications to be adjourned without a ruling.

"Our Justice Wilson has excelled himself for prevarication and cowardice," Alexander said. "We can only guess at what will happen next."

***

The next morning, before business hours commenced, we were disturbed by a sharp rap on our door. Sheriff Brady had two men with him, he looked both apologetic and ready to lose his temper given the slightest excuse, the contrasting expressions vying for supremacy in his long, ugly face. He begged my pardon, but he needed to speak with my husband. When Alexander presented himself, Brady announced that he'd a warrant for the delivery of the full proceeds on a policy of life insurance issued to Emil Fritz (deceased) into his custody forthwith.

"Who issued a warrant like that?" my husband demanded.

"It's my warrant," Brady told him.

"You don't have authority to issue warrants. You're an executive officer of the law, not a judicial functionary, as you well know."

"Argue it in court Mr. McSween. Meanwhile I'm obliged to repeat my request that you hand over these funds to me."

Alexander laughed in his face, which was probably not wise given that Brady was growing more twitchy and irritable by the moment, as if he'd partly known the audience would proceed in this way, and now anger and frustration were in the ascendancy over embarrassment.

"Do you really suppose," McSween asked him, "that I'd keep the money here in cash, at the mercy of your boss Murphy on whatever trumped-up pretext might occur to him. The monies are deposited in a bank outside this county in an account that is clearly denominated as being for the benefit of the Fritz estate."

"I'm guessing you've got money locked in your own bank safe Mr McSween. Open it up. I'll take what's due and we can all get on with our lives."

Alexander stopped smiling. "Those funds have nothing to do with Fritz or Murphy. They were deposited in good faith by our neighbours, yours and mine. If you want to add bank robbery to your crimes go ahead. I believe it is still a hanging offence. Of course you'll have to shoot me first but they can hardly hang you twice."

I suppose Brady considered he was beat. "Listen to me. This warrant won't go away. If you don't have that money here, you get it fast. I'll be back to collect it. Good day to you sir."

"I suppose you consider that went well?" I asked my husband.

"It could have been worse," he replied. "He didn't actually shoot me."

Chapter Five - 1877-8

A few days later, Brady rode across to the Feliz ranch accompanied by a band of armed thugs recently sworn in as his deputies. The purpose of his visit was to serve John Tunstall with a warrant authorising the sheriff to distrain goods to the value of ten thousand dollars from Tunstall's property in satisfaction of a debt that the partnership of Tunstall and McSween owed to the house of Murphy. Tunstall had by this time developed a substantial beef herd and it may be inferred that the villains intended to make off with some or all of this, cattle thieving being a larcenous mode of enrichment familiar to them. The response of Mr. Tunstall was to the effect he understood no debt was admitted by McSween and that no judgement had been issued by any court - further that any monies which may be due could only be owed as the debt of McSween and Co., a firm of attorneys-at-law in which he had no interest. Tunstall pointed out that he, not being authorised to practice law by the bar of any state, was legally incapable of being a partner in a law firm.

He said he'd stand indebted for any true amount that was owed by the partnership he had with McSween, but that partnership was limited to the business of the bank, against which Murphy had no claim. Needless to say, McSween had previously rehearsed these arguments with Tunstall against the eventuality of such a claim being lodged on him.

Brady declared he'd noted Tunstall was unwilling to settle the warrant, and that he'd return presently for the goods, one way or another. Tunstall replied Brady would hear from his attorney directly. What happened next is notorious and therefore subject to false report. I had this version from one of the witnesses who was present and I believe it to be substantially correct.

It was well known that Mr. Tunstall loved to hunt a species of bird that he called quail (actually I believe they were a kind of partridge) that inhabited his lands, having the hounds first scare them up and then taking them in flight with one or other of his treasured Italian shotguns. Some days after the discussion with Brady, he set off to wander the hollows and inclines of his estate, accompanied by some of his retinue. The boys were set to be his bodyguard, though he never could think of them in that way.

Having discharged his piece and brought down two unfortunate birds that had been beaten up from a hidey place at some elevated distance from the path, Tunstall invited the boys to collect what he had shot, and if they fancied, attempt to bring down their own bird, though he cautioned them to be mindful not to shoot a dog or each other. No doubt he could well imagine their attempts to nail a flying bird with a handgun, and relished the prospect of instructing such notorious gunfighters in the art of shooting after they should have exhausted their own futile efforts. Meanwhile, he himself continued along the path in the direction of the ranch to which they should presently return.

Whilst the boys were thus engaged, a party of strangers waylaid him. If it seems more than chance that the unknown riders should appear just as Tunstall was left alone by his bodyguard, let me say that Tunstall was partly to blame being so negligent in regard to the known risks he faced. I do not now believe there was treachery or blame on the part of the regulators, though such was widely suspected at the time. Those concerned proved staunch friends of the McSween faction later on. Probably the trespassers had the shooting party, which was by no means seeking to conceal its activities, under surveillance for a period, awaiting their chance.

Some of the boys were close enough to see what happened next, but too far away to intervene. Tunstall was carrying his unloaded weapon broken open in the crook of his arm. The lead rider, identified to me as one Jesse Evans, halted and said some words to Tunstall without dismounting. A short conversation ensued. A few moments later Tunstall, still making no attempt to flee, raised his voice and his words rang out clearly - 'I say. You don't mean to kill me do you?'. At this the rider drew his pistol and fired on the unarmed Tunstall, after which and following his example some of the other riders discharged their weapons into the prone body of Tunstall who had fallen lifeless at the first round. The riders then turned and galloped back down the path in the direction they had come.

Poor Tunstall, who had only beneficient designs for the county, would not live to see any of them realised. There was ever some ever childlike quality about him that would not come to maturity now, and for this I mourned him more and felt a deeper guilt on my own account over his fate. But there would be little time to dwell on such thoughts in the days that followed this first murder.

When the body was brought into town and I saw what had been done to my friend, I wept - one of the few times then or since. I had to arrange the laying-out, though I needed assistance. I knew in theory what was required to prepare the body for burial, but I had never before undertaken such a procedure. Some of the ladies of the town who were kind enough to come to my aid were sadly proficient in the business- I suppose through hard experience. We arranged the body in an open casket so that those who wished might pay their respects prior to the interment, as was the custom of the country. One of the cowards who had fired into the body after Evans shot his victim had also broken Tunstall's face with the butt of his rifle. We could not get the jaw to set right and the caved in features no longer resembled the man I had known. HIs box was set on trestles in our front room. Unfortunately no amount of cleaning can give the appearance of peaceful repose to one who has been shot full of holes and battered around the head. I forced myself to look at the corpse and willed myself to think clearly. What next?

There'd be a last will and testament somewhere, I supposed, relatives to be informed, the horses to be cared for and the Feliz ranch to be sold. So much put in motion, and so much halted for all time, in the second it took a finger to curl around a trigger and squeeze.

By the time Tunstall was put in the ground, there had already been more killings. Whether his assassination was the planned signal for an orchestrated culling of the regulators, or it was only that events took their own violent course is a matter for conjecture. There is no reason to suppose, when I look back after a passage of years, that the Murphy faction controlled the wild elements it had brought into play any more than our own side could effectively direct the subsequent activities of the regulators. These wild men were beyond the jurisdiction of law or reason. They certainly held little regard for the wishes of those who imagined them held subordinate by the offer of a few dollars pay. We had unleashed the monster among us and now it would have its play.

Sheriff Brady was now leading a posse of men sworn in for the purpose of exterminating the regulators, who were fugitive. It was evening time when the survivors of that group made their way to our store, being careful to tether their horses out of sight.

Although Tunstall's foreman Dick Brewer was notionally in charge, young Billy seemed to be their leader now, which was the latest in a series of events I was then too exhausted to be astonished by. I could have fallen asleep standing in our kitchen as I prepared food for the men from what we had in store. There was too much happening at once for me to take in. Back in the front room, the men hunched over the table with the open coffin of my dear friend standing on trestles in the background were talking only of revenge.

Alexander advised me we should let them talk. They were frightened probably, and the morning would show things in a different light, he said. I believe I asked him with some bitterness if he planned to compose another letter requesting assistance from the Governor. Perhaps I was sobbing quietly too, though I did not give way to bawling out the grief and rage I felt.

I told my husband plainly that I held him partly responsible for these events. I wished I had never heard of the ten thousand dollar policy - in any case ten thousand dollars was a paltry sum compared to what the dispute had cost. He asked what I would have him do - give up the claim and abandon the struggle to bring law and civil order to Lincoln. I told him that was exactly what I would have him do. Lincoln cared nothing for law and order and all his struggle had achieved so far was chaos and the death of a good man. McSween spoke of the expectations of our decent neighbours.

He said a man could not abandon a crusade once he'd embarked upon it.

"My ancestor was with Barbarossa, the Holy Roman Emperor, on a real crusade, seven hundred years ago," I replied. "Like most of that army, he never came back. Let me tell you about a real crusade. Thousands of men flocked to follow the Emperor - a man of enthusiasm like you - leaving their wives and children, the villages and farms they were supposed to manage, crossing Europe, through Asia Minor to Palestine. It took years. They fought the Turks, the Moors and each other. After Frederick was mysteriously drowned, the French took over, with that crazy English King Richard who got himself captured going home and bankrupted a kingdom with his ransom. Not one of these men gave any thought for what their actions cost their dependents. Eventually Jerusalem was taken, by a miracle they said. And so where is the Cathedral of Jerusalem now? It doesn't exist. No-one had considered Jerusalem itself or what they might do with it - the only plan was to take the city and kill anyone who stood in the way. It turns out that the whole idea of the crusade was a trick by the Pope to get rid of troublesome nobles and increase his own power and lands That is history Mr. McSween - that's how it works - not with nobility and high purpose but by stupidity and trickery. Your fine words will not deliver Jerusalem, and we do not need it. Our hopes for civilisation depend not on idiots taking up swords to escape responsibility, but on those who stay behind making sure the crops get planted and harvested, the children have their lessons and the old and sick are cared for."

I stopped then thinking that perhaps I'd gone too far. McSween was the orator, not I, and our situation was desperate enough without my adding to our woes. In fact, Alexander did not argue or make any reply. I believe he was close to nervous exhaustion himself. It was clear we couldn't send the boys away.

There was nowhere for them to go where they'd not be hunted down. Bosque Grande was too far away and there was no reason to suppose that Chisum, if he was home, was any better prepared to withstand a siege than we ourselves were.

It says something about my husband that he was up and about on the streets early next morning, hunting out Wilson and requiring him to seal a document appointing the surviving regulators as deputies. It says something about Wilson that he was as ready to deputise the regulators as he'd been to legitimise the pack of hounds following Brady. Alexander explained to the boys that if there was shooting and they were only private citizens they'd have to stand trial for any homicides they occasioned, but as deputies they'd be upholding the law should they need to fire upon those disturbing the peace. Alexander meant well, though his best intentions caused him to risk his life for a piece of paper of doubtful value. As he distributed the appointments, I was put in mind of those papal indulgences that old Pope Urban issued the crusaders, guaranteeing a free ride to paradise regardless of their sins if only they had first slaughtered a sufficiency of Saracens and other heathens they might encounter.

***

Mr. McSween was determined that the murderers of J.H. Tunstall should be apprehended and face trial. Since the office of law enforcement had been subverted in our county (Sheriff Brady being in league with the supposed killers) he proposed that the newly deputised Regulators should be the engine of what justice demanded. We had a long meeting with Dick Brewer, Tunstall's foreman who was now the nearest thing to chief of police that we had. Chisum had recommended Brewer as a steady man, and steadiness was to be hoped for in these desperate times.

Dick Brewer admitted that the young men in his charge were hot-headed. The worst was William Bonney, since it was his nature to regard life as a huge farce - he was up for any escapade at whatever moment. Bonney would take orders from no man and though in appearance he was little more than a child, the others were apt to follow his lead, mindful that he'd survived many adventures and had more than one homicide credited to his name. McSween suggested we might dispense with the services of such a boy, but Brewer advised if he were left without employment he'd likely find work with the Murphy faction directly. He was acquainted with members of the Jesse Evans gang and had once been friends with many of them. Besides this, Brewer told us Bonney was the best shot of any of them and without him the others might lose their nerve.

The gang that killed Mr. Tunstall were known in the territory and there was no problem of identifying suspects. Dick Brewer had a strong suspicion of where two of them, Baker and Morton, might be found, in the Rio Penasco region, not far from Mr. Chisum's ranch. McSween charged him to locate these two and bring them back to face the magistrates. The Regulators quickly departed and my husband and myself attempted to resume our daily lives in the business of the town, which for the moment seemed little disturbed by the murderous events but recently occurred. As we waited anxiously for news, more than once I regretted the course we had embarked upon and wished that the Brewer party could be recalled. I knew that my husband had a noble character and was serious in his conviction that the law must be upheld impartially, but the condition of the territory and the character of the men to whom we'd entrusted the expedition of justice left me with no confidence that the affair would not descend quickly into a blood feud. Juan Patron knew the country better than my husband and he'd advised me that our people were not so much hungry for some civilising ideal of justice, as ruled by passions that were apt to turn murderous. Our civilisation had so far only scratched at roots buried deep in the ancient earth.

    Some days later, Brewer and his men returned to Lincoln, without Baker and Morton in their company. The riders were dusty and hungry, and Brewer looked the most tired of all. When he lifted his hat to greet me, the lined forehead it had covered was tolerably clean in contrast to the face below, on which the sun had dried his grime soaked sweat. Mr. Brewer seemed to have aged since last I saw him. While the girl prepared food for the men and such of them as desired had the opportunity to clean themselves somewhat, Mr Brewer came to my husband's private office and made his report to us.

    The suspects had proved easy to discover, having no notion that they were being pursued. Having apprehended them without a struggle, Brewer and his associates made their business known to the authorities of the place and made a temporary refuge at the Bosque Grande ranch, which was a place that could be counted secure. A local man named McCloskey was appointed at the public expense to ensure safe passage of the prisoners until they should be delivered into official custody. Frank Baker was a half-indian who had been on friendly terms with William Bonney, and Billy Morton was Baker's friend, also known to the party. Both men boasted that they'd surrendered knowing they had nothing to fear from the judicial system of Lincoln County.

Bonney had suggested a somewhat circuitous route for the return of the party, on which the other men insisted despite Brewer's own reservations. The path was little used with many isolated sections. He told us that all the morning as they rode, the boys were in communication between themselves in that whispering, sniggering way that he did not like. He suspected that some among them had whiskey in their bags.

When the party reached a certain point, the riders halted as if by agreement, though Brewer assured us he had given no order. Baker and Morton were got down from their horses and by then they must have suspected what would happen next, for Brewer reported that they immediately began to plead with the Regulators that nothing bad should be done with them. Some of the men were openly passing around bottles by this point, but perhaps none of them would have acted except that William Bonney, tired of hearing the prayers that the prisoners, now kneeling in the dirt, were making for their lives, stepped forward and shot first one and then quickly after the other in the backs of their heads, so that each one fell forwards, broken faces staining the earth with their blood.

"It was as close to an execution as if a hangman had opened the trap," Brewer reported. His voice was no longer steady.

What happened after was that McNab, of the Regulators, shot the innocent and appalled McCloskey who'd been witness to the events, remarking that dead men told no tales. He could not confirm that Bonney had given the order for that assault. The bodies were buried along the trail with no marking of the spot. It transpired that some of the party had shovels with them, which Brewer claimed he had not previously noted. The foreman seemed genuinely distressed by what he had to report, and I was inclined to regard him as sincere. McSween told him to get cleaned up and join the others at their meal. My husband and I remained to discuss what we had learned.

Of course, McSween was distraught, less for the rough justice meted to Morton and Baker than the fate of the blameless McCloskey. But still we should have to account for the two men taken into our custody. He kept up a murmuring to himself that our hands were no longer clean, that we had hands stained with blood.

I was less amazed than Alexander at the turn of events. I had no wish to cast myself as Lady McBeth to his reluctant usurper, but the fact was that we were now embarked on a course that he had determined. Having begun, I urged him, it would be infinitely more perilous to halt. If we should throw up our bloodied hands in horror and repudiation of what we had unwittingly caused and cast ourselves on the mercy of our enemies, then it could be foreseen with tolerable clarity what should be our fate. There was not much more to say. McSween remained in his office for some time, whilst I had to oversee the feeding of the returned deputies and by my presence assert our tenuous authority over their doings.

Over their meal, the boys were cheerful and boisterous, though I noticed Brewer hardly joined their conversation and seemed to avoid my eye. They spoke in the over loud way of young men who wish to persuade each other they have done nothing shameful. There was much talk of Mr. Tunstall and his fine qualities, and suggestions that the poor man might now rest easier. The Regulators seemed to me like children brutalised by fear, driving each other on to do collectively what individually they would not dare, requiring discipline but resentful of authority, as much a danger to themselves as to others. In other words, I reflected, they resembled every other army that has ever fought a battle.

They were talking now of knowing where they stood. The county would be called upon to take sides. Somehow the name of Buckshot Roberts came into their conversation.

"Who is that man?" I asked Dick Brewer.

When Brewer described Roberts, I realised I had seen him about town - an old man with shotgun pellets lodged in his shoulder from an old wound, so deep he could barely lift his arm.

"Surely Roberts is no danger to anyone?" I said.

"I believe the Kid fears him," Brewer replied, "though don't mention I said so. Roberts was with the Texas Rangers, and against them for a time too. He can shoot a rifle from the hip as well as most can manage from the shoulder. Bonney claims he's the deadliest man of the county and we must know his mind."

"Mr. Brewer," I told him, "we are greatly reliant upon your experience. A man of your maturity, who is used to command, must assert himself in the company of such youths, for they want a leader with discretion. Either you lead or you put yourself at the head of a rabble."

"I'll do my best ma'am," he replied.

The next day, McSween put word out that robust types were wanted for hire, and quickly our ranks were swelled by around forty Mexicans, mostly from the surrounding villages. Some of them brought their own weapons and McSween procured arms for the rest. Of course, not even the compliant Wilson would swear in a Mexican as deputy, but these men were required to stand guard, over the bank and our store and in the case of the party sent across to the Rio Feliz ranch, over the late Mr. Tunstall's estate. McSween rented a nearby house to accommodate the ones stationed in town.

My friend Juan Peron warned me that we should not rely too heavily on the Mexicans.

"Surely you are not one of those who holds they are an inferior race?" I asked.

Juan had many qualities, but directness of speech was not among them. A favourite expression was that history had outdistanced his once great Spanish nation and now he was left with the consolation of his reflections. 'In my own case,' he told me more than once, 'I was fortunate, being descended from the younger son of an old family, who would have been destined for the church before we Castilians chanced upon our great Empire.' Now, he reminded me that the Aztec were long gone and the Conquistadores too, and commented that all Mexicans were half indio. Which was to say, he added, that the first Spanish men had devoted as much energy to fornication as to battle, for they had sired a new nation within a few generations of conquest (he permitted himself a degree of freedom in our talks that he would have avoided if there'd been Spanish ladies present, for he knew I would not be offended).

Just now I needed answers, so I cut him short. "Are you saying our Mexicans will not fight?" I demanded.

"The Mexican will fight as well as anyone, when he has a reason. In this he does not differ from you or I. The difference is that you are fighting for your family, your deputies are fighting for their lives and because it is what they know, and Mr. McSween is fighting for an ideal - the most dangerous reason of all. The poor men of the pueblo have no quarrel of their own. They are offering to fight only for pay."

In the end, some of the men fighting for pay proved true friends, but I was not to know that then, and I was thankful that the hired Mexicans would only be required to be station themselves in front of our properties, shotgun in hand, to deter looters.

***

I requested to meet Major Murphy without knowing if he'd be prepared to see me or in what mood I might find him. He received me at his home, in the afternoon, greeting me at the door himself with cordial tones of welcome. I knew that he'd been ill, but I thought perhaps he'd begun to rally, for he seemed more at ease within his body and not so bent over as I'd witnessed previously.

He declared that he was always pleased to see me, but wondered if he might enquire whether my inviting myself over had some particular purpose.

"Dear Major," I told him, "you did say that I might call in any afternoon to try my poor skill upon your piano, given that the tuning of my own is at such a questionable pitch."

"So I did," he remembered, "and here's me thinking you might be coming to discuss terms of surrender."

"Are we at war, Major Murphy?" I asked him. He made no direct reply but ushered me into the downstairs parlour of his establishment, where stood an instrument of reasonable quality with every sign of having being well cared for.

"I hardly use it myself," he claimed, " and the desperate hammering of our saloon players I do not count as music. Perhaps the keys will respond to a more sympathetic hand."

I had brought some scores with me and first essayed a short piece by Herr Bach, one of my favourites. To my surprise, the Major recognised and could name it. I continued with two further works before pausing. Murphy listened with what seemed like rapt attention. When I'd finished the third piece, I repeated the question I'd asked him in the hallway.

"You tell me, Susan," he suggested. "Do you consider we are at war?"

"Wars are declared by states and fought by armies, subject to rules of decency," I replied. Murphy shrugged.

"I served in the Indian Wars," he said, "if you tell me there is such a thing as warfare with decency, I'm inclined to disagree. As to armies and states, it is true that here we have no state as yet, and our people fight for their own reasons, good or bad, not because some petty official tells them they must enlist. You may say this is uncivilised and I say the better for it."

"Perhaps we needn't fight at all," I said.

"Tell that to your husband, Mrs. McSween. I do not love conflict. I must bear the cost of sustaining it from my own purse, while Chisum is I know the paymaster of your own force, for reasons that strike you as honourable, although I know his true motivation. I profit nothing by war and I have studied it's effects more closely than you have so far had opportunity to do. We've but lately finished our Pecos War that was brought on by the rivalry of my own interest and Mr. Chisum's. Somehow one of the Harald boys got himself killed in a skirmish, and the three brothers set us on a trail of revenge and counter revenge that threatened to extinguish the town."

"Then let us have peace."

Murphy asked whether I minded if he smoked, prior to igniting a large cigar using a phosphorous match of prodigious length, from which he then shook out the flame vigorously.

"Peace at what price, Susan?" he asked me. "The Pecos War is done, and Chisum stands monarch of the Pecos River where there is nothing but grass and cows. I am King in Lincoln, where we shall build a bigger town and perhaps in time a city. It will bear the name of the founder of the nation, but there'll be a Murphy Hall, a street named for Murphy, perhaps even a statue."

"Your ambition runs high."

"Do you think that McSween hopes for any less for himself? You have European ancestors Susan - you know that no king got his throne except by conquest, and none ever kept their kingdom that was not prepared to fight to retain and expand it. To me, your husband is only Chisum's proxy, and even if I were prepared to overlook his treachery in turning against the man that gave him his start, bringing that fool Englishman Tunstall here with his bank and his science - even if I let that pass, I cannot but defend my kingdom."

I waited to see if he'd finished. He drew deeply on the cigar though its effect seemed more like something to be endured than enjoyed.

"McSween should have been here earlier," he continued, "before the territory was carved out, or he should have been prepared to serve and receive generous reward. Now he must either bow the knee, or else be ushered beyond the limits of my kingdom."

"You know he will never bend the knee."

"Then you married a fool, Susan. Our people like to hear McSween declaim, but when his words are done, my subjects remain loyal to me. Chisum claims the small ranchers steal his beef. The ranchers say that his drives sweep up every cow in their path without regard to brand, like Moses leading the chosen people out of Egypt. The conflict is natural and the ranchers have no champion but me. I gave most of them their stake. I own these people, bought and paid for, like Chisum owns his cattle. Bonds of loyalty Susan, not loans at a commercial rate. I do not love banks. If Tunstall's bank should prevail, we'd have every Cohen and Shylock flooding the territory with usury before you could turn around. We did not escape the grasp of the British Empire to be ruled over by Israelites."

I made no reply. Instead, I sorted through the sheet music I'd brought. He had me flustered and I would find it difficult to play correctly. I settled on a spirited toccata that had some rippling moments in the most animated sections which were beyond the suppleness of my fingers to accurately convey. Nevertheless, Murphy applauded bravely when it was done.

"Major Murphy," I said, "you are not an unintelligent or uncultivated man. To be frank their are few among our neighbours so alike as ourselves. You must remember what Homer teaches us about the ruinous conflict of the Greeks and the Trojans."

"I recall that Homer's Trojans warn us to beware of Greeks bearing gifts," he replied, "though I'm grateful for the gift of music that you bring today. In matters of the classics, I prefer the lessons of the old Romans. Those senators were of a more pragmatic cast of mind. Though I have to say, I'm mindful that the democracies of both these ancient states depended on slavery, and as the exiled son of an oppressed race, the institution of slavery is one I've long despised. Your own German ancestors were for fighting Rome in the forests, admitting no Empire. In some ways, our heritage is not different, for you've something of the cultured savage in you Susan, if you allow it."

Perhaps he intended to say more, but of a sudden his body gave an involuntary spasm, as if he'd been struck by a sharp pain.

"Major Murphy, are you quite well?" I asked him. He recovered a little to speak.

"The doctors have me on a strong medication. As the effect begins to diminish I am somewhat at the mercy of pain. It is nothing, or at least, it will soon pass."

"I should leave you to rest. First tell me what we must do to end this quarrel."

He walked to the fireplace and leaned one arm against it, turning his face away from mine so that I should not see the expression of his pain. He spoke with great deliberation.

"The legal issue between Alexander McSween and myself is the matter of the ten thousand dollar proceeds of an insurance policy on the life of my former partner, which must be paid to me as holder of the policy. The full ten thousand, not whatever crumbs McSween deigns to leave over."

"My husband is not a wealthy man, Major. He has his own costs of serving the estate. More than that was the cost of travelling east to negotiate with the insurers, and he had to pay out a man that held a legal mortgage on the policy for your partner's debt from his own funds to secure the payout of the due amount. Your demand would sentence us to destitution."

"Then I repeat ma'am, you married a fool. Does it seem to you like the course of a prudent man to wager his own substance and what he hasn't yet got against my own fortune? He must take the lesson of this experience as his payment."

"Major, Mr. McSween will not consent to any resolution of this matter that concludes in our ruin, nor would I ask him to do so"

"Mrs. McSween, I know of the petitions your husband directs to Santa Fe and beyond, blackening my name, and I know what the men who read his letters think of his whining. There is no succour awaiting you in that direction. If it should come to battle, you have a dozen boys and some few armed Mexicans of which I take no account against my army. There is only one possible outcome. On the frontier, we learn that sometimes getting out with your skin intact and able to begin again is the best to be hoped for."

"You are trying to frighten me."

"I'm urging you to consider your situation in its true light. I'm turning this matter over to Dolan. You know I made the lawyer my partner. You'll find he is of a much less affable disposition than myself," He moved away from the fireplace as if it was costing him a great effort and stood erect, facing me with an expression he made pleasant by an effort of will. "Mrs. McSween, you play beautifully and I have enjoyed our discussion, even when the principal subject is difficult for us. I hope that you will come again, but for now I must beg your pardon. I'm greatly tired and somewhat indisposed."

He rang the bell and his girl showed me out. If I tell the truth, I did not know whether to despise the Major or sympathise with him. It made little difference - his cancer took him before the month end and we did not speak again.

***

Later, I had the report of what happened at the Baxter sawmill from Charlie Bowdre, one of the Regulators that had a decent upbringing. I seem to remember I met his mother once, though I cannot call her face to mind. I'd asked Charlie previously what he was doing, running with these rough boys when he'd his father's ranch left untended. My recollection of Charlie is a gangling youth with thick, straight hair that was overlong and not often washed. His eyes were oversized for his face. He'd have looked entirely at home in a pair of farm overalls, pitching hay. Instead he wore a suit that fit him loosely and was always dusty from the trail, and in it he seemed anxious, as if he'd been fitted with clothes that were a few sizes too big and remained impatient to fill out into them.

Charlie had told me before that ranching was hard work and for too long it seemed that you had nothing to show for it. Riding with Bonney, there was excitement every day, he claimed. They got their living easily. They had good horses and might go where they should choose. I remarked on the danger and the inevitability of a bad end, should he persist in the life of a shooter. He took this as a doubting of his skill or nerve, I suppose.

"I can't hit a target like Billy," he replied, "but no-one can. I'm a tolerable good shot with a rifle and fast enough with a pistol."

Fast enough to get yourself killed young, I thought, but there was no cause to say more.

The Regulators were now billeted at our property when they were not riding out in search of Evans and the others that had killed Mr. Tunstall. We endured their conversations which were mostly of the blood-curdling kind, for they had by now convinced each other that they were desperadoes of the classic sort. It was difficult to separate fantasy from whatever they might actually attempt. I was greatly disappointed by Mr. Brewer's attempts to rein them in, for while his presence seemed to be tolerated and acknowledged as titular chief, there was no question of his exercising genuine authority.

In the matter of Baxter's mill, it transpired that Bonney had determined that they should know the mind of Roberts, who he must have considered a threat. Dick Brewer was dragged into the affair as a reluctant captain. A message was got to Roberts indicating that his friend needed help at the spot. Charlie thought that Roberts must have suspected some artifice (the mill was an isolated place with just a few families living there) for he turned up provided with his full complement of weapons. When he espied the dozen Regulators waiting for him, he must have feared the worst, but for some reason he despised the notion of flight.

The boys had tied their horses at the rear of the house. Roberts dismounted from his mule and they spoke on the porch. Dick Brewer told him that the county was divided and they meant to know which side he would take. The old man replied that he'd done

enough fighting in his life and wanted no part of either side's dispute. That response was insufficient for Billy, who told Roberts that if he was not with them, they needs must assume that he was against them. Roberts only shrugged in reply, declining to make any answer to the Kid.

The party of Regulators then left Roberts on the porch, quietly awaiting what they'd do next. The boys went around to the rear of the house, as if they were going for their horses, but Charlie supposed that both sides understood that they were not about to leave peacefully.

"Nobody said much. Brewer didn't want any shooting near the house, but when our friend George Coe failed to persuade Roberts to give up his weapons, it was clear there would be a scrap. We just stood looking at one another as if to harden our hearts to what needed to be done and to know that we were of the same mind. I don't remember which one first drew his pistol."

The boys came round the house together and charged Roberts. It did not occur to them to split up and encircle the porch. Roberts was waiting for them with his shotgun levelled, braced against his hip with the arm that he could not raise, and his revolver in the other hand. Everyone fired at once and the noise in the small space was terrific.

"More than a dozen men firing within a few feet of each other and yet it seemed like no-one could hit," Charlie marvelled. I supposed (or at least I hoped) that it was more difficult to aim deliberately for the heart of another human being than the boastful words of our Regulators suggested.

"We'd two wounded in a few seconds, but everyone kept blazing away. Jack Middleton is shot through the lungs this night. Old Roberts took an unexpected step forward and planted his shotgun against Billy's gut before he could move away. He pulled the trigger but nothing happened, just the click of a misfire. It's as if Billy can't be hurt like a normal person can. I got off two shots while that was happening and one of them tore into Robert's belly, but he never ceased firing for a moment - just backed against one of the posts for support. I think we'd seen enough and we turned and ran back behind the house with no-one wanting to be the last that might be picked off by Mr. Robert's fire."

Charlie said there was discussion of what to do next. "I told Billy that I thought I'd wounded Roberts pretty badly." None of them wanted to go back round front and make a direct assault. They circled the property and found cover overlooking the house at what felt like a safe distance, behind the great logs that had been set out for planing at the mill.

"Meantime, Roberts had dragged himself into the house and set a mattress against the door, taking up a fresh rifle from the family that lived there. Brewer called to Dr. Baxter that he should send Roberts out, else others might be harmed. The Doctor was somewhere in the house and shouted back that he was not so much a coward as to turn out a wounded man. I suppose Dick Brewer thought he was safe behind that log, for we were at some distance from the house, but he raised his head a fraction too much as he was attempting to parley. It was enough for Roberts, who made a miraculous shot with the rifle he'd borrowed, and blew off the top of Dick's head. He dropped stone dead in an instant right before us. We could see Billy had been right to have his anxieties about the old man."

The boys had seen enough and they fled, getting back to their horses as quickly as they could. I later had it from Johnny Patten, who was cook up at the mill, that a doctor was quickly sent to Fort Stanton for, while the terrorised inhabitants did what they could for Roberts. It took him thirty-six hours to die from being shot in the stomach - a more agonising death could not be imagined. Patten had been in the army before turning cook, so he knew what he was talking about. He told me that he fashioned coffins for the slain men, for there was ample planking at the mill, and they were interred side by side.

I told Charlie Bowdre that Roberts was dead. "My god, I've killed a man," was his reply. He seemed shocked and surprised, as if he had not considered the action of aiming his pistol at another man and pulling the trigger might have fatal consequences.

***

By this time, Alexander McSween seemed almost incapable of making sense of the events that were going on around us. He was sunk in a profound gloom, punctuated by short periods of unnatural energy in which he exerted himself to great efforts for no useful purpose that I could discern. He was obsessed with his correspondence, directed to the office of the governor and to the seat of the federal government itself. Matters of such everyday significance as the disposal of men charged to safeguard our assets or continuing the fragile business of our bank were delegated entirely to myself.

I had to request that he desist in his habit of lecturing the Regulators, when he could find them together, in the manner of delivering a Sunday sermon. The boys continued to show him deference, but I could see that they detested the moral instruction Alexander thought they needed, and were only baffled by his words. William Bonney was now their unquestioned leader, and nothing that my husband might say found a resonance in the hearts of these young men who were now marching to a different beat.

I hesitated even to explain to Alexander what had occurred at the Baxter mill, for I understood how he must take the news. Roberts was an innocent man, who'd had no interest in the conflict of Murphy and MsSween and wanted only to be left alone. McCloskey and now Roberts - two innocent men killed by those who supported us and claimed to act in our name. My report aroused him to a temporary lucidity, though he seemed like a man in pain, so much that I feared for his always delicate health.

"We have become no better than our enemies. What does it matter if we prevail? We must send these boys away now," he complained, "for the help they bring is no help to us at all."

"We are too far in," I told him as gently as I could. I might have added that it was his insistence on continuing the fight that had brought us to this pass. "If we stop now, we shall be exterminated by our enemies."

His response was to put his head in his hands, in a gesture that was becoming depressingly familiar to me.

"Alexander," I told him. "You are not like Murphy and the others. You have a great deal to contribute to this community. If it is true that our hands are bloodied now, we can admit that we are caught in a war, and it is a fact that war spills the blood of innocent as well as guilty. For now, what matters is that we should survive. Afterward, you can make good what has been lost and prove to yourself and others your intentions to promote the general good, but whatever true motive we had in coming to the conflict will be defeated entirely if we lay down and allow our enemies to claim victory now."

In fact, I was no longer certain that I believed in Alexander McSween, but I could see that all hope should be lost if he ceased to believe in himself.

***

Bonney and the others left our house in the early morning, before I was properly awake. They were very quiet about it and I wondered if perhaps their hot words about revenge had cooled and they were set on making an escape. I judged that this would be the best course for themselves. Perhaps we should be safer with their presence removed. My anxiety was somewhat eased.

Over the course of the day, the peace of the town was greatly disturbed by the wild elements that had been introduced among us, namely the Jesse Evans gang and the other bands of lawless men that Murphy had invited to advance his interests, notionally representing law and order and under the supposed command of Sheriff Brady. I did not venture out and forbade that McSween should do so. From time to time we heard shooting, guns being fired off, into the air as we hoped. Now and then from one direction or another we heard hoofbeats and then saw horses galloped at full speed down main street, the riders whooping and calling to one another. I heard later that the men exploited their status as presumed lawmen to make off with whatever appealed to them from the town's stores, including a quantity of whiskey that should have been better concealed.

McSween took the view that for such men terrorising our town would quickly lose its fascination. They'd become bored and move on. The best course was to wait out this perilous time. I was concerned that eventually Brady would rouse a sufficient number of them to purposeful activity that they could begin hunting out the Regulators, which would doubtless bring them to our door, although we had no notion of where Tunstall's former guardians might presently be. The stores were closed and the streets remained empty - anyone who could stayed at their ranch or went to visit friends out of town. Those who had no safer place to flee to kept their doors locked. Of course, the saloon keepers had no option but to accede to the interlopers' demands that their premises be made available for use. It was a tense time and we were powerless to help our own cause.

By late afternoon the irregular firing and charging of horses had subsided and we could hope that the storm had abated. Suddenly, as if from a distance of just a few streets away, we heard gunshots once more, but now the nature of the shooting was different. There was first a great racket as of a volley being fired by a squadron of troopers, and then sporadic firing punctuated by the cries of men that eventually died away. We caught the scuffling noise of persons running in our direction, calling out to one another. The running men passed our establishment and the sound faded, but soon I heard a noise at our back door and someone knocking with soft urgency. McSween went to lift the latch and returned to our parlour accompanied by the Regulators, who were flushed and smiling, like boys that have accomplished a secret adventure in a forbidden orchard for a dare. Mr. McSween asked them what had happened.

"Brady's dead," Charlie Bowdre told us. "He's lying out there on the street like a dead dog and he is not the only one."

He said that Bonney had planned an ambuscade. The boys waited patiently in hiding as Brady rounded up sufficient outlaw deputies to begin a house to house search for their person. I suppose they watched the proceedings develop with a growing sense of excitement and childish glee. Eventually Brady corralled sufficient men and led them unwittingly past the spot where the Regulators were waiting, whence Bonney and the others emerged and discharged their pistols with great enthusiasm on the unsuspecting vigilantes, prior to fleeing as reinforcements appeared.

The boys were very pleased with their work, but Mr. McSween was distraught, saying that now we'd put ourselves on the wrong side of the authorities and matters would escalate to a full scale conflict, in which we'd be held responsible for the death of an appointed law officer. I had not previously seen him in such a condition of despair in relation to any setback. He seemed at least temporarily broken by the events.

So far as I could see there was no longer any law existing in our community that we could be on either side of. It was clear that Brady meant to assassinate these boys, as he'd already accomplished with some of their number. I had no doubt he had orchestrated the murder of my friend Mr. Tunstall, and I did not mourn him or regret his passing, though I did worry that we should now see renewed hostilities of which the outcome could not be foreseen. McSween held the boys greatly to blame though he would not require them to leave us or dissociate themselves from us. I think even he was aware of the likelihood that without their continued presence he'd be murdered as surely as Mr. Tunstall.

Unfortunately, my husband had now no idea which way to move in any direction. He seemed dazed. McSween was never a man of violence. He put his faith in ideas and the power of his voice to move hearers to his argument, but now the argument would be settled with firearms and no one was listening to him. My own temperament is of a more pragmatic cast. I suggested to William Bonney that the boys should take precautions to fortify the store, since it appeared highly probable that our enemies would surmise that they would be found here. Bonney at once directed them with energy and some foresight to make preparations. He still had the appearance of a mischevious and not very intelligent adolescent, but it was surprising what a change came over him when urgent matters of self-defence were in issue.

I learned afterwards that the killing of the Sheriff and others was greatly deplored in the county, and turned some of its citizens against our cause. The reason for this greatly amazed me on the hearing and speaks eloquently of the nature of our territory in those days. Sheriff Brady was shot in the back, and this more than the status of his office inclined the populace to blame Bonney. The fact that Brady was leading a band of cutthroats on a murderous quest, using his badge as a flag of convenience was disregarded in the public mind. What mattered, as I learned after, was that where there was to be an issue resolved by a trial of combat, a true man should offer his adversary an 'even break'. In summary, this code of latter day chivalry required that each man have leisure to take his station and enjoy a simultaneous opportunity to commence firing.

Unlike my Teutonic ancestors, my neighbours had no illusions that God would favour the righteous party or that a true knight could never be defeated. Indeed, on further enquiry it was clear that many combatants availed themselves of stratagems to gain advantage in these trials, which were well known and related to me with no sense of dishonour attaching to the successful cheat. Clearly it was the look of the thing that was most important. It was never adequately explained to my satisfaction why, in the absence of a conventionally supposed divine intervention, any man would submit to such a trial against another who was known to be faster and more deadly, though certainly male self-regard will exceed the bounds of prudence on many occasions.

I cannot offer an opinion on whether the notion of an honourable duel arose spontaneously in our community, or whether it was an imported notion. I think it probable that the fashion was spread, if not originated, by the myth-making agency or our dime novel authors who sought their fortunes in the transforming of events at the frontier into the heavily fictionalised stuff of legend, almost contemporaneously with their actual occurrence. The dime novels were consumed as avidly by those who lived in the place and had the reality under their noses as by the people of the East who knew no better. Whether my neighbours looked for sensational entertainment or hints as to what kind of a people they might be is unknowable, but it is a fact that over time the behaviour of some began to impersonate the caricatures they read. As regards the even break, it is also notable that a homicide who submitted to the authorities and successfully pleaded this defence would normally have an acquittal, whereas a less generous killer was invariably hanged.

I felt no connection to these sentiments. Supposedly we were engaged in a war, or at the very least a struggle for existence. My outlook remained somewhat European. Should Wellington have ceded his defensive position to Napoleon so that the two armies could meet on equal terms? Ought Bonaparte to have waited for the Prussians to arrive before commencing the battle? If Brady allowed his force to be outflanked and so surprised, was he not to blame for defective generalship? Whatever be the rights and wrongs of this dilemma, the situation for ourselves, fortified within the McSween store and anxiously awaiting the turn of events, was that we were effectively besieged.

***

McSween lost no time in persuading Mr. Copeland to stand as sheriff in place of Brady. He swore in Copeland himself - I did not care to enquire under what questionable statute he assumed that authority. Predictably, Dolan disregarded the appointment entirely and swore in his own man, Peppin, with similarly dubious legality. Copeland and Peppin were not outlaws, but neither could pretend to impartiality. They were universally regarded as providing a veneer of respectability to the rival gangs of hired guns of which they found themselves titular leaders. In the case of Mr. Copeland, his response to this situation was to largely absent himself from the town, abandoning the field to his rival, although Peppin himself got little profit by it, since I understand that Dolan neglected to make any arrangement for the payment of his salary.

Our own force was thus out-manoeuvred as well as out-gunned, and we could hope for little relief of our troubles through main force. The Regulators stayed with us because they had nowhere else to go and we could not turn them out. Without them, I have little doubt we should have been murdered in our beds. Our principle hopes turned on the circuit court and the correspondence that McSween continued to direct to the higher authorities which might come to our aid. The circuit judge was the personal incarnation of federal law who travelled the territory hearing cases that were serious enough to require it. When Judge Bristol's schedule brought him to Lincoln, he would surely recognise the condition of lawlessness to which we had descended and alert government to the imperative of swift restitution of public order.

When we heard that Judge Bristol had written to Sheriff Peppin (thereby implicitly confirming his position and further undermining our own) instructing him to open and adjourn the session of the circuit court as Bristol was once more indisposed to attend in person, I frankly despaired. Clearly the judge knew already of the state of the county and his reaction was that he wanted no part of it. The disorder and riot in our streets increased with every day that its occupation by the opposing forces of mercenaries continued. It was a wonder that not more people had been injured, though those of an honest type were mostly locked within their homes and stores in the hours that were most dangerous, after spirits had been consumed. Judge Bristol might have had good reason to fear for his safety.

One morning Mr. McSween returned from collecting his post exultant, bearing a paper that he waved with great enthusiasm, as if to disseminate its import to the open air. He told us it was confirmation from the federal authority that in view of certain neglect of duty including his partiality in appointing and maintaining the late Sheriff Brady, Governor Axtell was to be replaced by Lew Wallace with immediate effect. McSween said that Wallace was no pawn of the Santa Fe men and now at last we'd see some action to clean up the territory.

I supposed this was good news, although in truth I had by this time seen too much written and heard too much said that sounded fine but did nothing to improve our condition. I said that Governor Wallace might make a difference if he should bring himself to Lincoln, with a sufficient number of constables accompanying to impose upon the gunmen. Our own Regulators laughed and snorted at this touching belief of Alexander's that a change of politician might alter anything of real importance in the world.

"We must keep our guns cleaned and oiled boys," Billy told them, "for if Dolan gets any notion of this news, he'll surely desire to put an end to us before authority should visit the town."

Sure enough, four days later, those of Murphy's remaining thugs who had assumed the role of sheriff's deputy duly surrounded our place, as we knew they must, and then I suppose our situation could be regarded as fairly hopeless, although so far as the law was concerned, my husband and myself were technically private citizens who had committed no crime and should be entitled to the protection the state, regardless of whether those stationed with us be regarded as fugitives or outnumbered deputies seeking refuge. McSween's legal mind might have formulated a compelling argument for the resolution of these tangled events in our favour, but I highly doubted that the gunmen ranged about our establishment were of a mind to consider his submissions.

We were well provisioned from our stores, though I feared that the issue of this contest would be resolved in hours not days. William Bonney had seen that his men were well supplied with ammunition, but it would not last forever. Their horses were stabled nearby, where a more patient adversary might have located and confiscated them to cut off any possibility of escape. I don't suppose any of the parties believed that the battle might endure for three days, which is what occurred

Our enemies were sufficiently close that their communications were audible to us, and ours to them. It seemed that most of their force was posted in the street, with others ranged across the elevated land behind our property, covering the back door exit. William Bonney directed some of our party to occupy the upper floor so that the men on the hill should not have the undisputed advantage of higher ground.

For a while the two sides merely harangued one another, trading insults across the short space between them. I don't recall that any order was given before firing commenced. Probably someone became impatient or thought they had a clear shot and then events took a natural course. I do recall the terrific noise of so many weapons being discharged - it made you want to cover your ears and curl up in a ball. The first exchange seemed to go on forever. After, it would stop and then there'd be another shot somewhere and everyone would begin blasting away once more.

McSween and myself remained seated at our kitchen table. Alexander had refused the offer of a weapon. I would have taken a rifle if one had been offered, although in those days I had no notion of how to shoot. McSween made no willed movement, but he seemed overcome by panic. His face was very pale and he trembled without restraint.

"What should we do?" I asked him, contending with the racket around us.

"We must shoot it out," he wailed, "for they intend to murder every last one of us."

At length the taste of even these men for continued mayhem must have exhausted itself, for there was a lull in the bombardment. We had but one fatality. A boy I did not know who had been set against the marksmen on the hill was struck by a rifle bullet and killed instantly. I did not go upstairs, but they told me he was dead and there was nothing to be done. I marvelled that so much munition could be so energetically deployed on both sides without doing more damage.

The afternoon dragged on to evening without any decisive issue. I cooked food from our store with the two Mexican women that were with us, and we used up what bandages we had and tore up bedding to improvise more. The night was quiet, but the next morning we quickly saw that the siege continued.

Late morning of the second day and there was but little firing, I began to dare hope that the parties would exhaust themselves eventually. Two boys on the upper floor had been lightly wounded by rifle fire from the hill behind the town, but still it seemed incredible to me that so many bullets, however badly aimed, should not by the law of averages have produced more fatal results. Billy said that he was sick to death of cowardly sniping from men hidden on that hill.

"Get Fernando up here," he called down. Fernando Herrera was an old man with a slight stoop and grey moustaches. In the time he'd been among us I had seen him do nothing but take naps and demand extra rations of the re-fried beans that the senoritas prepared. He was known only for having beautiful daughters. One of the Regulators had taken an elder girl as his woman and Charlie Bowdre had married another when she was twelve (he took the relationship seriously as far as I could see). I assumed that this relationship explained Fernando's presence in our store.

The old man roused himself from the couch. When the problem was explained, he nodded silently and went back to the couch, returning with an ancient and battered firearm that might have been left over at the Alamo. He didn't bother to go upstairs, but positioned himself at one of the windows, not right at the window where he'd make a target but slightly inside the room. He put the rifle to his shoulder and sighted along the long barrel, staring up at the hill. For minutes he did not move at all and I began to think this must be another of Billy's practical jokes. I was staring up at the hill myself and I could not see a trace of humanity upon it. Something must have caught Fernando's eye. He fired and we heard screaming up there. The old man kept his barrel raised and his eye fixed on the hill. The silence that had come over us in the store remained unbroken for some time. Eventually someone whispered 'that was more than nine hundred yards'. The boy on the hill was still screaming, calling out for water. He took an hour to die, but none of the others dared bring him water in case Fernando was still watching with his rifle, even long after the old man had returned silently to his couch.

Not much else happened on the second day. The night was as quiet as the first. Early the next morning, we heard a voice outside calling to the others. It was the characteristic tone of Andy Boyle, the English soldier who'd been one of the first to join Murphy's band of killers. Perhaps he wanted us to hear him.

"This is no good," he shouted. "I'm away to Fort Stanton. I've a good friend who's a sergeant there and will lend me a cannon or a Gatling at least. That will flush out these rascals in a minute."

We watched him ride away with increased anxiety in our hearts.

***

Some hours later, little had altered. The sound of gunfire never really ceased, but it was mostly sporadic, with occasional bursts of intensity. I found it was not possible to maintain the heightened pitch of terror that the firing initially induced - I suppose one becomes hardened to anything sooner than may be imagined. McSween had retreated into a kind of stupor. No one else had much to say. It did not seem that there was much to be said. We had some more with wounds, but there was little I could do for them but fashion bandages to limit the bleeding.

I thought I must be dreaming when I heard bugles. Both sides stopped firing. Then in the limited field of view I had to the back of the house, I saw pennants and then blue clad riders - the cavalry of the United States army, riding out from Fort Stanton to save us, just in time like they always were in the dime novels, or so I thought. I imagined that they had intercepted Andy Boyle or else one of our neighbours had dared to escape and raise the alarm.

For the moment, the troop remained aloof from the combatants, making a show of force by lining the ridge above the placements where our assailants' riflemen were stationed. It was a substantial company - think they had at least one Gatling gun and a pair of cannons with them. I assumed that their officer would make a declaration of his authority to the besiegers and set his troopers to disarming them. I warned my own small contingent that no-one was to fire on any account and when called upon by the soldiers they must be prepared to lay down their weapons.

But still nothing happened. I could see the commanding officer, still sitting on his horse and reviewing the scene, as if merely awaiting further developments. With no order to desist to keep them in check, some of the Murphy faction resumed firing, in fits and starts as if testing the intention of the cavalry. I could see that the situation might deteriorate rapidly. Something must be done to plead our case.

"I'm going outside," I said. There was no-one else to prevent me, and Mr. McSween was incapable.

As I stepped out of the house and cautiously picked out the course that would bring me around to the soldiers without needing the pass the deputies on the hill, I had no false illusion that I was safe. The whine of an occasional bullet still flew by as I walked, with each step costing an effort of will. The noise was not so loud in the open air but of course the firing was even more deadly. I knew that some of these men would not scruple to kill a woman - if it happened each side would later blame the other. I attempted to prevent myself flinching at every report, reasoning that I could not know whether any particular bullet was intended for me. At length I found myself arrived at the front rank of the cavalry and somewhat amazed that I had not been shot. The officer commanding the troop was a Colonel Dudley.

"Why have you not acted to break up this confrontation," I demanded. "What are you waiting for?"

"Those men on the hill below us claim they are sworn in as deputies," he replied. "Their leader claims to be sheriff." I could not deny it, although the legality of Peppin's appointment was dubious.

"The men within the house are also sworn in," I told Dudley. "With them is my husband, who is an attorney-at-law and stands accused of no crime, but is detained by these men who are set here to murder him."

"My orders do not extend to interference with the civilian jurisdiction," he told me.

"Do your orders extend to preventing a massacre?" I asked him. "Or will you stand by and watch innocent citizens of the country you're sworn to serve being murdered in their homes."

Colonel Dudley did not reply. "You need only disarm both sides to restore order and leave the civil jurisdiction to resolve the rights and wrongs after," I suggested. He continued to stare down at the spectacle presented below him, his back very straight and every part of his appearance denoting a military bearing. To my eye, he cut a very ridiculous figure. I began to be afraid that he might be unable to make his mind to do anything at all.

"I must act within the confines of my orders ma'am. If the situation is so grave as you suggest, I may require to seek further orders."

"What are your orders Colonel, if you may confide them to me?"

"I may not ma'am. The military does not discuss its terms of engagement with civilians."

"If you decline to act now," I told him, "you'll be as guilty of murder as each of those thugs of Murphy and Co., more so for you have the means to prevent it all. The only explanations I can conceive for your current paralysis is that you too are on the payroll of Major Murphy's enterprise, or else you are frightened of these men."

"That is an impertinent comment madam."

"You think I care for your dignity Colonel? If your oath of commission means anything to you, if you have any vestige of manhood in you, you must act now."

He frowned and shifted in his saddle. "I will send to have my orders reviewed if you request it," he said.

"By whom will they be reviewed? Who is in command at the fort?"

"I have that honour madam."

"Then how can your orders be reviewed?"

He laughed in my face. "I meant that if you so request I shall request clarification of my orders from a higher authority."

"That is not good enough. We shall be dead before you have a reply."

For the first time he looked genuinely uneasy. "There is no call for you to return to the store ma'am," he told me. "It is not a place of safety."

"Thank you for advising me of that fact," I told him. "My husband is there, likely to be murdered at the hands of a gang of cut throats set upon him for his efforts on behalf of the public good. What should I do, abandon him?"

I turned without waiting for more and began to retrace my steps. I was too angry on the return journey to greatly fear that I should be struck down in my path. William Bonney opened the door for me.

"What did they say?" he asked.

"The Colonel will do nothing," I told him. "Either he is a useless martinet, paralysed by the requirement to show initiative, or else he answers to Murphy and Dolan rather than his commander in chief. Either way he is a coward."

Bonney nodded, as if that had been what he expected to hear. "We'll make a good show of it then," he smiled, "and sell them our lives dearly."

McSween had remained sitting at the table, with no sign that he was listening, but now his teeth began to chatter and he put his head down on the table. He was mouthing some words but I could not make out what they were. Perhaps I could have done more to comfort the stricken man, but I feared that if one of us did not continue to show resolve, our whole enterprise might collapse in a moment.

"Do nothing rash," I warned young Bonney. "This gang will not hold off long if they see that the troopers are impotent, but it could still happen that when Dudley witnesses their renewed assault, he'll be shamed into action."

"Especially seeing he knows there's a woman on the premises," he grinned. "Where there's life there's hope."

***

We did not see the men who put torches to our building, else we'd have made some desperate efforts to stop them. We only heard some rustling under the flooring like the sound a bird makes when it is building a nest, although whatever it was moving was too big for a bird. Next there was the sound of liquid being poured. No one had time to react to that before we looked out the window and saw Andy Boyle running away from our store. He was whooping and leaping in the air like a mad thing.

The negroes tell their children stories about Br'er Rabbit. An old black fellow who used to look after the horses explained to me once that these tales were really about an African god who would one day visit revenge on the white slave masters and meanwhile delighted in making fools of them. The characters were changed to animals in order that the stories could be passed on without fear of punishment. Well Andy Boyle ran away from our house having set fire to it, with that same wildness in him as if he were the trickster devil god himself. He danced away from the bullets and nothing hit, or else the shots magically passed through him without causing harm.

The next we knew was smoke curling from under the floor and the smell of charring wood. The timber was dry, and once it was lit there was no way to prevent a conflagration.

"She's on fire boys. Get down here now," Bonney called to the men above.

"What can we do?" I asked him.

"Don't waste time fighting it. Try to use it," he told me. "We're all trapped like rats in here anyway. When the smoke and flames get high enough, the boys can use it as a cover to make for the horses. You'd best escort Mr. McSween outside first. There's no legal quarrel with him and the troopers are present as witnesses if they're good for nothing else. He's not up to running so it's your best chance."

Some part of McSween that was still reasoning seemed to hear and comprehend what was said, for he roused himself from the seat he'd been occupying for some time and seemed to collect his thoughts momentarily. Bonney tore off a patch from the dirty white cloth that yet covered our best table and handed it to Alexander.

"Keep your arms up and wave that white 'kerchief over your head," he advised, "so they'll know you don't mean to fight."

"We'll go out together," I said, putting my arm around my trembling husband. He pushed me away gently.

"No, I'll go first. You follow."

We could now see flames coming up from below and it was coming harder to breathe. Mr. McSween stumbled to the door, then he paused and for a moment there was a look I'd often seen just before he began to make an address to the court. He stood as straight as ever. He examined the piece of white rag and he even smiled as he made a practice of waving it above his head. Then William Bonney cautiously opened our front door without exposing his own person in the door space and my husband stepped outside. I followed a second after.

Alexander had time to make perhaps three steps before shots rang out on every side. His body spasmed unnaturally from the different impacts as if he were making a little dance, then it fell to the hard earth like a bale of hay dropped from a rick, with the life pouring out of it in all directions.

I had blood on me, but so far as I could tell none was mine. The firing continued - the men inside the house were responding. I knelt at my husband's side, but he was already gone. For a moment I only wanted to lay on the ground next to him and let what may happen come, but his lifeless face and the sight of his wounds were so ghastly, and besides I knew that if I stayed put it would be the end of me. I began to crawl on my hands and knees away from the place, unmindful of the tears coursing down my face.

When I looked back, I had reached the far side of the street. My dress was stained with the filthy earth of the thoroughfare, the soot of the flames and my husband's blood. There was blood on my hands and on my face. I had come to rest propped up against the boardwalk, and now it seemed that the reserves of my determination were exhausted. I could watch, but I could neither move nor speak.

The Mexican girls and Alexander's young legal clerk, who was also unarmed, had been allowed to pass (the poor youth headed back east not long after). The fire had taken hold and my house was burning down. Neighbouring properties were at risk of being engulfed in the flames. The Regulators were still inside, darting into the window spaces from which all the glass had burst out to fire upon the Murphy faction and then dive back under cover. Every so often some new inflammable object was taken by the fire which flared up as it began to consume another part of our home. It was impossible that anyone could breathe inside. Smoke was pouring from every window.

Suddenly the door was kicked out and two of the boys ran into the street, their progress covered by a hail of shots from the remaining defenders. One of the boys fell. The other kept running - I did not see where. The attackers were shouting to each other and now they began to close in on the store, too excited to be mindful of the firing that was still coming from within. Another pair came out, firing as they ran and then two more. A number of the Murphy faction fell to the ground shot - wounded or killed I could not say.

Above the smoke I could make out the troop of cavalry still drawn up along the ridge at the back of our house, observing the scene impassively and uselessly. My husband's body lay in the street with the carnage going on around it, limbs twisted unnaturally about and his shattered face buried in the dust.

Still there was firing from inside the building, until it seemed that no living thing could have endured the smoke and flames without perishing already. The Evans gang closed in on the house cautiously, and then William Bonney emerged last of all, carrying a pistol in each hand. Instead of fleeing, he first calmly shot dead the two men nearest to him before holstering the extra pistol, keeping the other in his good left hand. This action caused the attackers a momentary dismay, for they broke ranks as each man gave consideration to his own personal survival. Bonney then whooped out some words of insult and was off down the road, turning every few moments to let fly at any pursuers. There were not many keen to be after him and he easily broke through to the stables. So ended what became known as the Lincoln County War, at least insofar as it had to do with my own person.

Chapter Six - 1878-9

The next morning the neighbours told me my husband was dead, as if I hadn't seen him gunned down not one yard from our own front door. They'd put me up at the Davidson house. The women looked after me - I don't believe I'd have been able to fend for myself. I asked for someone to take me to the house and I believe the Davidson girls accompanied me, each holding me by the hand. It must have been a frightening experience for them. The timbers of the house that was completely gutted were still smouldering. There was not one stick of furniture remaining. I was dazed, wandering the ruin remarking to myself where a staircase had been, which was the site of the parlour, which the kitchen. I managed to bear it until I came to the place where my piano had stood. There was a tangle of wires, twisted and rusted by the blaze, protruding from a pile of ash . Some of the keys had not been altogether consumed. I'm told I remained quiet through my tears. I paced out from the former staircase to where our bedroom furniture should have fallen through when the upper storey collapsed. There was no trace of my bureau. Of my few pieces of family jewellery, that were of mostly sentimental value, I recovered but one item that was not mangled beyond recognition, being a silver locket and chain. The small photographic reproduction within was scorched to charcoal - I let it fall among the ashes and put the locket inside my small bag. The girls must have brought me back to the Davidson place presently, though I have no memory of leaving the scene.

It transpires the law requires a corpse must be formally identified, even when a whole town knows the deceased. I was taken to some place I don't recall. They'd covered Alexander with a blanket, but there were blankets covering all the bodies there. I don't suppose our small town had developed a system for avoiding the confusion that arose, not having previously suffered an epidemic or mass slaughter of citizens. Whoever was managing the procedure looked under first one blanket then another, and I entertained the lunatic hope that I was to be told there had been a mistake - that Alexander was not dead after all.

Strange details stay in my memory, though my general recollection of these events is a blur. It is as if the mind declines to take in what it can not absorb and incorporate within the continuity of its previous experience. You might say that the thread of my life was broken. I'd seen death close up before - for in those days death was not kept so much hidden as if it were a thing of shame. However, a body from which the soul has been violently ripped presents a tableau quite different to an everyday cadaver. The departed may look serene or pained, but they don't ordinarily exhibit the shocked expression of life suddenly interrupted as I discovered in the blanched face of my late husband. He'd been shot several times, making ugly wounds, and I remember asking which one was lethal, as if it mattered. I desired to establish causation to the most precise detail, perhaps with the fantastic notion I could somehow beg fate to twist retrospectively only a fraction of a degree so that all might be well. Whoever was consulted opined that Alexander was so riddled with bullets that any one of a number of them would have been sufficient to guarantee a fatal outcome.

After that day, I was in the house of Juan Patron for a while. His people had been evicted by the Jesse Evans clan in the course of the siege and I recall there was considerable upheaval to be righted. Whilst I was there, I spoke with Ighenio Salazar, one of our loyal Mexicans who was recovering in the spare bedroom where Juan kept him hidden. Ighenio had been shot several times while trying to flee. He told me that after the massacre, the Evans gang walked around finishing off survivors. He heard someone saying that it wasn't worth wasting another bullet on a dead Mexican and then he was turned onto his back by that person's boot and kicked into a ditch, where he stayed until it was safe to crawl away. Colonel Dudley and his blue-coated company witnessed not only the massacre but the butchery that followed from their station on the hill, and still they did nothing. There might, I hope be a special place in Hell for those who swear an oath to protect their fellow citizens and then connive at their murder.

Before long, I was somehow managed away from the county altogether and found myself in Kansas, lodged in a rented place in a respectable neighbourhood at the expense of an unknown benefactor. At that time I had no money and no initiative to arrange things for myself. I spent my days looking back, discovering that I remembered nothing of my husband's funeral, though there must have been one. Eventually I started to leave the house and take short walks, if only to seek in my immediate surroundings some focus of attention that would enable me to neglect the past temporarily. I do not recall how long this state persisted. The battle was in August, so it must have been several weeks.

My immediate neighbours were a family by the name of Duesenberg. The patriarch would sometimes pass me in the street, invariably with a polite greeting. Though I must have struck the Duesenbergs as odd, there was no reason to suppose they were informed as to the root of my malaise and for this reason perhaps I found I was able to make some conversation of a trivial nature with them. I see now that I started to take an interest in the doings of this family mostly as a way to have some engagement with the world without thinking of my own life.

It strikes me that the Duesenberg clan must have been considerably odder than myself, and not only because I do not recall them exhibiting the slightest curiosity regarding my own condition. I won't say they had no concern for my welfare, only that they probably assumed I would tell them if there was anything I needed. The Duesenbergs were one of those families that seem perfectly normal at a superficial level, but with whom even a short acquaintance will confirm that they inhabit a parallel world, an hermetic system which they have constructed around themselves and which bars such of the external world as does not correspond to their own predetermined model. Before I am called to account for charging Mr. Duesenberg with the habits of a fanatic, I should acknowledge he and his family treated me with perfect kindness.

I had to undergo a process of coming back to life, even if life could never be the same. The few words I first exchanged with Mr. Duesenberg, graduating to his disquisitions on various subjects and my tentative introduction to his household, were nothing other than helpful to me. It was in the nature of Duesenberg's odd relationship with the world that he had no small talk. If you were incautious enough to open any topic with my neighbour, however inconsequentially, you would shortly be furnished with a precis of his thoughts and opinions on the same together with a closely argued rationale for those views. On the other hand, if there were no impersonal subject under discussion, but only for example a well-intentioned inquiry as to the health of his children and spouse, Duesenberg would respond with a few monosyllables and an air of bafflement that more seemed to be expected of him.

Mr. Duesenberg was a civic-minded, respectable and progressive man. He dressed soberly for his work, kept regular hours, and required that his three children should observe the decorum required of polite society. HIs wife was a quiet lady who spoke but little on any subject, though Mr. Duesenberg held sufficient opinions for two. My neighbour was not forthcoming as to the nature of his employment, but he had much to say on just about any other subject. I suppose he worked in some office in the heart of the City - he was always setting off early in the morning. When Duesenberg had a lecture to deliver on any subject, it was his wife's habit to stand a little away apart from him as if to make room for the expansiveness of his intellect, her gaze never leaving his face, occasionally nodding her approbation whilst he was holding forth, as if to say, yes that is what we think.

At weekends the family would take excursions into the near country, for Mr. Duesenberg held scientific notions as to the benefits of fresh air, especially for immature beings. Mrs. Duesenberg would have her parasol, and the children might be instructed to prospect for ancient artefacts that could still be picked up readily, since most citizens had little interest in arrowheads. Mr. Duesenberg was interested in the indigenous races, in a spirit of scientific enquiry. He held that the red Indian was greatly undervalued as a type. Though primitive in thought and lacking in the skills to develop complex tools, the savages had nonetheless developed a stable culture that sustained them for centuries, prior to the coming of civilisation and the extermination of the buffalo. They had understood the concept of nobility, which was to infer that their brains were of a capacity not markedly below that of your middling Anglo-Saxon specimen, and superior in many respects to certain types that were found in our contemporary world, for example that of the essentially parasitic modern Jew. Mr. Duesenberg opined that, through a scientific programme of education, the best of the race might be brought to contribute to the commonwealth of our nation, though of course we should not be so fanciful as to imagine that a redskin could be the equal of a white man.

I discovered from this same source that the science of eugenics was currently the great new thing among persons of an enquiring nature who gave their stamp to our national culture - progressives, as Mr. Duesenberg was apt to call them. As explained by him, the precise science of gene types was complex, but the basic principles of eugenics could be discovered by any person of common sense, for at root the discipline was no more than an extension of the precepts of agriculture to the problems of society. My instructor told me that anyone who had tried to raise cattle knew that the parenting of offspring was crucial to the improvement of the herd, and by this he meant not nurture, which was the care of the agriculturalist, but the qualities of parents that combined through the seeding of the bull to determine the nature of the calf. So it was with humans - only by breeding selectively might the quality of the race be improved, for science had conclusively demonstrated that humanity differed but little from the more developed species such as primates, of which the first man was but a precocious descendant.

Some of our prominent eugenicists were socialist in the matter of politics, holding that collectivism was the higher mode of social organisation to which the present state of our culture should aspire. This was surely a nonsense in Mr Duesenberg's opinion, serving only to illustrate that mankind in its current state was ill-equipped to develop a consistent philosophy. The essence of progress in the natural environment, I might say the engine by means of which species ascended, was obviously competition. He supposed that I was familiar with the term, 'survival of the fittest'. I owned I had not heard it previously.

The great worry of Mr. Duesenberg, and right-thinking men of science like him, was that modern society denied this fundamental principle. In our developed, non-natural state, the inferior had as much chance to breed as the competent - indeed the lower castes were apt to reproduce with greater fecundity since they were unrestrained in their habits by decency. In nature, the weak did not survive to produce offspring, in agriculture the wise hand of the farmer guided the improvement of the genus, but in human affairs there was neither the harsh judgement of nature nor the guiding hand, and this was alarming for my neighbour.

The species was headed for a crisis, and men of goodwill were required to act, according to scientific principle. Mr. Duesenberg pointed out that he himself had sired three children, this being the minimum required to support an increase in the population of the genetically viable and superior type. That effort would be in vain if more were not done to curb the proliferation of our inferior and defective types. The mentally deficient should be sterilised of course, as was already the policy in many states of the union, but the problem needed to be taken more seriously by those in authority.

I enquired whether Mr. Duesenberg and his wife were christians, and he confirmed that he and the family regularly attended service. I observed that if I was ever of a mind to take up the raising of cattle, I was sure that the lesson he'd read me would be of great utility. I'd no children of my own, I told him, and was not now likely to have. Privately, I reflected that my neighbour was a good man, by all the standards of our society, but that one might fear to what end a society of good men persuaded by convictions such as his might come. Already I felt puzzled by the conundrum of our modern times and felt that I was somehow apart from the society of men and women whose lives and ideas seemed not to connect with my own. The feeling would only intensify as the years passed. Even before I'd properly commenced to live a quiet life in Kansas, my heart was pining for the simple verities of the plain, with all its harsh exigence. The same nostalgia that I had previously discerned from the memoirs of certain sea captains, now marooned on the land but forever longing for the waves, was impelling my own spirit southerly, to the rolling contours and empty spaces of the territory of New Mexico.

My neighbour Mr. Duesenberg did me the good turn, though he didn't know it, of awakening a spirit dulled to indifference by tragedy and loss. This he achieved through the wholly impersonal lectures that he delivered impromptu in the name of conversation. On subsequent occasions I learned more from him of the emergent science of eugenics (he was also persuaded of the value of phrenology by which the capacities of an individual might be discerned from certain features in the shape of the skull, though he allowed our knowledge of such matters was in its infancy). He was a proud exponent of the principle of Manifest Destiny, which is to say the popular notion that the policy of our United States should be to extend its territories from sea to shining sea with all that lay between. He grew enthusiastic when telling me about the role of persons living at the frontier in forging the nation.

I asked what he thought we owed to the Indian nations whose existence on the land preceded our own. He was impatient with the Indian question, reminding me of the words of the Treaty of Ghent that ended the war of 1812 with the British (he informed me that in taking up arms on behalf of the native ab origines in opposition to the forces of progress, Britain had merely demonstrated how debased its notion of Empire had become, and that the conflict was only a spiteful revenge for our independence conducted under the pretext of honouring forgotten treaties with the Indians). Mr Duesenberg could recite passages of our nation's constitution and historical documentation verbatim and was not reluctant to do so when the occasion should permit.

"In 1812, John Quincey Adams himself wrote," he declaimed, "'The United States, while intending never to acquire lands from the Indians otherwise than peaceably and with their free consent, are fully determined in that manner, progressively and as their growing population may require, to reclaim from the state of nature and to bring into cultivation every part of the territory contained within their acknowledged boundaries'."

I said that I could not argue with Adams, but the Indians might have something to say about their freely consenting to the march of progress. Duesenberg said that violence was always regrettable but the difficulties were due to the unsuspected recalcitrance of the Indians and their stubborn unwillingness to integrate with the modern world. Were they not offered parcels of land gratis if they would but settle to farming and abandon their reservations?

I thought it indelicate to point out that one who had imagined that a whole territory as his birthright might consider the offer of a patch of ground too barren for white man's use to be a less than generous settlement. I told him something of what I'd observed regarding the fate of those unfortunates who abandoned their tribe in reliance on the promised land grant and fell prey to the likes of Dolan. The genial and unworldly Mr. Duesenberg had never seen an Indian or heard any word of the Trail of Tears. But still he had more to say on the subject.

"The Indians have the same chance as you or I," he told me. "The problem is, to quote President Andrew Jackson, that for the most part they possess 'neither the intelligence, the industry, the moral habits, nor the desire for improvements." They were simply an inferior species, he considered, doomed by feeble genetics and the law of survival of the fittest to extinction, except for such of them as might progress to occupy the lower ranks of our civilisation.

I found Mr. Duesenberg's Manifest Destiny a very close echo of the doctrines of the Prussian state which now prevailed in my own homeland. I was to remember him when the militaristic implications of that policy brought the world into calamitous warfare at the beginning of our present century, necessitating the expenditure of American blood and treasure to bring peace to the ruins of Europe. I expect that the Kaiser may have been a friendly, reasonable man like my neighbour. And even now, in my final years with the century in its third decade, with Germany devastated and exhausted, they have found a new leader whose message of the inherent superiority of his race and its obligation to realise destiny sounds to me just like the eugenic argument so beloved of our own progressives in Mr. Duesenberg's day. No doubt there'd be another European disaster resulting from this madness if it were not that Germany as a nation is broken past repair. It is a fearful thing to consider what industrious, sober-minded men may achieve when inspired by an ideal.

In any case, my neighbour's discourse served to revive my awareness of the concerns of the civilised world, the result of which was to impel me in an opposing direction - back to what he referred to as the untamed frontier.

***

My return to Lincoln later that year was a shock to Dolan and his cronies, I hope. Murphy was no more. The cancer claimed him, though he'd died in his bed, if not peacefully. I had sworn revenge on our persecutors, but he would be always beyond my reach. Though the thirst for vengeance reduces the one who is parched more than the one she feels wronged by, it is a passion that is easier to deny than subdue. The sensible course is to resist the indulgence of its promptings and not sink into that state of wilful ignorance where one's own motivations become clouded - even when it is not possible to forget. For example, my lawyers eventually succeeded in having Colonel Dudley arraigned, but the confusion between civil and military jurisdictions ensured he escaped without censure, let alone punishment. In time I have accepted this, but there is scarcely one week of my life goes by without my thinking of him at least once, sitting on his horse with his forces arrayed uselessly behind him, complacently scanning the scene from the elevation that abutted the town as its citizens were slaughtered by the hired thugs of Murphy and Co. I permit myself a sharp and sincere moment of hoping that his life has been devoid of advancement, prosperity or happiness (without ever allowing myself to stoop to enquiry of whether such has been the case) and when the moment is passed, I go about my business.

After calling on Juan Patron to thank him for his kindness in offering temporary accommodation and to entrust the greater part of my luggage to his loyal peons, my next visit took me beyond the town limits to the Bosque Grande ranch.

Chisum seemed older. Physically his appearance was not much changed, but his movement was more ponderous. He welcomed me warmly, remarking that he'd not hoped to see me again in the territory. I said I'd not been myself or he'd never have got me away in the first place, for I had divined that the accommodation and funds made available to me in Kansas and the costs of transportation must have been supplied by my friend. I had no means of my own at that time. I thanked him for his generosity.

"I owe you that and more," he replied. "I have the sense that your family has fought my own battles and paid the cost, and that was never my way."

I told him that the massacre was not his responsibility. In retrospect it was merely the climax of an orgy of looting, destruction, lawlessness and mayhem that the parties to the dispute of McSween and Murphy ushered in when they resorted to inviting low and criminal types to represent their interest. To a severe judgement, my husband had played his own part in raising the destructive whirlwind by his obdurate and sometimes intemperate words and deeds. Still I intended to see justice done.

"You might have used your own power more actively," I told him, "if you did not limit your life's concern to the raising and transportation of your precious bovines." I was always direct in my conversations with Mr. Chisum, which he seemed not to mind.

"Perhaps, but your husband would be guided by no man. There were times when I noted he seemed to be animated by a holy zeal, or carried on by his own words. When such a man is determined to hole his own boat, you may only leave him to his sinking." Chisum also liked to speak plainly.

"At least Alexander was right about something," the great man continued. "The order from President Hayes dismissing Governor Axell for his part in the graft and corruption affecting the state was made official two days after the battle. Your husband was counting on it, to start the breaking up of the Santa Fe interest. It shows he was right to hope that the nation's leaders would not remain indifferent to our woes forever. Someone at least was reading his letters and eventually investigating the matter."

"Too late of course."

"That's usually the way of things, and it is a bitter satisfaction," Chisum admitted. "Alex was at his best when he was patiently lawyering at a problem. He was a frail-seeming man who climbed many a mountain that way, one step at a time. He'd have likely climbed to a considerable height had he been spared."

I was in a hurry - there were so many threads to be picked up. Mr Chisum was shrewd enough to detect my mood and he answered my questions fully and succinctly. After that, we were all business that day.

As regards the bank, I owed providence a small debt that we had shifted its business to a separate, handsomely built banking hall shortly before the conflagration. I had already physically verified that the building was undamaged and secure. As my friend pointed out, the firm could not continue following the demise of its principals. HIs agents had supervised the return of deposits and the assignment of loans to one of our larger state banks that had means to absorb the business. The residual interest that was trickling in would be for the benefit of McSween's and Tunstall's heirs, but I'd need to supervise the administration of their estates before I could access the funds. For the moment the Bank of Lincoln was a locked up office with an empty safe inside.

I inquired about the Regulators. Mr. Chisum could not advise me as to their whereabouts and he counselled me against attempting to make contact with such as may yet be above ground. They were outside the law, he said, though the governor had pardoned the members of the Jesse Evans gang and other deputised gunmen who had fought for Murphy. I remarked that this was unacceptable. The appointment of our own supporters as deputies was equally valid in law as the handing out of badges to those thugs by Peppin. The Regulators were no more guilty than the men who had been pardoned, and I would make it my business to see that they were treated accordingly. I could not stand by when those who had defended my family were being unfairly persecuted for having done so.

Chisum advised me that William Bonney was now the head of the group and he'd led them out of the territory 'and if they have any sense, they'll stay away'. He remarked that Bonney was now claiming that one day he'd murder Chisum himself, the misunderstanding over wages due having magnified in the confused mind of the boy, to a degree that he now blamed the cattleman for his general misfortune.

"He said I owed him five hundred dollars and if I would not pay, he'd steal goods of mine to the value of the supposed debt. Later he's bragged he'll take my life into the bargain," Chisum said. "I don't take it personally, Billy was always of a boastful type. I'd say he has embraced his notoriety, dictating letters to the newspapers regarding his exploits that are duly published. Listing my name among his intended victims gets a better press than the unknown folks he's so far assassinated. Besides, he's set himself up against the world and society and I suppose I'm the most prominent member of society he's known. So long as he's posing as Robin Hood, I suppose he requires a wicked baron to contend with."

Chisum told me he did not anticipate Bonney would take any step to effect his threats, although given the reputed quickness of the boy with a pistol, I would understand if he was less than enthusiastic to make the case for his self-appointed nemesis to be granted the freedom of the county.

I asked after the Feliz ranch. He told me that some of Tunstall's people had stayed on. He was contributing to their subsistence but they needed to be told what to do next. The horses were secure but the cattle had mostly been driven off, and rebranded and sold on probably. I declared it would be my priority to set the ranch in order and asked if he could spare a man to assist and instruct me in the business. Then I must head to England, for Tunstall's relatives deserved to have an account of his doings and an explanation of his fate - besides that, I should need their authority to wind up his estate, and there was the matter of valuable legal work undertaken by McSween on behalf of Tunstall for which no final account had been rendered. I had hopes of persuading the family to make good what the deceased owed and contribute to my expenses of administration.

I conjectured that the legal work in which my husband was engaged at the time of his death would need to pass to some other firm so as to be brought to conclusion and the remittance of fees due. I had not yet made up my mind whether to rebuild the store but on the whole I thought I should not. There were some good people in the town but I had no wish in the longer term to remain and confront a daily reminder of what had occurred there.

"The town is not safe for you," Chisum warned me. "Murphy is gone, but Dolan is his long term associate and attorney. It's a moot point to consider how much of what Murphy did was Dolan's strategy from the off. He's a more circumspect man than the Major, not given to inflammatory talk, but he's no lesser a villain and he'll not hesitate to have you murdered, or anyone else who gets in his way."

"Nevertheless I mean to have satisfaction against him."

"How will you do that?"

"As Alexander would have - one step at a time through the patient application of the law."

I thanked my friend once more for his exertions on my behalf. I admitted I had more to ask of him. Those few resources that I should likely stand in possession of were few and not presently available to me. I would need a good attorney to develop and present my arguments against our enemy. I thought I had found one, by the name of Huston Chapman. I intended to see Dolan and Sheriff Peppin hanged and my husband's assets restored, but my attorney would need to be paid and I had to live in the meanwhile. I prayed that Mr. Chisum might advance sufficient funds to my personal estate to let the work continue.

"Are you sure about this Susan?" he asked me. "I had thought you would head east, begin a new life or resume a former one. Is this what you want, or what you feel you ought to try?"

I replied without hesitation that my life and work was here. "In that case," he told me, "your enterprise shall not fail for want of funding."

He said that we had some hopes. Dolan was clever but he did not inspire men as his predecessor could. The ranchers were moving away from him, some repulsed by the violent outrages in Lincoln. The federal authority was now alerted to the nefarious activities of the Santa Fe ring, which was far from saying that the ring might be quickly suppressed, but as a minimum the partners in crime would need to take some care to conceal their patterns of fraud and influence trading. McSween had uncovered something of the illicit connections between these supposed leaders of our community - a diligent attorney following his lead would uncover more. Further, the financial condition of the Murphy empire was parlous. The Major had purchased the amity of ranchers, in addition to the tribute he must pay to the men of Santa Fe. During the so-called war, Murphy had maintained not less than three notorious gangs on his payroll in addition to the various law enforcement officers and judiciary that were suborned to his cause. Chisum informed me that Peppin had quit the role of sheriff due to the matter of unpaid wages. Chisum had long maintained that if the conflict between his own interest and that of Murphy were long continued, then the wash of corrupt money would break upon the rock of the substantive wealth represented by the herds grazing the length of the Pecos river. His view had not changed.

I took my leave with my step lighter than it had been for some weeks. Enumerating to my friend the long list of what needed to be done had served to provide me with a clear sense of purpose and from that in turn my spirit seemed to derive energy. I was conscious of possessing the determination and pledged means to do what was required, together with something new - the captaincy of my vessel was now entrusted to my own two hands, and I accepted the command with grim resolve to prove a sturdy navigator.

***

On behalf of the poor boys, my attorney wrote letters and I paid visits to persons in authority to whom my recent misfortune granted access. Mr, Chapman's letters were logically and legally impeccable and sufficiently compelling to demonstrate to any person interested in the merits of the case that there could be no justification for a grant of immunity to one set of deputies on the basis that they were involved in a policing action, whilst denying the same privilege to sworn-in deputies who opposed them, particularly given that the state had determined as a matter of policy to make no inquiry or ruling as to the rights and wrongs between the opposing camps. I discovered that the most erudite and persuasive correspondence may easily be ignored or its contents wilfully misconstrued, but it is more difficult to ignore someone who is sitting across a desk from you and has the sympathy of her community. This is, I suppose, how the business of politics proceeds.

Eventually a strange compromise was proposed. All those participants in the Battle of Lincoln who had been lawfully deputised prior to the skirmish would receive a pardon, save for William Bonney. I suppose that the boy's fame worked against him - he was an embarrassment to the state and regarded as a notorious criminal (as he desired) even if he'd not been sentenced by any court at that time. It was also clear that the influence of the Dolan faction remained undiminished and opposed to any resolution that was genuinely even-handed.

Notwithstanding, our populace was roused to indignation at the clear partiality of this proposal, and the truth was that Billy had his supporters in our community, for reasons that I do not claim to understand - to me he was a foolish and insecure child, dangerous to himself and others, though that did not vitiate the duty I owed him. In the end, the Governor offered the final outlaw a pardon subject to terms, that he'd need to come to the Governor's own office on an appointed day to hear read. The political calculation leading to such an offer was naked - either Billy would fail to appear, in which case public opinion would be appeased, or else he'd make his entrance and be apprehended.

The politician had failed to count on a third possibility. In the event, Bonney duly presented himself on the specified day, with pistol and other weaponry prominently arrayed about his person. He heard out the proposed terms before politely declining an offer on terms that amounted to throwing himself on the mercy of the state (and for this I can not blame him) then he rode away. By this bold escapade he both added to the regard in which he was held in sections of our community, and shamed the public officials for their seeming impotence and cowardly reluctance to confront him. As I look back it is clear to me that it was for incidents such as this (and his self-justifying public epistles that the newspaper readers eagerly scanned) that his person became intolerable to authority, rather than for his crimes. Our territory was well supplied with killers of every kind and although Bonney was reputed a prolific assassin, this alone would not have sealed his fate.

When I judged that I had effected what I could for our friends in adversity, from which experience I emerged resolved to have no more to do with politicians of any stamp if I could avoid it, I furnished Chapman with detailed instructions and authorities to pursue the winding of of the bank and the various interests that were in my care before reserving my passage to England, where I planned to pay my respects and conclude business with the family of the late Mr. Tunstall.

***

My journey so far as New York was uncomfortable and uneventful. Under different circumstances, I should have found leisure to visit that great city, but my schedule admitted no such indulgence. In fact, it had taken me longer to traverse the continent than the sea voyage would last, since our steamship required but seven days and some hours to convey us to Liverpool, a fact of which our conveyors the Iman line boasted with inordinate pride.

'The City of Berlin' had been a record breaking vessel for the transatlantic route, but although she was still a new ship, I learned that record had already been broken, for new and ever faster vessels were being commissioned as fast as the shipyards of the Clyde and Belfast could rivet them together. I was informed that the Berlin was four hundred and eighty-eight feet in length (a ship as long as our main street at la Placita) weighed 5,400 tons - a displacement I was incapable of comprehending by reference to any thing in my experience, and could carry almost 1,200 passengers (never mind the crew) at a speed of sixteen knots. When they explained that a knot was a nautical mile, I was not much enlightened - it was enough to know this was a ship that travelled swiftly.

I had my concerns that the vessel would be cold, a sensation I've never been comfortable to accommodate. My apprehension was justified, at least above decks, though I found myself incapable of remaining below and away from fresh air for very long. Though my friend had provided me with funds for the voyage, I did not wish to presume upon his generosity by booking a first class berth. The elite passengers, some two hundred souls, appeared to enjoy luxury beyond the imagining of we third class inmates huddled below. The Berlin had a capacity nine hundred common travellers. On the voyage to England, the space allotted to us seemed enough to be conducive to our ease. I was warned that conditions for the return journey would be vastly more cramped, and I can attest that it was so. Well, the cattle trucks that you meet at the rail head at the end of a drive have come across half the breadth of the United States empty - for steers require but a one way visa. And so it was with most of the transatlantic voyagers. Those heading to Europe were rich tourists in pursuit of culture plus a few curiosities like myself. Coming back it would be crammed with every kind of European (but in particular it seemed, the Irish) coming to people our New World.

I had heard the familiar stories about the horrors of the Atlantic crossings - emigrant families herded into cramped, dark and insanitary conditions, confined below decks. Perhaps these were legends rooted in a distant past that had swelled incrementally in the re-telling.I can only say that I found the City of Berlin to be a thoroughly modern vessel and a credit to the Iman line. The dining room could not have been more spacious, for it utilised the full width of the craft, a distance of some forty-four feet according to my informants. More, the darkness of our night hours was, if not banished, at least reduced to shadows, since the ship was supplied with electric lighting - allegedly the first vessel of its kind to be so equipped. This was an innovation of wonder, according to the proud crew members who failed to tire of reminding we passengers of our good fortune, often punctuating their lesson by shutting down and restarting the electric lighting in their own immediate vicinity, which seeming magic was achieved by the simple flicking of a switch in the interior ways and chambers that were fitted with the utility.

I found the monotony concomitant with travel by sea soothing, and I would have been happy for at least the outward journey to take more than a week. I was never vomitous, though I could not help but be incommoded by the not uncommon reek of those who were. I spent as much time as I could in the open, wrapped in all the blankets I could secure, reflecting on the nature of the open sea, which is unchanging, day after day, when viewed in general, though each constituent part of it undergoes an unresting turmoil of movement, driven on by the unseen hand of tide and weather. The oceans are so impressive that we can not look away from them, as if expecting to find some clue to the nature of our own existence - even if it is only that we are very small indeed. In fact the waters are huge and indifferent, and would continue their roil and sweep whether or not there was a human there to name them sea. From time to time I thought of the people of my acquaintance in New Mexico who might never have seen the ocean.

If the sea was implacable nature, the boat was humanity, driving on through squall and swell, the waves thudding against the hull and the dull throb of the turbines felt everywhere as the men in the engine room shovelled coal into the black furnace beneath us. It seems to me that while a sailing boat aspires to partner nature, a steamship ploughs forward in defiance of it. It is the very picture of the times with our spirits disdaining the constraints of the elemental world.

People were waiting at the dock in Liverpool to meet me. From there I was taken to some village that I suppose was the ancestral seat of the Tunstalls - I have no recollection of the name but it struck me as English by virtue of its peculiarity. I had half-expected that the Tunstall clan in its entirety would occupy a stately home with some familial crest hanging above a massive stone grate while hunting dogs dozed by the fire. And in fact, they were a wealthy family and the parents and some of their adult offspring lived in a big house which however made no claim to aristocratic origins. The family had money from ancient industry, and then the coal that was under some of their land. I was treated with perfect kindness, which is not invariably the experience of those who bring bad news or the horrid details of it. I was made to feel as if each of the Tunstalls cared about my own person, which was an impression I had always carried away from meeting my late friend their relative, however negligent he might have been in matters of formal decorum. I quickly satisfied myself that whatever motivation impelled Tunstall to seek his fortune out West (and which of us knows why we make our most fatal decisions?) it must have been a questing toward rather than a running from that landed him in Lincoln County.

I remained as guest for some days, at the family's insistence. There was a sister I took walks with. The English countryside was a curiosity - so much green, so many different kinds of trees. The topography altered with every half-mile we walked along metalled roads with high hedgerows. One could not walk for ten minutes without passing a house or some other indicator of human occupation of the land. It was a country in miniature and teeming with people.

Audrey was younger than I, and intensely curious about the world. She was not so reticent as the others of her country, indeed it was easy to suppose her direct manner might cause offence to someone other than a Germanic inhabitant of New Mexico. I became very fond of her. The first time we were alone she could barely wait to ask me about Alexander (the demeanour and behaviour of men in general were a source of fascination to her). I know she meant well. For these people it was very normal to speak of the deceased and perhaps it would have done me good to unburden some of what I was feeling at that time, though unreasoning rage followed by hollow misery is all I can remember feeling. In any case, I considered for a moment how I should begin to speak of Alexander and how it felt to be his widow. I felt choked, as if either no word could come out or else a torrent of cries and tears should follow. There are times when you can say nothing or everything, when I have learned to keep my mouth closed. Audrey

must have seen my expression and concluded she'd gone too far. She moved on quickly ahead of my reply, asking how far I was into my First Mourning. I had to ask her to explain what that meant.

"I suppose you have different rules," she began.

"Here there are four stages of mourning. For a widow it's supposed to last four years, though if a man loses his wife he only wears black for three months. My mourning is for a brother and yours for a husband, so I may add some colour to my dress in a month or two.

People will make allowances for you, since you're American. Really you should be wearing bombazine fabric covered in crepe for the first thirteen months. Your mourning bonnet is more or less correct but the cuffs and collar are not quite right."

I said I had not supposed that private grief could be a matter for such rigorous prescription.

"It seems awfully harsh," Audrey agreed. "Mummy says that in the past things were quite simple, but over the years they keep adding more and more elaborations. It's the fault of the Queen. Before, the rules were useful, since one knew what was expected and at the end of a decent period, the bereaved were expected and obliged to move on. Some people find it difficult to let go of the dead you see."

"Why should it be the Queen"s business how long you wear black?"

Audrey said that I must know that Victoria was Queen at the age of eighteen, wedded to her cousin at twenty and widowed with nine children at forty-two. Twenty years on she was still mourning her beloved Albert and so the whole country had to become obsessed by death. In Audrey's view, the monarch was greatly to blame. A private person might give in to any mania, but a queen must set the example for her people, otherwise what was the point in having a king or queen at all? The consequence of such gloomy manners was simply a great deal of fatuous cant in the public life of the nation and an epidemic of hypocrisy in its private doings. Those who were not yet fully moribund of spirit suffered most.

"Take my own case. I'm young but I shall not be so for long. I want life and vivacity, not this funereal atmosphere all around. At least Victoria had her own youth, but she denies her subjects theirs. Thank goodness we don't live in London or it would be worse."

We crossed a stile, which was a gap made in a wall with a little step to help us over. The passage was difficult enough in our confining dress, which I at least was unused to. We had to help one another across, into a field where a well trodden path led on to another wall that had a gate. I remained amazed at the enclosed state of the country, in which it seemed that every small patch of ground had been claimed for some purpose.

Audrey continued her theme, stating her opinion that if the Queen couldn't make up her mind to come back to life, she should have the decency to take the opposite course.

"Philip of Spain lingered on for so long after the Armada, that in the end it was said either Philip dies or Spain dies. I fear that England may come to the same state."

She was a quick scholar, like her brother. I had a vague understanding of the history of the Spanish Armada, but I took her point. She begged me not to repeat our conversation to any of the family or else, she said, they'd have to pretend to be shocked.

"You should marry again," she declared. "Go back to America where you're free to do as you please. Live in New York and marry a rich man."

We both laughed. "I'm serious though," she insisted. "We have all this talk about what he would have wanted or what she would have wanted. The truth is you can't want anything if you are dead. We are too serious. Although I hear that in the former colonies, you are so prim that even the table legs are hidden in lace for fear they should resemble an exposed ankle."

"That's funny," I replied. "We are told the same story of yourselves. In fact, I had the origin of the legend - it was a remark one of your sea captain authors, named Marryat, after a trip to New England. He intended it as a joke."

I further explained that dining table legs really were kept covered at home, not out of ill-conceived modesty, but because the near impossibility of obtaining good hardwood table necessitated that plain pine be kept from view. We were more ashamed of our unpolished furniture than concerned to keep our ankles hid, I advised my friend.

I had no wish to return to the theme of my future matrimonial expectations. Audrey had told me before that in England women gave up their property when they married, since the law regarded the couple as one person of which the husband was the head. I had no idea whether this was correct. If so, I suspected that the lawyers of families of substance would be kept busy devising settled trusts to keep assets from the hands of treasure seeking male suitors. At least, that was how I imagined McSween would have dealt with the problem. (I admit that even years later I would often fall into the habit of thinking in the poor man's shoes - 'what would Alex have thought of this?'). In any case, one would expect that even the rumour of such an outcome would be enough to scare any would-be bride from the altar, but still it seemed that in England matrimony was the favourite topic of discussion among ladies of every vintage and class. I understood that here a decent lady had scant opportunity to earn her own living in the world.

To change the subject, I asked Audrey to describe what Tunstall was like as a child. She replied that he'd been brave, serious but in a jolly way, a poor student except in the few subjects that interested him and precocious in those. Growing up he was always big for his age, and clumsy.

"I loved my brother, but you lost your husband," she said. "What was he like? I imagine they must have been friends as well as business partners."

How to describe my late husband? I was not sure I had attempted to encompass him previously, for myself or anyone else. I told her that McSween was a noble character who believed that people could be better than they currently were. As a husband he was steadfast - we had a partnership of our own, I told her, for all matters of importance to our commonwealth were discussed between us. Alexander didn't know his own nature very well, I opined, but then I was not sure that men should reflect too much on their own characters for it is their business to be doing and contemplation of self is the enemy of action. Audrey laughed and said that her brother never had an inkling of his own character or that of anyone else. He assumed that other people were like him - vaguely kind and disposed to do good and in severe need of being enlightened about whatever were his own enthusiasms of the moment.

"If he came across anyone wicked he'd suppose there was just something they need to have explained to them,"

Audrey said. "Though one doesn't come across many truly wicked individuals living here. Petty small-mindedness is as bad as it gets."

"I'm afraid we have a surfeit of bad men in New Mexico."

"But John loved the country, You can tell from his letters."

I wondered if I loved the country, or only couldn't escape its grip. The Tunstalls had gone so far as to hint I might make a new start in the Old World, but what should I do? I was hardly likely to make a good marriage. I might be a governess I supposed, scraping pennies together to pay for trips on my few days of leisure each year. I thought it was possible I did not even like children. Perhaps I had a future career as a companion to another lady of similar circumstance but greater wealth, whose complaints about her treatment by the world I'd have to endure, becoming increasingly enraged and never able to display it. I was not sure that I loved my home, but it was the only place I had a chance to make a life I might want to live.

The indelicate matter of legal fees outstanding from Tunstall's estate to my husband's was resolved quickly. When I mentioned the matter, I was asked to supply copies of invoices rendered and work in progress before the fateful day. The evening after I handed these over, Tunstall's father presented me with a banker's draft made out for the sum total. He thanked me for my diligence in seeing that everything was being done properly. He asked about the ranch, noting that his son loved his horses near as much as people and would want them to be cared for. I explained the current circumstance as best I could, expressing my confidence that Mr. John Chisum would see to it that the place did not fall into ruin. Mr. Tunstall senior requested that I should act in the winding up of his son's estate in the West and I consented to do so.

I sensed that the father went into great detail in regard to the practical aspects of the business, wanting to be informed of everything, mostly because the end of the discussion of business should signal the moment when he'd begin to reflect emotionally on the loss of his boy. I read in a journal not long ago the words of some expert to the effect that our declining levels of infant mortality have caused the loss of a child to become more traumatic. According to this social scientist, the parents of my own generation and earlier were hardened to the death of children, since it was common. I'm an old lady who says that maybe the public nature of grief has changed - for some reason we're persuaded these days that others want to know how we're feeling about everything, rather than keeping our own counsel - but I never met any parent that didn't think seeing their child die before them was the worst that could happen.

In any case, Mr. Tunstall the father was a gentleman, like his son, whether he got his money from commerce or could trace his ancestry back to Julius Caesar. I'd have stayed longer with the family and seen more of the country if I could, but my return passage was booked and I was sure that events in Lincoln County would not pause to await my coming.

Chapter Seven - 1879

When I reached New York, I found that Juan Patron had wired me to say that Huston Chapman had been shot. My attorney Huston Chapman was the least ingratiating man that could be imagined. When I left his office after our first meeting, I assumed he disapproved of or even disliked me. I found out later that most everyone who knew him had that initial reaction. He'd been

recommended to me as a person of integrity who wouldn't back down from a just cause and I can say that he did not fail me in either respect.

Huston was a stocky man of medium height with a short thick neck and a chest like a bull. Dark complexioned, with wiry black hair that was grey where he'd let the whiskers grow out at the sides, he was otherwise clean shaven and thinning on top. I never saw him without a suit and necktie, or missing a shine on his boots, though he was the opposite of a dandy. He'd a massive, deeply lined forehead that weighed down features I can only describe as stern. His constant expression was that kind of serious people describe as intense. I struggled to imagine what would be his reaction should any person have the temerity to relate a joke in his presence - but maybe that never happened.

We never exchanged small talk. I didn't even have the chance to ask him about the empty sleeve where his left arm should have been. I assumed he'd lost it in the Civil War, since I couldn't imagine a person of his temperament putting himself in the way of such an injury if it were not in the call of duty, but this was a thing never spoken of. When I imagined myself asking what happened to the arm, the only response I pictured was him looking at the place where the arm should be, as if he'd never noticed its absence previously. Which is to say that for Huston Chapman, 'what if' did not exist.

I've known my share of men who for good or ill were self-sufficient in the certainty of their own person. McSween had his convictions, based on the hours he'd spent pondering moral issues and the conclusions he drew regarding the advancement of his fellow man. He convinced himself that society required the rule of law and acted accordingly. I'm sure Huston Chapman embarked on no such introspection regarding his motives. He'd simply discovered that the law was his profession, and the law must be served. His was a fierce, Old Testament kind of faith that admitted neither doubt nor even the notion that he might shirk his duty. He had such a lack of imagination that it might be seen as an impediment to his effectiveness as an attorney, though this was more that compensated by his patient diligence and utter commitment.

In what it pleased him to call his leisure hours, Mr. Chapman was fond of playing the game of billiards, as if any less apt pastime for a man lacking an arm might be thought of. We had an establishment in town that had a table, and since the Mrs. Chapman that I sometimes heard of but never saw remained at home when he was in Lincoln, he would sometimes play there before returning to his hotel room. I need hardly say that Lincoln in this moment was a place to which no man even of average prudence and discretion would expose his spouse. In the case of the Chapmans, I imagine that any suggestion of the wife attending on her husband in his mission would have been dismissed in the moment it was proposed. As regards the matter of billiards, I had the chance to observe Chapman's skill only once, but it was a thing to behold.

Lacking the means to make what is called a bridge with his supporting hand, Huston took a grip on the cue in the conventional manner, resting the part closest to the tip on the baize cushion of the table or, when a longer shot was called for, on the spider extension that he would lay across the felt. It may be imagined that even expert spectators were confident he'd be unable to make his shot, for the cue gripped at such an extremity from the tip must surely waver without a secure brace. They did not account for the extreme steadiness of his arm or the delicacy with which he could address the ball without straying from the fragile support he had set.

Prior to taking his shot, it was Mr. Chapman's habit silently to trace out the paths of the balls he was about to hit with the tip of his cue in the air just above the table. This was done not in a spirit of bravado but with a studious air, as if he were working through a problem in his mind. From this habit, even a novice such as myself could discern that what he intended, he generally achieved. I speculate that an able-bodied man with a similar level of skill might have beaten him comfortably. The fact is he was more than good enough to defeat any of our saloon amateurs, though he seemed to delight more in the geometry and kinetics of the table than take notice of his score. With his manifest supposed infirmity, I suppose he'd have been able to make a living from the game if his temperament had been other than it was. Of course Mr Chapman would no more wager on the outcome of a game than he'd accompany its passage with the imbibing of liquors.

Watching Huston play told me something about the man. He must have spent an unimaginable number of hours mastering the challenges of the game for a man with one arm. Perhaps he'd played before he was maimed, and determined not to recognise his incapacity after. So there was patient determination, but more. The strength and steadiness in his one arm were unnatural, but without a good eye they would be useless. I watched his opponents make their line, then they'd squint down the cue and adjust to their second or third thoughts about where the white ball should rightly go. Once Huston had determined his line, I never once saw him deflect or guess against himself. It was to show the unshakeable faith that sustained him.

At this point, I'll say a word about Dolan as well. Dolan started as attorney and partner to Murphy, but he was a different kind of man to the King. Murphy was shrewd and unscrupulous - he determined his objective and moved toward it without reference to whomsoever might be standing in his path, but he was also a persuasive character with a degree of charm, ruled over by his passions. Murphy had brought his own enterprise to ruin, as Chisum knew he would, through an ever increasing expenditure on bribery, corruption and the hiring of brute force that could never yield a dividend sufficient to warrant the investment it required. Dolan would never have been driven by overweening pride and resentment to embark on such a reckless gambit, let alone maintain it to such an extremity.

Murphy knew and had accepted the reality of his nature. He considered he was damned - he'd made an accord with the devil and was determined to secure for himself the most favourable return on the deal. Dolan was that kind of criminal who persuades himself that he is no more than a species of businessman. His view of human nature was that it was invariably as twisted, selfish and deformed as his own character - the only reason he was above and others below was that he was smarter. Dolan would have a man killed, not because that man had offended him (or because he'd worked himself into a rage of pretending this was the case) but when he'd calculated it made good business sense. When people said that Dolan was worse than Murphy, I believe this is what they meant, even if they couldn't express it. And now Murphy was dead and Dolan was running the show.

The way Dolan saw things, if you had bought the judiciary and law enforcement, so that you were immune from prosecution, you had the option to kill someone who was in your way. And if there were ten people who were in the way, you could have them all killed. The additional expense was negligible once you had bought the law - just a few extra dollars for the men who made it happen .

Huston Chapman never represented to Dolan the kind of threat that Major Murphy feared from my husband. His ongoing inquiries and his submissions to the court on my behalf were an irritation, as well as encouraging others in the belief that Dolan might be challenged with impunity. In such circumstances, Dolan saw no requirement to foment a pretext for dispute, or summon a gang of outlaws that would want paying. HIs inconvenience was easily resolved by a man with a gun who emerged from the shadows and walked calmly away after firing, whose face no one saw or could recall. The face hardly mattered because although another squeezed the trigger, it would be known by everyone that the real killer was Dolan, and next time they'd think twice before crossing him.

As soon as I read that telegram, I made arrangements to return to Lincoln as soon as I could, dreading the situation I might find there. Chapman had already been decently interred. I had a letter waiting for me from his firm informing me that in the light of the sad loss of their colleague they would be unable to continue to represent my interest in the territory, which was to say, I suppose, that they had no other advocate on board who relished the opportunity of being gunned down in the open street. I sought an audience with our new Sheriff (the miserable Peppin having relinquished his office) to enquire what steps he was taking to apprehend the killer - his defeated and evasive words demonstrated amply for my benefit that in the matter of detection and taking of evidence, the responsibility for any enquiry would rest on my own shoulders. I looked for counsel from Juan Patron, the oldest living friend I had in la Placita.

Juan gave me the full story. Dolan had arranged a meeting under conditions of truce with William Bonney, which both attended armed and with two others as their guardians. Jimmy Dolan pointed out that there was nothing left for the parties to fight over. The enterprises of Tunstall and McSween were extinguished by the death of the principals. Murphy and Co was bankrupt and its successor Murphy, Dolan Riley and Co. had questionable prospects. The one unexploited resource of the land that was available to both sides was the Chisum herd, from which each side must hope to cut out sufficient stock to make good their losses, in accordance with previous practice. All present agreed that this arrangement made sense.

The meeting was held in a saloon of the town, so the discussion was public if subject to widely diverging report. The parties were drinking heavily and after their negotiations concluded the peace treaty was toasted with more drink. Legend allowed that after quitting the saloon, Dolan and his confederates were staggering away when they chanced upon Chapman who was unluckily just leaving his office. One of the party demanded in jest that the lawyer should dance for them and shot some lead into the ground nearby by way of encouragement. Chapman responded that he was a state attorney and he would not besmirch the dignity of his office by capering for a drunken fool, whereafter he was duly shot dead in front of the witnesses.

I did not believe one word about the supposed drunken prank gone wrong. I had heard of the practice of 'making the tenderfoot dance' from the same source as everyone else - it was a staple of the dime novels that romanticised our Western frontier. I never heard of any case outside of these fictions. Though our wilder elements were not above wasting ordinance in futile display, it was clear enough even to them that firing off in the direction of another was likely to have fatal consequences on one side or another. To be frank, the general standard of pistol accuracy in our territory would have made aiming near to the feet of another more hazardous than it might sound, and even a tenderfoot may have a pistol of his own. Besides which, if one shot might be accidental that did not explain why Chapman was shot three times, once through the heart - an organ at some remove from his boots.

For me it was clear that the tale was invented to explain why more than one shot was fired, to give the incident the colour of a near accident, and to provide a fatuous motive. With his long campaign drawing to a close, Dolan wanted the troublesome Chapman got rid of. His assassination was the first casualty of the peace. There would have been some pathetic argument of self-defence too, but for the fact of Chapman being crippled by having but one arm and there being no implement found about his corpse more deadly than an ink pen.

I told my friend Juan that I had frankly come to despair of our community. It seemed that the ordinary citizens of Lincoln were prepared to tolerate the presence of killers in their midst even when outrages were committed on our own streets. A few of our neighbours, who were otherwise sober working people, even gloried in the impotence of authority and the audaciousness of these bad men, though it would mean the death of the town, for how could a town prosper and grow in the diseased moral condition to which we had declined? I recalled that in the forties and fifties, when San Francisco was not much more than a goldrush town, the local worthy people had yet been able to band together in clandestine manner (for the police and judiciary were bought there as they were in LIncoln) and cleanse the city, first of the Australian gangs who'd landed from Sydney to terrorise the state and then of the more insidious canker of home grown corrupt vice. Was there no prospect of a similar vigilante movement arising in our own case, I wondered?

"The vigilantes of California began well," Don Juan recalled me, "but over time, their secret society came to perpetuate the abuses that its members were sworn to eliminate. Those people were bound together by what our late friend called the material interest, and for such a moment comes when it is too easy to use power in defence of one's personal ambitions, for example by driving off an upstart newcomer recently set up in trade and threatening to become a competitor. Eventually the morality of all masonic institutions based on secrecy decline in this way.

"Besides," he continued, "San Francisco is a city in which the representatives of the material interest are strongly concentrated. Our own pueblo is home to some cattle ranchers and the ancillary trades that spring up around their needs. We have neither heroes, nor men of property, save for your Mr. Chisum and his few friends, who like him think only of the care of their livestock."

"What will happen to us Juan?" there was no comfort for me in his words.

"Susan, I can only say that my own people have been on this land for almost two hundred years. We followed the Camino Reale when the trade route to the north was opened, and when Spain abandoned Mexico we remained behind, forgotten. In that time, we have seen many times that sickness that arises from the soil of this territory from time to time and afflicts men with the taste form murder. Once it takes hold, they find it progressively easier to kill and destroy. The restraint of society is eroded and what is left over is animal in nature. In the end some men are consumed by the lust for violence and need to be hunted down like mad dogs. Whilst the epidemic continues you may hear even respectable farmers enjoying the orgy of crime vicariously. It has happened here before and it will happen again. People like you and me can only do what my ancestors have done in such moments, watch and hope to survive until the fever subsides."

"I cannot wait, Juan. My situation leaves me no options beyond flight or fight."

"Then I will try to help you."

This was a revelation. How could Don Juan Patron assist in a struggle against the vested interest that threatened me? He was a respected person and patriarch of one of the first families, but the community of our Spanish speaking neighbours generally kept aloof from the rough business of the town, and its voice was rarely heard in matters of civic importance.

Juan Patron explained, somewhat apologetically, that he was lately appointed special representative for those in our territory who had Spanish origins and language. He said it would doubtless be better if our elected representatives and officials could regard themselves as the delegates of all who lived within their constituencies, or failing that a Spanish representative should be elected, for was that not the American way? Nevertheless when he'd been invited to assume the office, for what it was worth, he'd felt obliged to accept.

"It is a beginning at least."

"But what does it actually mean, Juan?"

"It means I am officially deputised to attend the legislature and make a nuisance of myself in matters affecting Mexicans," Juan replied, "even if you and I know that I have no connection to the peoples of that country beyond certain similarities in the way we speak. This is a distinction too fine for the politicians of Santa Fe to take into their cognoscence."

"Those politicians are dangerous."

"And monstrously unpleasant company," Juan Patron agreed. "But what am I to do? We cannot complain that our neighbours are complaisant in the face of mayhem and vice if we shirk our own duty when it comes knocking on the door. At least I can tell my friend that such small influence as I may have in this office will be at the disposal of her own just cause."

I found the notion of Juan Patron being mixed up in the swamp of larceny, graft and personal spite that we dignified with the name of politics horrifying. He was an old man now, full of dignity, honest without compromise. They'd spit him out broken or worse. I urged him to caution and not to assume the slightest risk on my account. I said it would be more than friendship could require if he would occasionally share with me intelligence as to the ongoing machinations he might witness. Juan Patron waved away my fears for himself. He said that the more years one had lived already, the less there was to be frightened of.

"It is you who should be cautious," he said. "Your husband was like a man of old Europe. He found security in deeds and sworn depositions. He was not the first. The French and the Spanish made treaties with the Independent States over land, even the British too. They signed papers and imagined their business to be sorted out for good - in America there was enough space for everyone and most of it was empty. They did not see that we Americans meant to have it all, and so the treaties were a waste of paper. Our borders were always destined to be the seaboards."

"What of Mexico and Canada?"

Juan showed his courteous smile. "When Sam Houston drove the Mexican army from Texas, he chased them south thinking maybe he'd take that land as well, following Cortez. The further they went the more his men were dismayed by the degraded nature of the country, till they concluded Mexico was neither a threat nor worth the trouble of conquest, and went home. I know very little about Canada except that it is very cold."

"They say Billy is with the Mexicans, in the pueblos," I commented.

"Those people love him, unaccountably," Juan replied.

"He was always charming and full of foolery, except when he was murderous."

"It is more than that," Juan Patron replied. "They say that he thinks no worse of a Mexican than he does of any other man. It is true that he boasts of the numbers of men he has killed excluding Mexicans and Indians, but this is no more than the accepted accounting method of these desperadoes. They also say he hates Bob Ollinger, who was once his friend, due to Ollinger's bragging of the Mexicans he's shot in the back or in the stomach when they were unarmed."

"I never heard of Ollinger."

"If you stay in town, you'll see him. He makes a striking figure - long hair and a face that could pass for handsome. He dresses as an old style frontiersman - with the buckskin jacket of a buffalo hunter - and he keeps his gun polished. Your likely to observe him making sudden tricks with the big knife he carries and has practiced throwing till he is able to impale a wooden post most effectively."

"What does such a one do in town?"

"Ollinger is one of the number that have been brought in recently by Dolan. I think Dolan may have handed him a deputies badge. His only work is to guarantee that the townspeople remain sufficiently cowed as to go along with whatever plans Dolan has for us."

Juan remarked that the town was not a safe place for me and I really must remain at his house, for a few days at least.

***

It is safe to say that Juan Patron did not limit his efforts on my behalf to whatever was within the bounds of prudence. Either that, or the blood lust that had taken hold of the county had reached a stage where even a small matter might prompt more killing. I can not say why my own person was spared if it be not for providence, the guiding hand of which I sincerely doubt. Women and children too were by now numbered among the victims of our discontent.

A few weeks after our conversation, Juan Patron was approached in the street by an unidentified stranger, who made some trivial enquiry of him before producing a knife from a coat pocket and proceeding to stab my friend in the heart. The stranger strolled away calmly, leaving the knife embedded in his victim's breast. From what I hear, Juan Patron collapsed to the boardwalk and lay crumpled on his back. Whatever last words his lips mouthed, his lungs possessed insufficient force to deliver, and so his life bubbled away speechless.

I can't say exactly why it hurt me so much - maybe even more than the death of my husband. When Alexander fell, it seemed like we were engaged in a war, and the participants in war or war's counterfeit needs must be accepting the risk of a fatal outcome. Not only was Don Juan outside of our petty squabbles, but he and his forbears pre-dated us in the territory, so that it was as if some part of the timeless land that could not be regained had been sacrificed to our vanity and spite.

Even the manner in which he'd been killed was an insult. The stabbing was Dolan's way of saying that a presumed Mexican was not worth a bullet. When I saw the open casket, it was as if they'd drained every last drop of blood out of the old man. He'd a pallor that the undertaker's rouge did no more than accent. Still there was a nobility in his dead face that was not like the expression of the other violently killed men I'd seen laid to alleged rest, which I attributed either to some characteristic of his ancient lineage or else the superior skill of the embalmer.

The figure in the box was smaller than the Juan Patron I remembered - death had shrunk him, or the living version had seemed bigger than it really was due to his fine clothes and imposing presence. Now, he seemed desiccated, like an Egyptian mummy without the bandages. His people kept vigil with candles burning all around even in the daytime.

The ceremony was one of the few Catholic masses I ever attended. Though the events of my life have not inclined me to credit the existence of a benevolent deity of any denomination, I was raised in the protestant faith (notwithstanding my distant German ancestors cleaved to the church of Rome) and so the funeral service I was used to hearing was a few words spoken to a congregation sitting on plain benches in a brightly lit barn. There'd be a little about death, to the effect that it came to everyone, and then more about Jesus and the life hereafter that was promised the faithful, then the simple melody of a hymn sung with more sincerity than musical skill, accompanied by a wheezing harmonium. In contrast, I recall the mass for Juan being said in Latin - in any event the specific words were incomprehensible to me, but served effectively and at length to communicate the solemn awfulness of death. The church was dark and smelling of incense. The music was beautiful rather than inclusive - I mean it was like something given to us, more than a noise we made for ourselves collectively.

The church was beautiful in its way - full of dusty representations of saints that the years had granted authority beyond what the skill of the original craftsman had been able to confer. I knew the papists for idolators and here was more proof, I understood the service well enough to hear repeated prayers to Mary and the names of various saints who were invoked as if they'd be able to intercede with the almighty on behalf of the deceased.

Despite this nonsense, I've been on the side of beauty all my life, even or especially when it's been hard to find the sense of life. I was told that a mass would be said for the repose of the soul of Juan Patron every year for as long as there were people alive who remembered him - this resembled a bid to augment one's spiritual capital posthumously, in case you'd not been quite good enough in personal life to warrant admission to paradise. I found aspects of the business dishonest. On the other hand, I reflected that if my neighbours could be induced to view mortality with the same respectful dread as these folk, perhaps they'd be less ready to blast holes in one another over trifles.

Whatever the reason, the death of Juan Patron has weighed heavy on me these long years, with a sense of responsibility, but then I'd no leisure to mourn him properly in my heart, for everywhere I turned there was some matter that required my urgent care and now it felt like I'd no soul to confide with, save my friend Mr. Chisum when I could meet him. I was not yet thirty-six years old and yet it felt like almost everyone in the world I cared about was dead.

***

I determined that I should bring the viper Dolan to the gallows, and by extreme perseverance and shaming of the supposed administrators of justice in our state I at length succeeded in having him arraigned for the homicide of Huston Chapman. Chapman had been a member of the state bar and a person of good family. Of course there was no chance that one so eminent as Dolan would stand trial for the killing of one of our Spanish speaking residents, however strong the circumstantial evidence linking him to the crime. Dolan himself facilitated my efforts, in that he took progressively fewer pains to conceal his murderous complicity in the ongoing violence. I suppose he judged himself immune from suit, and sought to terrorise the populace into obedience.

The outcome of the prosecution demonstrated my enemy's astute strategy as well as the extent of his influence. He contrived to have the case transferred to a court where the judge and the supposed randomly selected jury were individuals suborned to his cause. An acquittal was the inevitable verdict, though I enjoyed the minor satisfaction of having him stand in the dock and face his accusers. No impartial person who heard the evidence could have doubted that the killing was ordered by Dolan. It remains a source of continuing pain for me that this corrupt man later contrived to execute the judgement obtained in the Fritz case against the Tunstall estate and by this means to secure the Rio Feliz ranch for his personal abode. He died there in his bed, aged forty-nine years, succumbing to a deserved and overdue disease.

From Juan Patron, I now had the names of the parties comprising the membership of the Santa Fe Ring, together with a report of the abuses that each of its principals was chiefly interested in. The Murphy/Dolan faction continued to enjoy the support of our public administrators due to the patronage of the Ring, which I was shocked to discover comprised a majority of the most prominent citizens of our nascent state. Their chief business was to grab land cheap and sell it dear, supplemented by fraudulent dealing in federal contracts and cattle theft by proxy. The Ring was engaged in a bitter struggle with the railroad company, seeking to extract a ransom for each strip of land that must be acquired for the great project of linking the east and west seaboards by rail and the connecting lines that linked the cities en route. In this struggle they eventually overreached, for the directors of the joint stock company that was contracted to build the railway were bigger crooks than themselves. Perhaps my information was not so difficult to come by, since the business was on the way to being notorious, but I was conscious that a heavy price had been paid for it. More bitter than the extent of the corruption of our state was the realisation that every person of eminence to whom one might bring evidence of the wrongdoing was implicated and drawing a generous income from that same corrupt enterprise.

Meanwhile I had moved my basis of operations. It was finally clear to me that the Bank of Lincoln could not be revived. The town held no fond memories for me that were not tinged with bitterness and perhaps it was not even safe for me. In truth, when I passed any of my neighbours in the street I no longer felt I was seeing someone I knew - for too much had happened and too many of them had watched it happening and done nothing.

I moved to White Oaks, New Mexico, never such a pretty place, but in those days a thriving and bustling settlement, boasting many businesses and even its own opera house (for with the ashes and warped strings of my piano still untouched in the ruin of the McSween enterprise, a passion for music and the civilisation that it represented to a soul rooted in the Germany of my grandparents had never deserted me). White Oaks was full of life, even if it was noisy and a little vulgar. Hardly anyone knew me at first, and that felt like a blessing. What was left of me was an enfeebled stem, barely alive and not fated to prosper unless it be grafted on to a sturdier root.

White Oak was also close enough to Lincoln that I might continue my struggles to administer the estates of the dead, recover what was due, and hold the guilty accountable. Better yet, it was well provided with lawyers, for I should need a brave, determined and skilful attorney to continue the work. Gold was the reason White Oaks existed (in truth I should have seen that its great prospecting days were already passed by the time I relocated there). Where there is gold, the land has value, which in turn means that disputes will arise. For some reason, the citizens of White Oaks had developed the custom of resolving disputes by adjudication rather than the more direct methods preferred by my former neighbours (who tended to put their faith in the alleged peacemaking qualities of products of Messrs. Sharps, Winchester and Colt). The result was that you could not fall over in the street in White Oaks without some lawyer helping you to your feet and offering to assist in litigating whatever injuries you might have sustained. The steady decline of our community these last forty years is attributed by commentators more shrewd than I to the impossibility of undertaking any project here without attracting the litigious attention of some party - for many in this locality the lottery of the courtroom came to be preferred to honest labour as a source of income.

Even back then, there were already three prominent law firms - exceeding the capacity of the local economy to make positive use of them. For me it meant that I could secure the services of one who'd be willing to run the risk of taking on a claim in Lincoln - maybe I'd even be able to haggle over the rate. I confess that I already had my eye on a legal clerk I'd come across who seemed to meet my requirements. He was not yet qualified as attorney and already looking to set up for himself, so he'd ambition bordering on recklessness and he'd want to make his name - meaning he'd work cheap. George Barber was a young man when I came across him in the office of his then employer, younger than me, but he was handsome and strong and not too intelligent. I believe I may already have had a notion that we might unite more than our commercial interest when I suggested that he might leave his employer and dedicate himself full time to my cause.

***

I lay no claim to being counted an expert on matters of the heart. I cannot say with any confidence whether the mutual affection between Alexander McSween and myself was the same emotion that noted authors (and it seems anyone else who can get an audience) mean to describe when they talk with such certainty about love - whatever we had, it seemed enough for us and I miss him still. On the other hand, I believe I can state without fear of contradiction that I never loved my second husband.

If I sound callous and it be suggested that I exploited George, think that I am describing with the benefit of hindsight. my contemporaneous assessment of our situations was not so coldly rational or lucid. Think also that then, as now, a woman without a husband must expend a ferocious quantity of energy to achieve what a man of lesser merit might do without first struggling to establish his credibility as a personage to be taken seriously. Whenever I should plead my own case, I was flying in the face of convention, and I had not yet learned that modern Americans are prepared to treat convention with the contempt it merits if only the matter is put to them in the right way.

Besides which, I was not yet such an old lady, and I'd known the charms of young married life and then lost them before the gloss should have faded. I was not ready to be an old widow. I refer here to the matter of sex, to put it bluntly. I have always read whatever books I can find, like many who live on the plains whose intellect is not wholly dormant. We have time on our hands in the evenings and few distractions. Out here, a man or woman might read the same book many times over, until they come to know it so well the words come to be the map of their life, and not always for the merit of the work but maybe because it's the only volume they have (unlucky if it is the Old Testament or some specious guide to self-improvement). I always had some books by me - works on the planting and rotation of crops, common ailments of the bovine sub-species and their remedies, condensed histories of the Greek and Roman eras. I consumed all of these readily, but I could never get to the finish of any of those insipid narratives that treat of romance where the business of a physical relationship is ignored, or hinted at as a mere procreative necessity or religious ordeal. I can stomach a made-up story if it might tell me something about life as I've found it to be, but those ladies' novels that are all affectation about people who could never exist in the flesh and blood world leave me oddly disgusted.

So although I did not consider I was likely to have children, I was yet a healthy woman. Alexander and I had begun with urgent fumbling, that it still pains me to remember, to satisfy an urge that was as compelling as it was vague (for what profit do we get from the act?) but we'd learned together to enjoy the act of physical union. Perhaps the loss of such joy is felt more keenly than its absence from the life of one to whom it remains unknown. Barber was a young and vigorous man and I hoped that we'd have a sexual relationship that would bring us together and perhaps then we would come to love one another truly. There was but one other in the world I could imagine making a better match for my spirit and that one being unavailable, the chances of meeting his like appeared negligible - it was Barber or no-one for me, it seemed.

I make this confession tentatively, since my proposition seems to contend with what I know through literature of how other women think, and yet from the few sincere conversations with women of intelligence that life has offered me, I do not believe that my experience is singular or monstrous. Perhaps the time will come when our ladies of letters will write frankly in this regard and the objective of mutual of gratification will become accepted as a commonplace, though what a blow this might strike against the self-confidence of our men is not to be thought of.

I digress and it is enough to say that though I did not love Barber when we married, I proceeded in hopeful anticipation that I should learn to love him in time, and meanwhile the uniting of our respective interests seemed to me a matter of common sense more than romance.

My husband commenced to work for Mr. Chisum, completing the labour of marking out and perfecting title that Alexander had begun. It was dangerous work and with urgency attached, for the Santa Fe interest was intent of swallowing up parcels of land that were unclaimed or where the only claim rested on custom and might therefore be put in dispute. At the same time, by our mutual patient endeavour and in despite of obstruction from Dolan and his clients we managed gradually to administer the estates of McSween and Tunstall and I was eventually able to render a final account and send it with the balance due remitted to Tunstall's family, though it was a poor recompense for their loss. The result of these endeavours was that I found myself by no means wealthy, but at least possessed of funds that raised my state above that of a beggar who is dependent on her friend. The capital I had was not great, but I judged it might be sufficient for the seeding of some practical venture in order that I might begin to make my own way in the world.

"I wish it to be noted for the record that I am wholeheartedly opposed to your proposition," John Chisum's tone suggested that if he'd been speaking to a man he'd have used more direct language, though 'damn' was the only expletive I heard him employ in my presence.

I had just informed him that I had made up my mind to try at ranching, that I had found the location and determined a business name (it would be the 'Three Rivers' ranch and brand) and that I should welcome any advice he might be able to give as an honorary consultant to the venture.

"You know nothing of the business," he accused me.

"I've been studying. Also I have been living among ranchers for what seems like half my life which is to say that the principal topic of conversation wherever I've been was the raising of cattle and their transmutation to beef."

"Reading is not the same as doing."

"A good point of which I'm painfully conscious. And yet reading suggests some improvements that may have been overlooked by those exclusively governed by precedent. Also I've had ample opportunity to take the measure of the ranchers of our territory who you might class as my competition and having regard to the general competence of these individuals, I think I might do well."

"I hope you don't include myself in that peremptory judgement Susan. I'll acknowledge myself a man ruled by precedent, or the school of life as I'd prefer to call it."

"Dear Mr. Chisum. In regard to livestock there is no higher authority I know than yourself. In regard to life, you seem an innocent, and it is only because I know you well that I'm aware this is because you've seen into the human heart too well and prefer to see what it might be, rather than what it is."

"That one is too deep for me Susan. You've left me behind as usual. But if you won't let me dissuade you, at least I hope you'll let me help you."

I'd previously accused my friend of being the sort who prefers to think well of his fellow man even when he knows that to be to his cost. Chisum would respond that he was no saint, just a rich man who could afford to indulge his capriciousness in giving an uncertain man the benefit of the doubt. I said that it was a safe bet most rich men did not see the world in the same way. Mr. Chisum shrugged.

"I got more money making friends than I should have by making enemies," he said. "A lesson worth remembering maybe." I tried to remember all the lessons my friend offered, even when I could not entirely agree with him.

The Three Rivers Ranch began trading with an asset of forty head of cattle all certificated pure bred and donated by John Chisum who said that was as many cows as a novice to the business could hope to properly care for, at least for a season or two. I'd assumed I would need to rely on credit from the bank - I cannot describe my feelings when Chisum's men drove the steers up to the half-finished ranch house and explained that now they were in my care. Mr. Chisum sent word that by his reckoning he'd delivered not a present, but the minimum he owed for a debt that didn't appear in any books of account.

By now, Mr. Barber had his own practice in town and with all the competition between the attorneys of White Oaks the business kept him away from the ranch, but I was rather glad of that. From the beginning, I wanted it to be known that the ranch was my own enterprise and whether it failed or prospered the outcome would be in my hands.

***

I have been frequently asked how I managed in those first years as a woman in business, and I can only answer honestly that I don't know. I had no grand design, only a general purpose that broadened out in the way a tiny path becomes a trail that leads on to a highway that will bring you in time to a city. Day to day, there was just one problem to be solved, then another. I was always conscious that I should be in a hurry and I was determined that the business should grow, for a rancher in a small way was at the mercy of such men as Dolan and Murphy. I had no more consideration to spare for the matter of revenge (and I'd abandoned the concept of justice as applying to our commonwealth in its present condition). More accurate perhaps to say I was determined the success of the Three Rivers ranch should be my vengeance upon the Murphy faction and its heirs.

What leisure I had was devoted to study, not the indulgence of the senses in appreciation of music and philosophy which I so cared for, but practical learning about the rearing of cattle, the improvement of land and commercial aspects of the business. To extend my herd meant I should have to increase the scale of my holding, and I had much to discover regarding the choosing of property, its qualities and the types of haggling associated with its acquisition. I reflected early on in my education that the grazing of cattle on land exploited but a small part of what the ground might yield, and thus I made up my mind to find out what might be made to grow in the soil of which locations and how to prospect for minerals or metals that might be bound up in the rock. Recalling that White Oaks was a city founded on the discovery of gold in a seeming unlikely place, I entertained some hopes of my own acres yielding up some store of treasure.

I was lucky not to be saddled with excessive debt, and of course my friend Mr. Chisum was my guide and principal source of learning for anything to do with the Longhorn steer, but I held to my resolution that the management of the business should be in my own hands. I needed to be free to make my own mistakes.

Looking back at those first days, it seems to me Chisum helped me even more with his knowledge of men than with what he knew of cattle. Not every man for hire was steady, dependable and knowing in the trade, and of those that were, few were agreeable to taking orders from a woman who'd less experience in the business than themselves. I was at risk of being let down or worse, but my friend helped me pick subordinates who proved willing and loyal, over and above what I was entitled to expect for the wages I paid them.

Barber helped with the land dealings of course, but he and I quickly discovered that our respective lives were becoming increasingly remote. He'd ride out from town to stay at the ranch and his talk would be all of the squabbles and rivalries of his business (which was prospering). While I have ever been eager to hear stories of the doings of people, I will admit that I found his narrative dull, even depressing. I wondered why his clients would put themselves to such trouble and expense over trifles and the bickering between advocates themselves (most of whom were personally unknown to me) seemed vindictive and petty, I would say unmanly. As we shared supper and Mr. Barber continued to update me, I'd find my thoughts moving on to my own concerns and probably my eyes took on a glazed expression.

I remember on one occasion I became so exasperated by his tales of wrangling over parcels of land I made a comment to the effect that if enjoyment of property for a settled term of years was the criterion for granting title, then all the land around us had been stolen from the Apache, although they had got it by dispossessing the earlier tribes who'd been settled since time immemorial. Mr. Barber replied that he had not previously been aware of my attachment to the feudal system of conquest and holding the land, which he supposed was how my ancestors in their castles of the German forests went about things. I had to allow that his sarcasm toward me that evening was merited. Gradually the nights when Barber did not find time to return to the ranch at the end of his working day became increasingly frequent, and I cannot say that i missed his company.

Management of the ranch required that I should ride. I had thought myself an adequate horsewoman previously, but I found it was a different matter to be on a horse from morning to evening, so that I spent more of my day riding than walking or sitting. I wore boots and trousers for practicality and a man's hat because it was necessary to have protection from the glare of the sun and a bonnet would not do. Before long, attire that was generally considered masculine was what I was comfortable wearing. I was aware that my husband disliked this wardrobe and perhaps considered it a challenge to his patriarchal authority. I dressed so not to spite him, but because I had a business to run. Barber would have preferred that I should tour my holdings in a pony and trap I suppose, although the greater part of my land was not accessible to such transport. In the moments that he became peevish regarding his opinion on what was proper for the wife of an attorney-at-law to wear, my own reaction veered increasingly to indifference.

I will admit, notwithstanding I was among people (and animals) all day, I was developing a sense of isolation. In my experience, loneliness becomes a habit that once put on is difficult or impossible to entirely quit. It bears compensations as well as discontents. I was head of an enterprise snd a childless woman living on her own apart from society. Of course I was lonely, but I had no thought of wishing to exchange my life for any other.

My heart was so warmed when Mr. Chisum rode across to visit, for I could hardly spare the time to go to him. On one occasion he arrived with a small entourage that followed in a wagon. His people began unloading as I greeted him.

"You'll need to direct my Mexicans in the planting of these," he gestured in the direction of the wagon. "You're more expert than I in such matters, I judge."

They were fruit trees - the same as those in his garden that I'd admired for their appearance some time before, noting also that the climate and soil of the territory would be perfect for a more widespread cultivation of the species. He'd sourced a number of saplings that he brought in hooped barrels to my place. The thoughtfulness of the gift made my eyes watery, though I was careful not to let Chisum see that. Whenever he had to leave, I was sorry that his visit was ended, worse I experienced an emptiness in the hours that followed which I was always careful to dispel by undertaking some challenging matter directly, anxious that the mood might if indulged prove itself a precursor to depression of the spirit. During my time in Lincoln, I'd had occasion to witness the effect of prolonged melancholy. Many a ranching family had failed in their enterprise for want of continuing resolve rather than by any physical misfortune.

***

In this period the exploits of William Bonney impinged on my life once more, though thankfully not in a direct sense. There were increasing calls for some end to be put to his career, that was judged by some to be a mockery of our pretensions to a civilised state.

Billy had not been able to keep away from New Mexico, or even the part of it that we occupied, for very long, though his personal security decreed that exile should be the prudent course. He retained with him some companions of his days as a Regulator, Charlie Bowdre for example, and others who'd shunned the terms of their pardons and cast in their lot with Billy as captain. This band led a shadowy existence in the pueblos around the old Fort Sumner, nominally fugitive but posing no threat to the property of the territory with the few petty crimes that they bestirred themselves to undertake in order to get their living. The theft of horses was a business that was disapproved by our society out of proportion to the damage it did, but the gang robbed no banks nor held up any rail locomotive, and our law enforcement executive was not so eager to exert itself to confront so dangerous a band when they could be counted only a nuisance. In fact there were several enterprises in the town of White Oaks that catered for the subsistence of miners and other single men which benefitted from the activities of the gang, through being furnished with cheap beef that had once borne the mark of Chisum if anyone had troubled to check.

William Bonney was as stubborn as the late Alexander McSween in his own way, and I had the impression that he remained among us as much to display his contempt for the notion that there might be a man good enough to take him down as for any great attachment he held for the county.

Matters changed after the gang robbed and murdered the Indian agent Bernstein, who was a government employee. It is a measure of their success as criminals that they were driven to rob what the government had supplied to keep the Indians barely alive. After they were pursued for this offence and following the shooting of Sheriff Carlyle, Billy had marked himself for extermination.

The circumstance of the Carlyle shooting was not clear, but it was known that the sheriff and his deputies had tracked and then pursued Billy and his friends across a distance of some forty miles on horseback. At length the gang took refuge in a shack, where for some reason Carlyle entered alone leaving the deputies guarding the place. After some time, Carlyle climbed out of a window and began running away from the building, at which point one side opened fire and the other reciprocated, the sheriff falling dead in the resulting crossfire. The lawmen claimed that Carlyle was shot in the back as he tried to escape the fugitives. Billy dictated his own history of events in contradiction of the official report that had somehow come to his attention in a Las Vegas newspaper, and this was sent by open letter to the Governor. According to the version of his letter that was eventually published in our own Golden Era as well as the Lincoln County Leader, the unfortunate Carlyle had invited him to discussion under flag of parley, suggesting the gang should submit to the process of law. Billy, being reluctant to comply, indicated that the Sheriff must remain with them until the next morning to guarantee a temporary truce, as all concerned were in need of sleep. Later the sheriff attempted to escape and was gunned down by his deputies who mistook him for an outlaw.

The rights and wrongs of this sorry incident would never be known with more certainty than that of hundreds of similar tragedies that blighted our civil society at that time. What was certain, by his unwillingness to remain away from the territory, his efforts to cultivate his own legend as a hero more sinned against than sinning, and his presumed culpability for the death of an officer of the law, Billy had roused the great and good of our territory to a stern resolve that he should be dealt with once and for all.

Not long after, my husband announced that we were invited to a social function in town. I was surprised he mentioned it, knowing the demands on my time and my general regard for the company of the supposed elite of our society. On these occasions, the businessmen held court while lawyers and other professionals fawned on them, competing for business, and the ladies talked polite nonsense until everyone was too bored to continue.

"You'll want to attend," Barber assured me. "It's an ordinary fund-raiser, but Pat Garrett is standing for county sheriff and he's agreed to attend so the local constituency can view their candidate."

I said I'd heard Garrett had always declined to put his name forward for election as sheriff, on the basis that if a community thought he was up to the job, they'd invite him to do it, not ask him to make speeches. Justice Wilson had told me Garrett regarded such elections as bragging contests.

"Times change," Barber observed. "In any case, Mr. Garrett has been guaranteed that he need make no speeches and if he should allow his name to be put forward, he'll be duly elected."

Leaving aside the questions of how such a result could be guaranteed and what was the point of an election under such conditions, I realised that there could be only one rationale for this development. It was known that Mr. Garrett's services did not come cheap. Worse, he was an honest man whose oath to uphold the law would not be applied selectively according to favour. If the men of influence voted Garrett as sheriff it was because they wished to be rid of a greater nuisance, namely Billy and his friends. I admit my heart sank at that moment. The so-called desperadoes were only boys, though their crimes were real enough. Some of them had been in the service of my family and had gained nothing by it. If Garrett was set after them, then it seemed to me they were surely doomed.

***

Everyone in White Oaks who considered that they counted for something in our community needs must attend the ball at which the sheriff elect was to be presented. Mr. Garrett had declined all invitations to make any kind of address and so the formal business of the evening proceeded as if he were not among us, though he must have sensed all eyes upon him for the duration of what I imagine was an uncomfortable evening. We were not officially introduced, but even without the fellows nudging their companions and pointing him out and others who openly stared, his was an impossible figure to mistake.

How to describe Mr. Garrett? In my later years, I get to the cinema whenever I can - it is truly miraculous for someone of my advanced years to view an entertainment form that was not even conceived of in my youth. The motion picture weds science and art - it may one day grow be a genuine form of art in its own right. I will admit to a weakness for cinema of the Western genre - its themes are close to my heart, even when events depicted are laughably improbable and the characters' vocalisations are derived from the conventions of dime novels rather than any language that was ever spoken by peoples of this earth.

There is a screen actor named Mr. Gary Cooper who is my particular favourite, seeming to embody the virtues of what even a veteran such as myself has come to think of as the Old West (sometimes it is hard to separate the memories of my own life from the mythology that has overtaken it, and I am struck by the realisation that my country is inventing itself through an imagined history of which lives actually lived are but the raw materials). I read that Mr. Cooper is to impersonate Wild Bill Hickok in an upcoming production, which I look forward to seeing if I should survive another winter, though not of course for any illumination it might offer as to the life and times of the real Mr. Hickok. Your western provides a stirring entertainment not to be taken seriously, though it is a great shame that we never see a more accurate depiction of the role of the alleged weaker sex in the life of the frontier - in film they appear to exist only as the pretext for brawls between the men or to scream in terror at the imminent attack of approaching savages.

I digress as old women will. I meant to say that Mr. Cooper reminds me of Garrett when he was younger. Mr. Garrett was even taller than the actor though nothing like him in the face, with his heavy eyebrows and whiskers. He did share that same long-limbed ease of movement and had an aura of integrity about him that the actor exudes. In the case of Garrett at least I can attest it was plain honesty that showed, rather than the lofty idealism of a McSween. Garrett's idealism was personal to himself, as though he were humble enough to accept he could not change the world, but proud enough to set his own standard of what was judged decent and then keep to that standard. As a leader, he'd be the kind to inspire a frightened man to do his part for fear he'd be shamed by what

Garrett would achieve alone if he was let down. I know for a fact Garrett more than once housed at his own expense prisoners whose subsistence had been neglected by the authority that hired him. He was famed for surviving many tense encounters, even if reports of them were distended by our customary sense of exaggeration.

In the early part of the evening, every lady's eye was on Garrett, while the men talked more loud and brash than usual as if to draw attention to themselves. Later on, the pitch of our collective interest subsided. Women had to talk about whatever gossip occupied them of late and men of business congregated in small groups to earnestly discuss matters of no lasting importance. I tracked Mr. Garrett to the verandah that lined the upper floor of the hall. The big doors were open since the weather was mild. He was away from the balustrade, leaning back against the wall, the better to avoid attention, smoking a cigarette and affecting contemplation of the stars, although I could suppose that his thoughts were occupied by more earthly matters. I ventured that it was a fine evening and congratulated him on finding respite from our polite society.

"I should be professionally skilled in the tactics of evasion and discovery by now Mrs. McSween, but you have hunted me out quite successfully."

I told him that I was Mrs. Barber now, but in fact I was surprised and perhaps a little flattered that he knew me at all. He said that the territory wanted for men like my late husband and the visionary Mr. Tunstall. Had they lived, their bank and other projects would have brought the county on greatly. The events of Lincoln he counted a tragedy. I noted that the human agents of that tragedy were still at loose and prosperous in their estate.

"I infer that you mean to know whether I should proceed against those elements if I should be so lucky as to be elected?" Garrett stated. I admitted curiosity.

"I'm neither blind nor deaf, Mrs Barber. I hear the stories, but we do not hang villains on account of tale telling yet, even in New Mexico. If I see a man commit a crime, or there's evidence, or a judge tells me, I'll go after that man whoever he be. That's my expertise, you see, I'm a thief-taker and tolerable good at it. I'm not equipped to investigate the invisible men you oppose, even if I'm less than comfortable that my paymasters may be among them. If there's violence or mayhem in the street after I'm elected, you may be sure I shall put the culprit in my jail whatever faction he may support, but I cannot in honesty guarantee you to deal with the man who set that offender to his crime. That's business for a public prosecutor."

I thanked him for his candour. I asked if the stories about himself were true, and he replied that he had never actually fought a bear. I cannot say whether his neglecting to deny the more substantial legends of his times was due to modesty, or only that he had the good sense to know a candidate should not be his own debunker. When I asked for his views on matters of criminology, I confess that I was interested to discover what mercy my former Regulators might expect at the hand of this man.

"I'm no theorist," Garrett admitted. "In my youth, I was a wild boy and travelled the extent of the union with other rough comrades. I spent some time in jail for vagrancy, lodged with some more accomplished transgressors. We had leisure for discussion and from them I learned where I'd been going wrong in my efforts at roping cattle, for I'd already tried my hand at being a cowboy. Then they proceeded to instruct me in the art of brand blotching - how I might brand with an iron at low temperature with a dampened cloth between the metal and the hide and keeping the iron pressed longer, so that afterwards the false brand would not appear new.

"From this experience," he continued, " I draw the moral that jail does not reform the criminal but provides his academy. Also that a young man deviated from the right path has the chance to reform himself, though beyond a certain point in life, a criminal will remain true to his calling till he's hanged. We must have punishment for such men, but the only virtue of prison is that it restricts their liberty to offend further whilst they are confined. I never yet met a man that was improved by prison, though I heard stories of one or two."

"What are your intentions in regard to William Bonney?" I asked him plainly.

"If Billy is wise, he'll keep away from the territory, for I've no warrant to pursue him beyond. The men with him will follow his lead. But I fear that he's become infatuated with his own story and won't be satisfied to settle quietly where he's not known. He'll be unable to tear himself from the county and then I suppose one of us shall be compelled to kill the other. I've no personal feelings of animosity toward the boy. I shall gain little credit either way, for if the Kid dies the county may decide my own wages are superfluous, and if I should kill him, for a certainty it will be put about that I shot him in the back or when he was unarmed - the territory is so besotted with the legends of its truly bad men. I shall be forever looking behind me for the man who wants to be famed for killing the one who shot the Kid. "

He was so calm and matter of fact in the way he expressed these thoughts that I could not but feel sympathy for the gang that would have to face him.

Chapter Eight - 1881

Later, I visited William Bonney when he was being held at Lincoln He'd been tried by a court and jury and duly sentenced. Since there was no prison, he was being held in an improvised cell in the upper floor of the old Murphy store, across the street from the office of the local sheriff, prior to being hanged within the jurisdiction of the scene of his crime. Sheriff Garrett assigned two officers to guard him constantly. Many people had requested audience with the prisoner but of these applications some were denied by the authorities while Billy declared he had no wish to see others. His favourite visitors were journalists and other scribes who he regaled with the exploits of his life to date.

Garrett had found him easy enough to track down, since Bonney made no great secret of his whereabouts. The sheriff's pursuit of one of Bonney's associates, Tom Folliard, brought him to the gang's hideout, since Folliard's flight led the posse directly to his friends. Garrett despatched Folliard with his rifle and the survivors barricaded themselves in a shack. Their horses were nearby in a stable, and before calling on them to surrender, Mr. Garrett determined to cut off their means of escape. He took up his rifle again and with one shot cut through the reins of the lead horse, which escaped. His second killed the next unfortunate animal which blocked the entrance to the stable with its corpse. Our many self-proclaimed experts would state as incontrovertible fact years later that the first shot was the truest aim ever made at a target in our territory, and I never heard Mr. Garrett protest that judgement, though privately I have wondered if he were not really aiming for the beast's head. In any event, the stratagem of blocking the stable ensured the surrender of the gang after a brief and futile exchange of gunfire in which my former neighbour Charlie Bowdre also killed, finding an outlaw's grave alongside Folliard.

When I saw young Bonney, I was shocked. He'd been badly beaten and sat hunched over from some injury, his face covered with cuts and bruises. He declared that he'd been treated civilly by all following his apprehension until handed over to the custody of deputies Ollinger and Bell. He said that it mattered little, for he'd kill Bob Ollinger of a certainty, though it was a shame he'd need to deal with Bell in the process, for he was a decent enough sort. He was still such a young boy, kept permanently shackled and due to be hanged. I had no admonishment to offer for these words of empty bravado.

In spite of his injuries, Billy was in good spirits. He'd been the object of much attention at his trial for the death of Sheriff Carlyle and after the guilty verdict was duly recorded he was besieged by those who wished to profit from his authentic narrative. He was always ready to oblige a request for a story, with a flourish of his rough wit. They assured him he was something of a hero to many, and he was more than ready to believe it. He politely thanked me for not forgetting him and said that he was pleased to see me, if only I was not come to persuade him to entrust his soul to the divine mercy of Jesus, since he'd already had visitors of that type and wanted no more. It had not crossed my mind to preach to him - I had too many doubts of my own on that score, having seen but little evidence for the existence of a divine creator that cared in any way about the doings of humans. I asked if he did not believe in god.

"I never thought to question what they tell us about heaven and hell," he answered. "I suppose it is all as people say. Except the likes of me are going straight to hell for sure, for I've a weight of sin on me. We outlaws laugh at the notion that a man might make conversion at the last extremity and get to paradise by such a trick. It makes no sense. Those who recant and fall to their knees praising Jesus at their end are the ones that piss their pants even before the rope is around their neck, begging your pardon for my turn of phrase."

Bonney had some opinions about hanging, which he spoke of as if it were as much a joke as any other subject of his conversation. He was confident he'd not be one of those cowards who died begging for their lives, if it should come to that. He confided that the men who leaped from their box before they were pushed toward the drop, as if to defy their fate were probably no less frightened than the rest.

"Once you've seen a few hangings," he assured me, "it's clear you want the rope to break your neck, for you're a long time strangling to death otherwise." This I already knew from stories of old Europe, where the acquaintances of criminal types became known as hangers-on, because they could be counted on to add their weight to the rope and so terminate a friend's ordeal when the inevitable moment of retribution should come. I said nothing of this to Billy.

It seemed the prospect of hell failed to inspire terror in the young man. He appeared to think it wouldn't be much different to the life he was now living. I was tending more to a belief that death might be a final end, but I thought it best to leave the condemned man whatever comfort the prospect of an eternity of damnation offered, so we spoke no more about metaphysics. Instead, I asked him if he recalled much about his childhood (which we suppose to be our happier times). He reminded me that he was but twenty years old - his youth was not so distant as to be forgotten.

"I meant, when you were really small, what can you think of?" perhaps it was my own maternal instinct coming out.

"I know that my mother was Irish, by the name of McCarty. She named me Henry, and she used to say that I'd the looks of one risen from a peat bog, with my long face and buck teeth. I was always small and got by making people laugh. My mother was the first - she said I cheered her. She was nothing like me - all plump and rounded out. I don't know how she got fat when we were so poor - I've always been skinny. I do know she got money from men. I didn't meet my father, and I never saw much of my mother. When we were little all the boys stuck together. You had to be part of the gang if you wanted to manage. We looked out for each other, but first you had to show yourself a worthy companion."

"Did you go to school?"

"If I did, I don't remember it. And then you know, when I was twelve I killed my first man." He was more comfortable yarning on his times as a desperado than describing his childhood. That was a polished tale he'd told many times, but I wasn't interested to hear it. I asked him why he'd first taken the life of another human being.

"Well, I tell everyone I killed him," he confessed, shamefacedly. "I didn't stay long enough to find out after I put my little knife in him. He was beating one of my boys over some trifle, but he was a big man, strong, and he'd fully lost his temper. He would have killed my friend and was not far off achieving it, so I used my blade and then we ran away and never looked back."

"You've been running since, I suppose." Somehow he got hold of a pistol and discovered he was uncommon quick and accurate with it. He'd always got into scrapes but now he no longer needed to save himself by acting the fool or running away. He said that those who told him that it was an awful difficult thing to kill a man were mistaken, you only needed the weapon in your hand and to blast away. In his opinion what held others back was fear of being killed themselves, which he anticipated would be his fate one day.

"Everyone dies in the end don't they?"

He told me the story of how the boys had been tracked by Garrett, how he and his men allowed them no rest till they sheltered in a hut they found, with their own horses and a few they'd managed to steal tied up outside. Old Long Legs called down he had the place surrounded and they may as well surrender and then the firing started.

"They say that after Charlie Bowdre was wounded you put a gun in his hand and pushed him outside saying he was dead anyway and may as well kill Garrett. It's being called a cowardly action," I advised him.

"Charlie was my friend," Billy told me, "but he was gut shot and would not survive. You've not seen, but it is a long and painful death. Imagine how famed he'd be if he'd have shot Garrett. I'll admit I thought the diversion may give us time to make our escape, but if it had been me shot I'd have done the same."

He seemed to bear Patrick Garrett no ill-will and perhaps it was gratifying to him that he'd been taken by such a notable lawman. He claimed he'd have surrendered to no other.

"We two are old friends," he reminded me. "In Pat's wild years we both ran cattle for old Pete Maxwell. Every week we'd lose the wages Pedro gave us betting at cards. We were so much in each other's company they used to call us Big Casino and Little Casino."

The reflection that these times were past and not to return seemed to cause him melancholy, but only for a moment. He related the details of the trial as if it were some elaborate entertainment planned for his amusement. After, he said, there were some hairy moments when the townspeople wanted a lynching, only so they could claim to have put an end to the legendary outlaw. Garrett had the train ready to take them away, but the mob besieged the railway, threatening the sheriff as well as his prisoner.

"We were in the car but not moving," he told me. "The sheriff had several pistols with him. He advised me that if the crowd made a more determined assault on our position, he'd need to remove my irons and hand me one of the pistols, on condition I agreed to be bound to surrender to his custody when the scuffle was done. I gave my consent and I'd have honoured my promise, probably."

It was lucky that some quick thinking officer of the railway got the train started and moved out of the sidings, for the driver and guard were too much frightened to do their duty. The incident had served to convince Billy that somehow he and Garrett were kindred spirits.

"Though I'll one day kill him, or him me," he concluded.

There was nothing I could do for him. He gave no thought to his imminent execution but seemed preoccupied with fantasies of the life he'd lived and revenge he'd one day take on those he felt deserved it. I could make more sense of my cattle and frankly I was glad to return to them. I was sorry that a man like Bob Ollinger had been detailed to guard the prisoner. I'd heard Mr. Garrett remark that he did not allow Ollinger to get behind him when he'd a weapon about his person, even if he was the sheriff's own deputy, so he had few illusions about the man. Perhaps entrusting him with guarding a prisoner was a miscalculation by Garrett, but then he'd few enough good men to spare and perhaps he felt safer with Ollinger (whom he'd no motivation to exempt from any onerous duty) removed from his own presence and confined to the role of goaler.

***

There is no necessity for me to relate at length the sordid narrative of William Bonney's escape and subsequent fate for the bare facts are well known, though clustered about with an embroidery of invented details. No outlaw band rode into town to free their leader. Deputies Ollinger and Hall were killed with their own weapons, shot by their captive as a result of their own culpable negligence. Probably the detestable Ollinger became careless, imagining he'd broken Billy's spirit through the beatings administered on him as easily as he'd cowed our citizens by dressing up as General Custer and practising knife tricks in the street. The deputy was a bully and such are apt to be surprised eventually. When the shooting finished, the people of town dared not impede the convicted man's escape notwithstanding he'd not yet freed himself of the irons that fettered him and so he rode away nonchalantly on Ollinger's horse. Now Sheriff Garrett must track him down wherever he fled.

After the Kid was shot, Mr. Garrett's words to me proved prophetic. Those who'd contended over their coffee and cigars that Bonney was the better man maintained that he'd been surprised and gunned down when unarmed and unaware, or he had only a knife on him, or else he was shot in the back. Not long after, it began to be whispered that Garrett's salary was awful high and a heavy and perhaps unnecessary burden upon the public purse.

Garrett's own report was short and to the point. He came to a certain pueblo with two deputies whom he stationed at the outskirts of the settlement, while he rode in cautiously and alone. He came to the dwelling of one Pedro Menard Maxwell, one of our marginal citizens who resided among the Mexicans and for whom Garrett and Billy had worked as cowboys many years earlier. Whilst he was at this man's bedside, interrogating him as to the whereabouts of Bonney, the Kid himself entered the shack for reasons unknown. He'd a five-shot .41 calibre pistol in his buckled on holster and a hunting knife in his hand, possibly to cut meat he intended to beg of his neighbour. The Kid uttered the words 'Quien es?' twice, before both men moved, but Garrett had the advantage, being crouched by the cot of Maxwell and having some suspicion in advance that Bonney was in the locality. He counted himself fortunate, though other assessments of his conduct were not so charitable (the word 'assassin' was spoken, and it was observed that the state had avoided the expense of a further trial, in terms that suggested this circumstance had arisen by design).

 I cannot say that I mourned William Bonney. He had become a totem for lawlessness in our community and he would surely have committed further outrages had he lived. I am certain that mothers weep for wayward sons who have gone wrong beyond redemption when they meet their deserved fate, and I had some part of that feeling though I was reluctant to acknowledge it. For a long time, I wondered if I had done all I should to help the boy before he went past help, but I now believe he chose his own trajectory, resigned in principle to the violent end it would entail but always imagining his course had just a little longer to run. Perhaps my feelings of guilt had to do with the sense of relief I also experienced, for it seemed to my mind that the Lincoln War was now finally over. I would busy myself with my herd and begin what remained of my life anew.

 I divorced Barber not long after, and while his behaviour provided a pretext for that, I am sure that each of us knew that our partnership was dissolved long before. Since neither of us made claim on the other in matters of finance, and there was no issue of our union, the formal separation was relatively painless even though legal procedure of this nature was still rare in the state. I had no care for what our polite society might think of my status, since I saw no need to respect the opinions of frivolous people. That is not to say I kept away from town, for I have always enjoyed the energy and bustle of cities and I was an especially frequent visitor to the opera house and its musical entertainments - but above all there was the Three Rivers ranch depending on my care.

 I started with four hundred cattle, then four thousand and after that tens of thousands. I'm told that we finally grew the herd to 40,000 though my own reckoning suggests a figure considerably less than that. In any case the commentators were right to say that I grew rich. The cattle roamed freely across my land, near half the number of Mr. Chisum's own herd. Of course my mentor remained my truest friend, but Mr. Chisum was a man who knew how to give advice when it was asked for and keep his own counsel when it was not. I sent the other so-called experts, would be suitors, and advisers posing as friends on their way. I knew that I did not want another husband and I did not trust any adviser over my own judgement. I knew also that I would never turn the Three Rivers over to a manager - if I was not there to run it, it should be sold, for I could not bear the prospect of an incompetent or unreliable man running down what I had built and enriching himself in the process.

The newspapermen wanted to see me often. The Cattle Queen of New Mexico was what they called me, in the way that newspapers have to make every thing bigger than life. They wanted to see the fruit orchard I'd developed from John Chisum's gift of a few trees, the silver mine I'd prospected myself (it was a slender seam in truth, but economic to extract and a useful increment to our annual revenues). They desired to observe my cattle roaming the acres of Three Rivers and hear me tell how we'd improved the herd and what would be my next development. I thought it a healthy signal for the territory that our scribblers were now more interested in commerce than the progressively declining incidence of gunfighting in our towns.

Most of all they wanted to see the ranch itself - the palace of the Cattle Queen, I suppose. I was proud enough of it myself. The house was a single storey construction in keeping with our local tradition, with white adobe walls. In its plan I had utilised my memories of the graceful dwelling of my old friend Juan Patron - contriving comfortable shade and spaces that were private and apart from the areas where business was conducted. I'd planted trees around, carefully selected, and the walls were covered with creeping vines and potted plants that delighted my eye. Inside was mostly timbered, with dark woods in the Spanish style, though I'd designed the windows to let the light flood in as a contrast to the sombre interior. I had a phonograph that was imported and I liked to keep the air sweet with the music of the orchestral recordings I'd been able to obtain. Pride of place was granted to my harmonium. I'd realised that a piano frame was unsuited to the territory in its current state. The harmonium was more resistant to the abuses of unskilled transporters and had the virtue that its notes remained true without the attentions of a professional tuner who might prove difficult to locate. I had a piano too, to remind me of my lost favourite, but it was the other keyboard I mostly favoured.

As for the business, the few good men I had with me from the beginning remained my trusted lieutenants, though they now had others working for them. I no longer needed to impose my authority before I could begin to issue orders, since it was generally accepted that woman or no I knew what I was talking about. The few new men who had difficulties with that state of affairs did not stay with us long. I knew, from study at least, that a moment of greatest difficulty for any successful business would be when the founder was no longer able to direct it, either through age or infirmity or because the scale of the business had developed beyond what he or she could grasp, but for the moment I had few anxieties on that score for I hardly considered relinquishing the Three Rivers that was my personal triumph.

***

One day, I rode across to see Mr. Chisum. Some period had elapsed since our last meeting. I was shocked at the change which had overtaken him in so short a space of time. He seemed shrunken into himself. When I was announced, he barely raised himself in greeting and flopped down weakly into his chair straight after. He even had a blanket covering his knees which was a thing I'd never seen before.

"It's cancer," he told me before I could ask about his health. "The same sickness that took Murphy and now it's taking me. Perhaps there is some death in the soil of this place as Juan Patron used to maintain."

"Are they sure?"

"I knew myself before the doctors confirmed it. Hurts like a bitch, if you don't mind me saying. If I was a horse they'd do me the mercy of putting a bullet in my head."

I do not know of any reason why anger should have been an appropriate response to hearing this, but anger was what I felt.

"You must fight it, Mr. Chisum. You cannot give in when the country has such need of you still."

"The country doesn't depend on any one man," Chisum replied, "and while I might have meant more to it ten years ago, my time has passed. My great work was to open up the trail and guide the great herds north so that our business here should have a market. Now any fool can drive his cattle to the nearest rail head and the main business is to fatten them first. I'm fast becoming as superfluous as the old longhorn itself."

It was true that the hardy but tough longhorn that could withstand the natural harshness of the country and the vicissitudes of the trail no longer held a monopoly in our territory, and I had remarked to him myself that other breeds would have their day eventually, though I do not recall Mr. Chisum evincing any great enthusiasm for that notion. Modified versions of the Hereford and Angus breeds of the British Isles were already making their appearance as Mr. Tunstall had predicted. I had some in my own herd.

"I need you John," I told him. "I can't be without you."

"You require no advice from me," he replied, "for you've surpassed me in the business whether or not my herd remains the greater. My time has quite passed I think.

"I have a confession," he continued in a less hearty tone. "I've lost half my wealth. I allowed myself to be swindled by some men who came to me from the meat packing business, looking for investment. I could see that the days of the trail were over and finally, too late, I was looking to diversify. Meat packers! What do I know of packing beef you may ask, and I answer nothing. I've proved that by allowing these gentlemen to fleece me. I was accustomed to boast that I cared for nothing beyond the open range and the life of the trail, and how that assertion has come back to bite me."

I was appalled. "Can your loss be so bad that it has broken you?"

"Half my fortune. I'm still a rich man I suppose. I cannot say I started with nothing, though I worked as county clerk and at other employments before coming into my patrimony, so that I should know something of what life was about. In any case, I've multiplied the estate I took from my father many times over, even allowing for this setback. I should be at peace with what I achieved. I mind the money less than having been taken in. And I'm tired Susan. You would not believe how wearying constant pain proves. You speak about fighting my condition, but there is no enemy to confront. One does not fight an illness, one can merely hope to endure it stoically - which becomes more of a strain when my doctors won't come out and say what they mean. You would imagine that speaking the word cancer was equivalent to summoning the devil for all the trouble they take to confuse the issue."

I closed my eyes. "How long?"

"Oh, they don't give me a straight answer to questions of that nature. Murphy held out for years. Perhaps the vitriol in his nature made him cling to existence with particular fervour."

"You can't stay here John. You need to be where you can be cared for and made comfortable."

"If being made comfortable is all I have to look forward to, perhaps I should put the bullet in my own brain."

It was not easy to persuade such a proud man to see reason. Even if he could no longer manage Bosque Grande, he was reluctant to quit the territory. The state of Kansas was the extent of easterly migration that he was prepared to discuss. Kansas was where the eight hundred mile trail ended when the cattle completed their three month trek, where the herd of longhorn cattle that spread out over three miles was loaded into the rail trucks at Abilene. Any further east was civilisation, where my friend sensed he'd be a man irretrievably out of place. The trucks might set out for Chicago and the stock yards, but beyond Kansas my friend could not follow. Whatever else, he'd not end his days on the wrong side of the Missouri River.

"I have relatives in Kansas," I told him. "It was where we lived after leaving Pennsylvania. I should revive my relations with them. If you were to settle there, you'd have good doctors available, and our paths might cross often."

"Tell me something about the place, Susan," he replied. "I'll give it consideration."

I stood and approached him, resting one hand on his his broad shoulder. With the other I smoothed the sparse grey hair that covered his old head. Then I dared to stoop and very lightly kiss the wrinkled temple of my friends forehead. This was the closest approach to physical intimacy that I had ever permitted myself.

"Or you could stay here, and I'd nurse you," I suggested.

He smiled, and I suppose a smile is meaningful. The difficulty is that the meaning is not always clear, and you may go awful wrong if you assume that a friend's smile means precisely what you would like it to mean. There's a conundrum here that's all the more maddening when neither can say words that might confirm your perfect mutual understanding or expose your horrible mistake. Most of the time we got along well together without much speaking, and now it was too late for words.

Eventually Mr. Chisum said something about it being foolish talk to speak of me nursing an invalid, when the only result would be that two enterprises that demanded full time care would be neglected instead of just his own interest. We didn't speak of it again.

The morning after that interview with Mr. Chisum, I got out of bed as usual, fetched the basin of water into my chamber, and began to sponge my body clean. Though I had provided myself with every comfort, there were few mirrors at Three Rivers. The one that stood in my chamber was the only full length glass in the house, and I was in the habit of keeping it slightly turned away from where I would stand, so that I did not have to see my own image - perhaps there was something of the puritan in me after all. But now, prompted by an urging I could not name, I tilted this mirror back so that I was fully reflected in it. I let my night dress fall and stared at my naked reflection as if I might discover the answer to some secret riddle of which I did not yet know the question.

I discovered that my face was deeply lined and tanned by the sun from being outdoors. There was a whiter section between forehead and scalp where my hat would normally be. My face I considered for a moment only, for I could not avoid seeing that reflection habitually, and I had grown used to it. The softer wrinkles of my pale body, congregated around the joints which articulated movement, were more of a shock. It seemed that my skin had become too big for me, or else it had stayed the same and I was shrunken. I turned slightly to the side, noting where my breasts were sagging. I had a dread of becoming fat, since the old ladies of my tribe had large bellies and legs that were spindly and lined with blue veins that denoted a failure of circulation and failure of hope too. So far, I was spared the worst - it seemed that the exigencies of an active life agreed with me, but just then I was thinking less of that and more of the change since I'd last appraised myself in this way - it must have been years earlier. It was then that I realised that tears were rolling down my cheeks uncontrollably, though I was not sobbing at all. Whether they were tears for John Chisum or for myself I could not say.

Before long, my friend moved to Eureka Springs, Arkansas, in the Ozark mountains, leaving me with powers of attorney in his name (though he didn't give up the famous canister that had stored in it all his authorities from the days of the Old Trail). I'd go there to visit him, all dressed in my constraining ladies outfit with sleeves so tight you could barely move your arms and a skirt that flared behind me as I walked - bits of lace and a high buttoned collar and even an old poke bonnet that made me look like I'd come from church and feel like a horse with blinders set upon its face. I had been informed that tightly curled locks were the fashion, though I did not find either the process or the subsequent wearing of that style to my taste. My own hair could no longer be called luxuriant and I refused point blank to have that of some other person fixed on my head, regardless of whether that was the mode. Nevertheless, I resolved to present myself as a lady at ease in the society of the mid-west at least - it was hardly New York.

Eureka Springs was already a fashionable place, attracting wealthy visitors and residents owing to the supposed healing properties of Dr. Saunders' patent waters and the fine alpine scenery. It would not do to admit that some of the matriarchs in my own neighbourhood still wore trousers under their petticoat dresses during the week for the convenience of effecting farm chores. I have to say that I discovered in the neat boulevards and gracious buildings, as well as the smooth manners of the place, an easing of my own spirit.

There were many places in our United States named

Eureka, after the words of the Greek philosopher who was supposed to have declared 'I have found it'. My own former home in Kansas went by that name. In our United States, the meaning was normally that gold had been found, though such a place name might signify precious metals had been located within fifty miles, or only that the town promoters hoped to attract gullible or overly optimistic settlers who might come to stake a claim. In the case of Eureka Springs, it was the spa water that had been found, which turned out to be more lasting than gold, since water is not so quickly exhausted as a seam of metal. The town remains a busy and thriving settlement to this day.

  I journeyed to Kansas also, and re-made the acquaintance of my nephew, Edgar Shields, by now a grown-up young man of the sort a mother could have been proud of. He enjoyed hearing stories of my life, or at least he was a patient listener. On the return journey to Three Rivers, I would find myself reflecting that I'd been afflicted by the same story telling compulsion as seemed to animate a majority of the persons in our territory. Half the time they had nothing to say and no one to tell it to, and the rest was taken up with spinning tales of people they might never have met. The best storytellers always remembered to invent some redundant detail, for the authenticity it should give the tale, but by now I had learned scepticism. Once, as a girl, I used to read those old histories of the crusades that my German ancestors fought in Asia Minor and Palestine as if they had been plain chronicles of fact - now I wonder if any of that old legend was ever true.

  Fortunately I had a cure for the melancholy that my return from these trips occasioned (and for my concern regarding the gradual but inexorable decline of my good friend that made each visit to him more painful than the last). The ranch was my refuge and the heavy wheel I needed to keep turning. There was always something needing to be done, and I was glad of it.

Chapter Nine - 1884

George Barber requested to see me. It was a matter of some importance, or so he claimed, concerning the railroad. We met in town at the coffee house, since I had no wish to visit his office or entertain him at my own establishment. Though there was no animosity between us, the nature of our former relationship and subsequent estrangement made social relations somewhat uncomfortable. We talked initially about some trifling things before he came to his theme.

"What do you know about the Atchison, Topeka and Santa Fe Railway Company?" he asked me.

It was a strange question. I knew that the company had been formed some years earlier and was one of the principal railroads of our nation, that it had constructed one of the great east/west lines under a charter from the federal government. There had been some conflict with a rival company when it came to the passage through the western mountains, since both had surveyed and intended to build the same route. In the way of our country, that dispute came to be known as a war, which was finally resolved by the intermediation of government. Like all the big railroads, the Santa Fe continued to open new routes, laying down miles of track each year. What else should I know?

"A railway is more than a locomotive pulling some carriages along a track," Barber observed. "It is the engine of progress." He said that by connecting point A to point B, when A was a flourishing city in the East and B was little more than an idea, the route the locomotives should take would also determine which communities along the way should thrive and which become extinct.

I said that I already knew that every frontier town was desperate to attract a railroad and it was rumoured that the price paid by some ambitious hamlets was ruinous. Everyone, from the first surveyor to the Chairman of the railroad expected to be treated for their favourable consideration of any place where a station might be sited. This was not my own idea of progress.

"There's more to it than you know," Barber informed me. As usual, it seemed that real estate was the main issue.

"You're aware of how we get legal title in the territory. The first settlers had it by custom and use. Your friend Mr. Chisum paid barely a cent for his broad acres. His estate is founded on the hunger of a great number of cattle and his astuteness in hiring your late husband to perfect the deeds to his land before the voracious speculators of our state should lay claim to it. Then we have the Act of 1862, which ruled that a family which has land under cultivation for five years minimum may lay claim to it, and that a newcomer may purchase designated plots for a price that may be considered nominal."

"McSween told me the legislation was intended to encourage settlement and find homes for the many dispossessed of our Civil War as well as the veterans of the conflict."

"True enough," Barber continued, " but to facilitate the purchase by veterans, Washington also legislated for the issue of bonds on the financial exchange, so that a man might make his investment before travelling to inspect the property he might presently settle. The proceeds from the bonds were invested to set aside more land to be available for purchase at the subsidised rate."

"This sounds like a complicated way to settle a country."

"the law has greatly affected your own fortunes Susan, whether or not you know it. Predictably, the bonds were acquired in great numbers by speculators rather than veterans and prospective settlers. These men who are behind the likes of Murphy and Dolan have made great fortunes by first controlling the price at which land is acquired by the government and then ensuring that no-one shall bid against their own nominees so that they have it back at a tremendous discount. That land is then sold on at profit to genuine settlers who have no other means to get their hands on any title. Of course, the system depends on corruption in the heart of government and intimidation on the ground, but it has so far proved resistant to reform."

"I have renounced my dreams of bringing down Dolan and the rest," I informed him. "Such types are as impossible to eradicate as the weevil or other common parasite." It was painful for me to rake over the ashes of our time in Lincoln, and it seemed that the more I should discover the more dispirited I should become.

Mr. Barber was not so insensitive as not to notice my reaction. "I don't say this to stir up painful memories Susan," he explained, "but for you to understand how paramount is the holding of land in our territory, and what men will do to get profit from it."

"With the coming of the railroad," he continued, " the rules are changed. The federal government approves the projects that the railroad companies propose, and then pumps them with money sufficient to achieve the purpose. Costs are inflated, and congressmen and senators grow fat on the schemes they have voted into being. There may come a time when we have more railroad lines than fences. But the government is aware that a railway in isolation will not serve to develop the country, and the carriages must carry passengers to collect fares. There must be settlement, so in addition to the funds they are allotted, the railways have generous grants of land adjacent to their track, which they sell in lots as the extension of the line proceeds. You may see farmsteads sprung up along the great routes, peopled by Swedes and Danes that the railways consider to be industrious, steady people. The railroad agents are at work in those northern countries, offering subsidised passage and implements of farming on easy terms. Once the Irish and Chinese complete the heavy labour of engineering, the Scandinavians take root and begin to farm."

I considered this for a moment. "It would seem that this system is open to abuse by speculation as much as the other, but on the whole the effect should be beneficial for the country, don't you think."

"I am not thinking of the country. I am thinking of White Oaks, New Mexico. The Santa Fe line is extending in our direction. Either it will rest here and our town will prosper, or it will pass us by and the town will die. There's no more gold in our hills. The town must have a reason to exist - it should be the regional capital for a wider constituency. This is why I am standing for mayor."

I think I actually burst out laughing on hearing this last, though why it should seem so funny that my ex-husband might run for elected office I could not say. He was not the most charismatic of men and the prettiness of his features when I first knew him had faded quickly through the long office hours kept by an attorney-at-law. Nevertheless, the existing office holders were proof that with us, the lack of an impressive personality was no disqualification to an aspiring politician. But why would Mr. Barber want to be mayor, and what did it have to do with me, I wondered.

"It's for the good of the community, Susan," he told me. "The officials of the railroad and the government will treat with the representatives of the community in their negotiations, which means the mayor's office. The election is imminent and it will be hotly contested. Not all the candidates will be favourably disposed toward our community, which is to say that some of them have been bought."

He shifted in his seat. I thought he looked uncomfortable. "I'm respected in town, but I'm not famous like you. Plus I've been divorced, which would be less of an issue if my ex-wife was by my side supporting me in the campaign. The fact is Susan, politics costs money, that I don't have. You might think of it as an investment, but we'd be working for the good of the town and our neighbours."

He told me I wouldn't need to make any speeches, just be seen at his side on the public occasions - that and the money of course. I think the reason I became so flustered was that I had not anticipated making any further impact on the world beyond the management of my own enterprise. It was true that the journalists and sketch writers would still beat an occasional path to my door, and perhaps I enjoyed reading their reports on my achievements, but I knew that the perilous waters of business were as a millpond compared to the predator-infested creek of politics and I had doubts of my competence to navigate such a channel. I told Mr. Barber that I would consider his proposal and give him my response in a few days. He must have wondered that I took my leave of him so hurriedly.

***

There is a book written by a Mr. Thoreau of Massachusetts that enjoys a great vogue among us. In it he describes the social experiment of his attempting to live in a state of natural simplicity for a year in the vicinity of Walden pond. I had always thought that the account suffered from excessive romanticism and it was no great surprise to me to discover that Mr. Thoreau had his land gifted him by the essayist Mr. Emerson, who was his great friend and silent partner in the business and no doubt aided him in other ways. Similarly, it transpired the would-be noble savage visited his nearby mother's house most every Sunday during his sojourn, which no doubt appeared to him a filial duty, although I am sure that Mrs. Thoreau took the opportunity to ensure that her boy had at least one good meal per week. I could regard the author in the same light as one of those counterfeit cowboys that come among us from time to time having resolved to settle at the frontier and becoming first kitted out in what they imagine to be the authentic Western dress. Such types are despised, but the success of Mr Thoreau's work demonstrates that he at least hit upon some resonance in the mostly urban souls of his readers, who perhaps hungered for a more basic and true mode of existence than that which they experienced in the cities. They were prepared to credit the bucolic idyll he imagined, particularly when they could experience it vicariously through his book rather than attempting to live it themselves.

I offer this reflection not in a spirit of sarcasm, but as a proof of the contrast between the romantic ideal of a life in the wilderness (being in the case of Walden a short hike away from civilisation) and its reality. I may go further and suggest that the literary representation illustrates a fundamental gap in perception that exists between men and women. The men of our territory shared the same deluded view of their estate as Mr. Thoreau's narrative depicts - they imagined themselves lone pioneers engaged in an epic struggle with nature. Whereas in fact, I do not know one rancher in our vicinity that was not dependent on a wife to labour at his side and produce children that were themselves set at a young age to full-time labour in the service of agriculture (often to the prejudice of their education and development). Ranching and farming of any kind are collective enterprises that require both a family and a network of support from neighbouring families. The latter is sustained by a pattern of social intercourse that men call trivial and not worth their time, though without it they would perish at the first difficulty. In the years since the buffalo hunters and trappers slaughtered the available wild game, our many bachelors are either confined to town or else become miners working claims that are apt to drive them out of their wits through solitude and frustrated hope. Here, loneliness has defeated as many men as nature has put down. Society is more important to those who have but few neighbours, and it is the work of women to build and maintain its framework, for no book of statutes will do it.

The noble savage who the writer Thoreau imitates lives in a tribe, that is a community in which cooperation rather than competition is the key to prevailing against a harsh environment. There are male Indians that live alone, like young lions driven from the pride by the alpha male, but they are wandering outcasts living hand to mouth in vagabondage. The man that lives alone fails when he has some task that can not be achieved by a solitary, and any mild complaint that affects his health sufficient to keep him from getting his subsistence for a few days may have a fatal consequence.

Our men that are proud self-sufficient individuals in their own eyes are dependent on good relations with their neighbours when it comes to raising a barn, digging a well or caring for the sick, even returning straying cattle to a neighbour's herd. They must have a network of amicable relationships, and it is this that women have to cultivate as much as the soil. Taking tea with the neighbours, attending church, and all the silly social occasions that ladies contrive to ease their idleness, as the men claim (I don't know any idle ladies) is how the many tiny stitches that knit our community together are cast. Each single stitch is trivial, but if they were all unravelled then our individual and collective existences should quickly fall apart.

If I digress more than usually at this point, it is to explain my becoming involved in politics, which was the last thing I thought I should do. For it was reflections such as these, rather than any eloquence on the part of Barber, that induced me to accept his proposal - more duty than ambition, although I determined from the start that if I should fund his campaign I would be no puppet at his side meekly endorsing his candidature. In fact I was not sure how far I might depend on Mr. Barber the mayor to remember his disinterested motives. The incessant bickering between himself and the other advocates of the town (who were so numerous they resorted to stirring up discord where there was none, in order to feast on the litigious consequences) I could in no way interpret as being beneficial to our community, but if Barber might be regarded as the least bad candidate of a poor bunch, then at least I should be able to direct his policy on a virtuous path while ever he depended on my support.

***

My recollection progresses to the occasion of a supper and fundraising for the supporters of Barber's mayoral bid. I have always been careful of my appearance in public outside of the working day of the ranch, but that evening I took particular pains with my wardrobe. I wore a new, tightly waisted jacket with a little cap that well matched it, and a gown that fitted to my own proportions at the sides, but flared out behind over a crinolet and bustle.

    I should offer a word of explanation. It will be recalled that a crinoline was a hooped structure of light steel or whalebone over which an underskirt of cotton and linen was stretched, which caused the dress worn over it to protrude some distance in all directions from the body. The ensemble took up a considerable space and tended to confound the wearer's sensation of her own body space. For this reason and because it was a requirement that any adult woman with pretensions to decency however remote should adopt the style (even if engaged in full-time work) the crinoline was a notoriously dangerous garment. Projecting from reported incidences of fatality, a respected statistician, whose work was widely reported in the popular press of the day, estimated that at the height of the fashion more than 30,000 crinolined women died in Europe and the Americas, mostly due to their dress catching some spark and the resultant candle effect of the structure. The design was also wonderful for catching unexpectedly on some passing object, for example the revolving wheel of a nearby carriage. The crinolet was a reduced form of the garment, lately evolved, which projected only behind the wearer lending an elegant tail to her gown. The effect was no less dangerous but enabled ladies to proceed stately but in relative comfort, and not so much in need of a tug to guide us to berthing when we should require to make port.

    In all honesty, I cannot say that I minded these old fashions at the time, though I look back at them with amusement. Our gowns were elegant, and our gentlemen were so too, in my recollection. I preferred the style of suit that Mr. McSween wore, with a frock coat and high collar, and a narrow tie secured with a four-in-hand knot. Mr. Barber, by contrast, wore a business suit of thick worsted cloth with but four buttons on the jacket and a waistcoat with no collar. It was the modern way, but I felt we had left some style behind.

    I declined to be escorted to the venue by Mr Barber, making my own way into town in my carriage. The hall was the same where I had met with Mr. Garrett. Barber was already there when I arrived, working the room and noticing everything with his shrewd lawyer's eye. The proceedings dragged on, until eventually we were seated together at the head of the room with some prominent citizens who would support the campaign. Mr. Barber began a long speech extolling the benefits of our community, declaring his gratitude for the confidence reposed in his person, and explaining the points that would be in issue in the contest. His locution was exact and precise, full of subordinate phrases and digressions that I suppose were witty, though I found my attention wandering. When he'd finished, I stood up without stopping to confer with Barber, and said I'd a few words to offer. I remarked that they all knew who I was, and those I was acquainted with would know that I only had the interests of our town at heart. I believed that George Barber, whom I knew to be a good man, had those same interests as his motivation, and that's why I was supporting him for mayor.

Judging by the applause, I got a better reception than George himself, and I cannot claim that displeased me. Afterwards Mr. Barber told me that my plain speaking had been well received and I was an 'asset' to his campaign, by which he meant that I should make substantially the same declaration to a wider audience. Already I was glad that the election was just a few short weeks away. I felt that I had landed fairly and squarely in the morass of politics, and was not sure I could tolerate the reek of it for long.

***

I was in town not long after for some reason when I was accosted by Justice Wilson. This pliable official had somehow transported himself to White Oaks and had himself appointed to our jurisdiction. I tended to shun Wilson when I could do so without being too obvious, but he was a good source of information. Where he got it, when his chief occupation was sitting at table in a favoured establishment with a coffee before him, was difficult to say. Wilson sat me down and ordered a cup for me. He was the type of man that cannot bear to be alone and is always looking for company. I noted that these days he laced his coffee with a judicious measure of whisky produced from some inner pocket of his jacket. Otherwise he seemed unchanged.

"I must compliment you on your appearance the other night Mrs. McSween, or is it Mrs. Barber? You looked very handsome and made quite an impression in your finery."

There was some facetious note to any comment Wilson made. I elected to ignore the compliment and his question regarding my appellation.

"I did not know you were there."

"Oh of course, I was present. At the back where I should not be noticed. You know I'm not one to put myself forward in the affairs of important men. They swim around each other, thrashing their tails and flexing their fins, while I am more like the remora that picks away the morsels that have become fixed between their teeth and so avoids being bit."

"Does that mean Mr Barber's campaign can rely on your support?"

"The campaign of every candidate may rely upon my support."

He was so unembarrassed by his own duplicity that it was difficult to get angry with Wilson. He was not worth the trouble. Besides, he took no side so far as anyone could judge and he was constitutionally incapable of keeping a secret, even if it should be to his own advantage. Now he leaned towards me and his voice took on a confiding tone.

"You do know what Barber, Hewitt and Ferguson are squabbling over I suppose?" The other two were rival attorneys-at-law who had also put their names down for mayor.

"Mr. Barber has informed me that one or more of the candidates has been suborned by the interests of those who wish to divert the course of the rail line to their own advantage, which is why the negotiations must be undertaken with the true interests of the town at heart."

Wilson scoffed. "That makes for a good story, I'll admit."

I demanded he explain himself. Wilson said that each of the three candidates had signed agreements with a multiplicity of speculators to deliver specified parcels of land at discounted prices once the coming of the railroad was confirmed. The agreements were conditional on the party in question being in a position to deliver conveyances of the relevant parcels.

"They all want the railroad to come," he told me, "in fact they're desperate for it. Each one is only determined that they and not their rivals shall be the one to profit by its coming. Plus they are holding out for personal terms from the Atchison, Topeka and Santa Fe Railway Company for delivering the town to the convenience of its engineers and realtors."

I willed myself to remain calm as I asked him how he could possibly know this.

"The remora fish, remember," he said making a short and repulsive gesture of pretending to make small quick bites. "The agreements must be notarised in order to be binding beyond doubt - and our friends do not like doubt. The local notary is me. My fees are modest, but they do mount up in a gratifying way in such moments of our history "

If there was any part of Wilson's story that did not hang together, I could not find it out, in spite of my sincere desire to do so. It was all too clear he was giving me the truth. I went directly from the coffee house to Mr. Barber's office, where his legal clerk, a pale stick of a man too old for his junior position, rose at my coming to inform me that Barber was with a client. I ignored the clerk who stepped aside as I proceeded to the consulting office.

Barber was alone, reading through some papers he quickly gathered and covered over when he saw me. He made the beginnings of a smile and greeting, although my mood must have been obvious to him.

I cut him short. "I know you've been making deals with the speculators," I told him.

My ex-husband shrugged. "What of it? Do you imagine that Hewitt and Ferguson are doing any different."

"I know they are doing the same and that you are as bad as each other. That does not excuse your actions. In fact your own case is worse since you hold yourself out as the honest broker, and you've exploited my position in the town to further your interest."

Barber stood and paced across the small room to firmly shut the door that I'd left open. He returned to his chair and invited me to sit.

"Your argument gains no force by raising your voice," he observed. "I suggest we consider the situation dispassionately. You know from the work I did for Chisum I'm a tolerably accurate surveyor. I've studied the land and I can tell you the new branch of the rail line has to come through here. Either the Santa Fe or the El Paso will build it and we can play one against the other. We'll have the railway and the town will thrive from it. Also some men will get rich in the process, and I mean to be one of them. My neighbours do not lose by my industry, as some other person is bound to get the profit if not me. I do not understand your objection to my conduct."

"You are a fraud and you mean to swindle your way to riches."

"Not every man is for the public good in so disinterested a manner as the late Mr. McSween," Barber informed me. "We have few saints on the frontier and it often transpires that those few that do appear cause more harm than good."

He shrugged his shoulders, as if in that one gesture he might rebut my objections and dismiss my evident indignation.

"I see from your face Susan, that we shall not reach agreement on this issue. So what is to be done. Might we not agree privately to disagree?"

"My association with your sordid campaign terminates as of this moment," I told him. "I advise you not to lay claim to any endorsement of your candidature from me. Further, I mean for it to be known that you and the other candidates have secret deals with outside interests that will pay illicit commissions on land deals to whichever of you becomes mayor."

"And how will you make that known, Susan? Think carefully. We have nigh on four thousand citizens in town now, not counting Chinamen and whores, and the election is days away. What are you going to do - start a rumour? Hire Starr's Opera House for a gala recital and public shaming? And what would you achieve by this?"

"I'm heading directly to the office of J.H. Wise. We'll see what people think about your harmless side-deals when they read about them in the Golden Era."

He laughed at that. "You think Jonathan cares so little for the town that he'd print that story? White Oaks is his bread and butter. We must have a free and fair press, but within the bounds of reason."

I could not tolerate his complacency. "I shall be holding a public meeting," I told him. "Right after I register myself as candidate for mayor. If there's no other honest person to hold the office, I suppose myself shall have to do it."

"That would be most unwise," he began to say, but I was already making my exit from the offices of Barber and Co.

***

The next morning, dressed sombrely and with some formality, I made my way to the establishment of Justice Wilson for the purpose of presenting my candidature. It may be imagined that I had little rest over the preceding night, bitterly regretting my rash words about seeking office, wondering how I should manage a campaign and how I might do if I should be unfortunate enough to be elected. Still, I had uttered words in the nature of a promise, if only to myself, and that must be honoured.

Wilson was not home of course. I had someone send to the coffee house for him. I waited outside, not caring to sit down and wishing that the sorry business might be concluded as swiftly as possible. I was surprised to note the portly figure of Wilson ambling in my direction and engaged in apparently amiable conversation with Mr. Barber.

"Good morning to you, Susan," Wilson said. "I have some intimation of your business today. It will raise some legal issues, in which regard you'll be aware I am no scholar, though I've been justice these long years. Mr. Barber has kindly agreed to assist us in matters of that nature. Why don't we go inside and I'll have Martha prepare some tea, which I know you both prefer to coffee, while we go over things."

We repaired to his study, where I suppose he considered his judgements. It was furnished with a good oak desk on which rested a few law books probably long out of date. The affectation of a flag of the union was hung on the wall behind. Wilson lounged in his swivel chair with the expression of one who expects to be entertained. Barber pulled a chair across to the side of the desk and I sat before the justice.

"I mean to register myself as a candidate for our upcoming election of mayor," I told Wilson as bravely as I could manage.

I think he chuckled. "Very good Mrs. McSween, or should I put you down as Barber, or Susan Hummer? We just have a few preliminaries that Mr. Barber has alerted me to. Perhaps you should explain attorney."

"You may not stand as mayor of a town in the territory of New Mexico," Barber said. His voice was impersonal and businesslike - the voice he used in court.

"Pray tell me why not?"

"You are not entitled to be entered on the electoral roll, by reason of being female."

"What are you talking about George? I've voted in elections these past years the same as every other citizen." It was true, although in the past few recent years I'd foregone my supposed democratic right in disgust at politicians and their doings.

Wilson looked at Barber. Barber replied. "You and other ladies may have voted in previous elections for sundry offices," he admitted. "That was allowed under a misapprehension. Your honour I refer you to the fifteenth amendment to the Constitution of our United States, which provides that every male who attains his majority shall be entitled to vote."

He took a small volume from his satchel and handed it to Wilson, opened at the appropriate page. Wilson scanned the relevant paragraph and nodded.

"It does seem to say that."

I recalled the Amendment. "You know very well that was the legislation that was passed to give black men the vote. It had nothing to do with taking votes from women in such states as allowed it."

"We are not a state as yet, only a territory," Wilson replied.

"Mrs. McSween is right in saying the Amendment was intended to benefit emancipated slaves by admitting male blacks the right to vote," Barber intoned.

"Just let's see those sons of bitches seek to exercise that right in this territory," Wilson muttered.

"However," Barber continued, "it was open to the legislature to include all adult persons regardless of race. Instead the statute provides that males share suffrage, and males only. The words are quite clear and our local jurisdiction may not choose but to follow them."

I was outraged. "You're using lawyer's words to twist the meaning," I complained.

"On the contrary," Barber was now warmed to his professional style. "The matter was debated prior to the amendment being passed. Your women's movement had their say." He consulted his notebook. "It's leader Miss Elizabeth Cady Staton complained that the measure would extend votes to, and I quote 'every Patrick and Sambo, Hans and Yung Tung' while disenfranchising decent women."

Wilson chuckled again. "I suppose that she disapproved of the manner in which those races customarily deal with their ladies."

I had married young and left home partly to avoid the strict patriarchy of a German household, and so I could see what the lady meant. But I had made my escape in order to become an American and free, not to find myself subordinate once more.

"It is impossible that the legislature should have intended to take away rights and liberties," I argued, "for our constitution is a declaration of rights not of their denial."

Wilson looked again to Barber. "Minor v. Happersett your honour, 1875 - confirmed that is precisely what the legislature intended."

"It goes against the founding fathers," I protested. "No taxation without representation. Your honour I ask that my tax return be put in evidence. I can assure you it's for a not inconsiderable sum."

"The State v. Stone, your honour 1872 - Miss Stone declined to pay her taxes until she be admitted to the roll for voting. The sheriff was authorised to detain goods of hers to the value of the outstanding debt."

I could think of no more to say. Apparently we could have women of business, women stockbrokers, even women lawyers, but politics alone was a male preserve. Barber leaned back in his chair looking smug. Mr. Wilson said he regretted in view of what his learned friend had to say he did not see any way in which he might allow that my name should be added to the list of candidates. I will not say that I did not cry tears of rage that night, but I also made myself a solemn vow that I would have no more to do with the debased circus of our public life and would comport myself as a private citizen hereafter. I had enough to do without concerning myself with society or with its notions of justice.

Chapter Ten - December 1930

I'm an old woman now. Every day I read the newspaper from cover to cover and measure out the time in cups of coffee while life happens to other people. When our paths should cross, I nod to those few acquaintances of my own vintage who remain above ground, and if we speak we remember to act more stupid than we really are. Heaven knows what we might say to one another if we began a serious conversation. If I've got anything to tell that doesn't fit my assigned role of kindly old lady, I normally keep it for nephew Edgar Shields, himself no longer a young man.

I don't get away from White Oaks much. Until what seems quite recently, my days were enlivened by infrequent trips to el Paso, where I'd go to haggle with practitioners in the lapidary trade. The last of my negotiable wealth was stored in diamonds and other stones you see, since I never got into the habit of trusting banks. But now the last of my jewellery is sold, there's not even the occasion for such excursions.

Murphy couldn't put me down for long, nor Dolan or any of the others. I survived droughts and depressions. What's fixed it for me in the end is my own unforeseen longevity. I sold up my enterprises and retired in confidence I had laid enough by to provide for more winters than I'd likely see, but fate, that has always seemed to oppose me, chose to play one more trick in that particular, and here I am still alive. In every thing I considered I had been prudent, for I'd judged the expenditure my tastes might warrant and limited my indulgence to what my pocket could stand, having regard to those few years that then remained to me under the normal terms of human mortality. Nevertheless, I'd be destitute and on the street now but for the kindness of Edgar, who sends me a monthly remittance. He reminds me I helped give him his start, more years ago than I can remember, and says he's glad to be able to return the favour. I know what he means. I'd have liked to help more people myself, back when I had means. It turned out harder than I'd expected to do the right thing by anyone, despite my best intentions.

Juan Patron told me that life becomes less personal as one ages. One must learn to be a good observer, he said, because such is the role of the aged. Poor Juan was practicing to be ancient most of his life, though he was cut short before he could even properly be called old. I imagine his shade still watching over me now, weary, resigned and full of courtly generalised benevolence as ever.

For his death and that of Huston Chapman, I have always felt most responsible. The McSween crusade on behalf of civilisation and the rule of law achieved only the demise of four good men, besides sending many others who were never destined to reach old age to early graves. From what I hear, even in 1930 business still buys influence, and there are more attorneys like Barber who serve themselves than those like Chapman who served the law. Tunstall's material interest is everywhere triumphant, but we're no better for it. Banks that were supposed to be the engine of progress bleed the rest of us for profit.

What's true is, everything comes and goes. Pleasure blooms and fades but once, while sorrow is a hardy annual. John Simpson Chisum died December 23, 1884 at Eureka Springs, Arkansas, aged sixty years, of cancer. At that time hIs holdings in cattle were greatly reduced from the reputed 100,000 head he'd maintained at the peak of his business, but still he was a wealthy man, leaving an estate of $500,000 even after his gambling debts were settled. It turned out his dependents included a former slave girl in Bolivar, Texas by whom he'd two children as well as the extended family dwelling at the South Springs Ranch at Roswell, Chaves County that I already knew of. He did not marry. I knew that the daughters at Roswell were fine girls, who'd see that the orphans were cared for.

I was a few days off my thirty-ninth birthday when he passed, and you might say in the prime of life. After, I continued to manage my ranch and other interests carefully, although I wondered increasingly as the years passed to what end I laboured. I have the feeling that, beyond that year of 1884 my ship sailed on with some of the wind gone out of my sails. It's frightening when I reflect I've lived almost another half-century since that time. I've been more watcher than doer for many years now, and I've discovered that for those who only bear witness, time is like a runaway carriage on a downward incline. Even though nothing seems to happen, you're running faster and faster over the final miles, heading for inevitable catastrophe. Even the days seem shorter, with no time to begin anything before they close. Before long, you give up on planning projects you won't complete. I've been old much longer than I was ever young, and though I'm grateful I've been spared to see the modern age and all its wonders, There's not so much to tell about those later decades.

    Speaking of runaway carriages, the Atchison, Topeka and Santa Fe railroad never extended to White Oaks, though it required a twelve mile detour to avoid the town and find another suitable route. The lawyers of our town overplayed their hand and continued ever afterwards to bicker over which of them was responsible. In fact the main line continued to bypass Santa Fe itself, whether for the difficulties revealed in surveying the land, as officially claimed, or because the management of the railway and its British investors had no taste for dealings with the notorious elements of that city who'd been licking their lips in anticipation of the tribute they'd exact from its coming.

    Yes, the new century brought us motor cars, and the construction of a few roads on which they might be driven. Now we have a new highway from Chicago to California (Governor Hannett, following the precedent of the railroad men, has ensured that it's route loops around Santa Fe so as to have nothing to do with the Santa Fe Ring that has to this day not been fully eradicated). Why anyone should attempt to drive two and a half thousand miles over dangerous roads in a motor car when train tickets remain comparatively inexpensive is beyond my imagining. Nevertheless, I'm assured by all that Route 66 is a marvel of the modern age.

    And at some point in this passage of time, as the horse gave way to the automobile, I grew old, almost without noticing. By which

I mean to say, I discovered that notwithstanding the continued acuity of my intelligence and most of my senses, I was increasingly burdened by an accumulation of minor symptoms that were never fully resolved, to the extent that where I'd once leaped from bed and dressed in a few minutes to confront the day, I must now rouse my will as a prelude to compelling my reluctant body to bring on the series of aches and pains that have become an invariable accompaniment to my levee, some of which I must be prepared to endure throughout my waking hours unless the day be a particularly blessed one.

    I knew after Barber I did not want another husband, and those I have called friends were persons of similar cultural inclinations to myself. We could talk of theatre and literature and music, but little of the business of the Three Rivers Ranch. In any case, I had always promised myself that I should entrust it's management to no other person on my behalf, but I admit it caused me a sharp and bitter pang to understand that if I should sell the undertaking and retire, I must give up the house I had developed and lavished such care over those long years. The place was imbued with such an accretion of my own true spirit and the events of my life besides, that I could not imagine thinking of any other place as home.

    There was no resolution for this dilemma but to admit that the house was very large and quite isolated and if I should survive many years it might not be long before I was not able to care for it properly. I'd rather have the house find a new owner than see it disintegrate around me. So I made my calculations and laid my plans accordingly. I have always seen myself as a practical woman and I meant to be practical in this painful business.

    I first sold the business of the ranch to Mr Monroe Harper, continuing to dwell in my home. Finally, in the year 1917, I gave up the house. I got a reasonable price from Mr. Albert Fall, and I moved into town, buying a modest but comfortable place that was cheap because even then it was clear that White Oaks was emptying of its citizens. I'd missed out on so much being so tied to the land and now I would travel and see life beyond the state line. The new house would be a base and a link to the familiarity of the past. I declined to invest in stocks and shares, mindful of the great panics of the past, and so I avoided the disaster of panics that recurred in subsequent years (foregoing golden opportunities to increase my estate by a factor dependent on the optimism or desperation of my would-be investment managers). Instead I bought more jewels and precious metals to supplement those I'd long kept about me since I vowed that I should always possess some negotiable wealth, whatever may befall. Among my baubles was the cheap and fire-scorched locket I picked up from the ruins of our house in Lincoln, with no photograph ever inserted to replace the one that was destroyed.

On my retirement, I was assured by well-wishers that I'd lived a remarkable life and the business I had built was an unprecedented success for a woman with no inherited treasure or position to begin from. After dispassionate consideration, I might allow these words were true. It is for others to decide what qualities I might have possessed that made for my commercial success. When people ask me how I did it, I generally tell them, one step at a time.

I can more easily tell them who I was not. I did not have the scientific enthusiasm of Mr Tunstall or the crusading zeal of McSween. I lacked the cold ruthlessness of Dolan and even the unruly, unscrupulous passion of Murphy. From Bonney and criminals like him, I learned only that there is a will to self-destruction that is bound up in the human spirit. The petty, mean-spirited greed of Barber and his colleagues I merely found depressing.

My truest friend was John Chisum, who helped chart my early course and set me on my way with a few good men he'd hand-picked. Chisum made his own mark by discovering what other men could not do and then accomplishing it, which is the best test of a man. From him I learned that it is easier to deal with others in terms of friendship than emnity, and that one who keeps his word makes it more difficult for others to break theirs.

The meat packers and speculators who took half his fortune preyed on his expansive nature. They achieved nothing by it, for they were men who preferred to spend what they could get from others rather than build any thing. That type is more common than the Chisums of this world, but by that I don't mean to say that my friend's values have been superseded. Rather, after his great success, John Chisum became complacent, which is perhaps what occurred in my own case, although I did not fall into the trap that rich men often make for themselves of assuming that fortunate success in one enterprise is a guarantee that their ventures of every kind will succeed.

My own enterprise was always more moderate than my friend's, though I was never so far from knowledge of my self-worth as to be guilty of false modesty. I began with what I could understand, and practiced to understand more. When I was sure of my ground, I prepared to take the next step. If I saw an opportunity to increase my estate, without undue risk, then I took it. Where there was space to improve what I held, for example by introducing a new strain to the herd or exploiting the silver that lay under my land, then I studied the matter diligently before proceeding to grasp at that chance. I have been called the Cattle Queen of New Mexico, but I did not set out to gain any crown, only with the determination to solve each problem as I encountered it and become a little better every day.

Outside of commerce I would not claim any great success in life. My hopes were greatly wounded by men - by their grand designs and their petty squabbles. It is my observation that they do not leave childhood behind easily, if ever. Among the females of my acquaintance I found some companionship but no true friends. The powerful wave that swept my little craft along left me washing about in seas very far away from the calmer waters where my sisters drifted. We could sight where our respective craft bobbed up from time to time but we were seldom within hailing distance, which is to say only that I had little in common with the lives of most of the women I knew. Of course they had children of their own, while I had not, but in honesty I have never discovered in that absence the great slough of unspoken regret or pit of hollow emptiness that is so often imagined for childless women by those who don't know any of them.

Now, perhaps I've told as much of my story as anyone would want to hear, though still I'm not sure how I should finish. It feels like there should be more to tell than just who said what to whom. My mind is full of other recollection - the cool quiet of mornings in the open air, sunsets so beautiful they make you sad for the passing of all things, the impossible clarity of water in a running stream after new rain. I don't have words for these things, many of which I hardly seemed to notice at the time, and yet now these impressions are most vivid for me.

Edgar suggested I might conclude with some words about my feelings. He claims I never say much about what I was going through inside when the great events of my life occurred. I suppose he's right. On the other hand, that wasn't the way we told our stories in the times I'm seeking to relate. You might hear it said someone was good or bad, but the complications that made them so, or the obscure parts of character that might be neither good or bad, were not discussed in so many words. Oh, we were interested in people and what made them as they were, as much as folk have always been. It's just that for us, what you might call character was something implied by what people said or more importantly did. We didn't so much chew over between ourselves thoughts that might have been going on in someone else's head, on account of it seeming impossible to know such a thing. Knowing someone is not the same as guessing their thoughts. You can't get inside the thinking of cattle, but if you're around them long enough and pay attention, you'll be able to judge their mood and what they might do next, and so it is with people, I believe.

Back then, it seemed the only person whose thoughts you could ever know for certain was Jesus, because every preacher of every denomination seemed to know exactly what was going on in his head and they were never reluctant to share that intelligence. I long ago ceased to find comfort in the words of such men, but It's been suggested to me that if you don't have faith, then dying must be an awful terrifying prospect. I find it difficult to explain to younger folk that when you're tired and worn out all day, the notion of perpetual rest eventually loses its terrors, and that it's enough for me to know life will go on, with all its difficulties and evasions, after I'm gone. I'm content I've played my own small part the best I could, and if it's time to quit the stage and let other players continue the drama, I'm no longer afraid. I'm still devoted to the sublime music of Herr Bach, but it's the tunes that hold me now, not the words of faith. For myself, I'm not even confident to describe my own emotions. It seems like sometimes, others have seen more clearly what I was feeling than I ever did. So in spite of what Edgar says, maybe I'll conclude instead with some words about all that has changed in my later years, for it's sure that I now inhabit a different world to the one I grew up in.

You may question why I'd want to list the changes I've seen in the story of my life. I'd say the richness of a life cannot be measured only in events. For example, I've not only sat in my chair reading the papers during my years of decline. I was able to indulge my taste for culture. Music has been my constant consolation, but I have been fortunate indeed to live in an age so productive in the arts. I heard Mr. Oscar Wilde lecture and saw Miss Sarah Bernhardt perform on stage and I count both these experiences among the most memorable of a life that is widely judged to have been remarkable. I confess to finding that some of Mr. Wilde's written works lack substance, although perhaps that is the point of them (too many of his famous aphorisms may be reversed to express their opposite with no loss of effect). When I heard him speak in Kansas City, the theme of his discourse, or rather it's point of departure, was the decorative arts. I remember little of what he said but his words left no-one present with any doubt as to his genius. As to Miss Bernhardt, she essayed a number of parts for us, including Hamlet, for her talent could not be confined to the subsidiary roles normally allotted to her sex. No-one can say by what alchemy this lady was able to speak the words of some long dead author that might have but little effect on the printed page, and yet make each person in the auditorium feel that some part of what she said was addressed directly to them and touched their personal experience. Miss Bernhardt brought us to tears without our knowing what we were crying for.

In the wider world. The Panic of the 1890's went on so long that we started to call it a Depression. That long, dry period put the Republican party in office, and then President McKinley was shot dead by a man who was driven crazy on losing his job. In the year 1901, Vice-President Roosevelt was sworn in to replace McKinley. Roosevelt was a writer, a war hero and a rancher who'd been a humble cowboy at one stage. The other politicians hated him - west of the Missouri we felt he was one of us. He was younger than me. More important, he was prepared to take on the spoilsmen who'd dominated our federal and state legislatures through their system of patronage and corruption since Andrew Jackson - nearly eighty years earlier. For nine years I felt as if the new century would put an end to those vices of the old that had caused so much suffering in my own life. And in the meantime New Mexico stopped being a territory and was officially named a state.

Mr Roosevelt was the first public man I ever heard to promote the preservation of nature. He understood the wilderness, and he understood that progress was not the same thing as despoiling it. Thanks to him we have national parks and nature reserves. I treasure these words of his in my old age and sometimes wonder if my old neighbour Mr. Duesenberg was around to hear and commit them to memory. 'I recognise the right and duty of this generation to develop the and use the natural resources of the land, but I do not recognise the right to waste them or to rob, by wasteful use, the generations that come after us." Unfortunately it is clear that the President was ahead or outside of his times, for such wisdom seems to move us but little at the current time. After nine years he handed over to a man he trusted, who proved unequal to keeping the established interests at bay. When the dismayed former president sought a return to office he was kept out by a combination of those interests.

Unfortunately, even Roosevelt briefly fell under the spell of Mr Duesenberg's precious eugenicists, though with him it was a question of keeping criminals and feeble-minded from reproducing, rather than a matter of race, and in any case he soon repudiated those ideas. However, the supposed science is very much the fashion with us now and I fear that trouble will come of it if the interest that is currently confined to progressive and scientific types should ever spread to the populace in general. Even Mr. Jack London, whose tales of the Klondyke I have so admired notwithstanding his ardent socialism, is an adherent to the faith. It must be hoped that common people will never be persuaded it is practical to breed humans for improvement the way we breed cattle, or that one race may be intrinsically superior to another. As things stand, every crackpot professor of the subject makes his way from

Europe to our shores, to be fawned over and have his lectures warmly applauded by those who should be aware that we Americans are a mongrel race and better for it. For myself, I no longer make so much of being descended from German aristocrats as I once did. The year of my final retirement, 1917, was the year our army sailed to war to enforce a peace on the shattered remains of Europe. I read that some Americans of German descent suffered at that time for the excesses of the Kaiser, though I never experienced any such prejudice myself.

By this time, some states were allowing women to vote, though the gentlemen of New Mexico and Texas and most of the south continued to maintain their sole competence in matters electoral. Eventually the work that women were needed to do for the war effort made the difference. The coward Woodrow Wilson who'd needed to be pushed into the war (even delaying for two years after the atrocity of the Lusitania) was also pushed into supporting the Nineteenth Amendment, which narrowly passed. Roosevelt had argued for it earlier but even he could not carry the country with him at that time. In 1920, the American constitution granted women the right to vote, though the amendment has not been ratified by some Southern states to this day and there are those like Mississippi and Florida that declare they will never pass it into law.

The war of 1917 made the difference for women. The men went away and lost their senses, died or won medals (or did all three) while women kept the country running. When it was over, I believe the male survivors expected women to return to housework, for now the men wanted jobs. It was what I expected too. I'd seen how quickly men who'd seen their woman as equal when both were yoked together at the work of opening the frontier began to hold them back once it was judged that civilisation had come to the territory. I recalled strong rancher's wives puzzled by the expectation they should become ladies of leisure. But in those two years of war, things changed. After, there weren't so many men to go round for the women, and those women who needed to earn their living knew their jobs and weren't shell shocked or wounded. I remember one of the women's movement leaders (they were always falling out among themselves and forming new groups) remarked that women rode to equality on the bicycle, by which she meant that at last they could get around on their own, but there were not many bicycles in New Mexico and they would not have been of much use, compared to a horse. For me it was the conflict more than the velocipede that brought us forward.

But the cost was high. When I think of the great war, it is those twelve hundred drowned on the Cunard ship Lusitania who come first to my mind, rather than the millions dead in the trenches. Perhaps this is a failure of imagination. I remember my own cruise aboard the 'City of Berlin' and I can picture the terror of those victims, a few miles out of Liverpool bay on a freezing night when the torpedo struck. I believe it was the cowardly nature of the action, exacerbated by the feeble Prussian excuse of having posted a warning to shipping at its Washington embassy, that so appalled. When I think of submarines loaded with torpedoes and ranks of men machine gunned like corn being threshed, I sometimes wonder what we mean by civilisation, and to me the old frontier codes like the 'even break' no longer seem so ridiculous as they once did. Perhaps once we knew, but have now forgotten that men must have conflict. The restraint of chivalry was an instinctive reaction to the knowledge that unfettered human combatants will descend to a level of savagery unknown to beasts. I might even suggest that something has been irretrievably lost here, were it not that I should be considered a nostalgic old woman, and perhaps rightly so.

I'm grateful to Elizabeth Cady Staton and Lucy Stone and all the other women remembered and forgotten who gave up so much in order for me to have the vote, which I make sure to use if only to thank them. I follow the political debates insofar as I need to be worthy of that right. What I've discovered from my political education is that the truth expressed in an amusing way is apt to be considered a joke, since it's evaluated for wit above meaning, while a false idea that's told in a turgid and convoluted manner will pass for truth by the time the hearer is too bored to question or has assumed that the complexity of the subject is beyond him. Our politicians have also learned this lesson, and accordingly cultivate dullness to a precocious degree. I've survived various panics and a full-blown great depression, each of which was supposed to wipe out our economy, and I have seen enough to recognise our politicians view great events as merely the terrain over which their glittering careers must extend, while their advisers have studied themselves foolish only to be able to proclaim learnedly that confidence is all that matters in the end.

Incidentally, the brewers and distillers were the last men to exert their influence against the female vote, for fear their profits would be affected, and sure enough not long after suffrage we had the rash and damaging experiment of prohibition. The women's amendment was also resisted to the last by the persons of unseen influence who directed our politics at city level in their own interests. They foresaw a dilution of their power and that the higher moral character of the female sex would be less tolerant of their corrupt practices. It is my fervent hope that their anxiety may prove justified as our emancipation proceeds.

Those war years were good for beef producers, more so for manufacturers and oil companies. When the conflict was done, they all imagined they would go on making profit exactly as before, but there were no armies to supply, fewer customers left alive and many of those who'd survived lived in countries that had been torn to pieces even before the great 'flu epidemic started. It was clear we were headed for another depression, though you wouldn't have known it for a while. I was lucky to get out of business before the trouble started, though not everything turned out as I planned and my investments suffered. It's not the Great Depression has made me poor so much as not dying before it got underway. I shall be eighty-five years old if I survive to my next birthday.

I've been personally introduced to authors too, in my dotage, principally through my acquaintance with Mr. Garrett, for gentlemen of that profession were ever about him. He eventually produced a version of his own recollections, co-authored with some person, but it did not have the success he hoped for. Garrett was never fortunate in matters of business. I recall in particular the visit of a Mr.

Hough, who'd worked as a lawyer in our territory and had some knowledge of the personae of the great frontier drama. He got most of his material listening to Garrett spin his reminiscences, and they toured the sites of famous events together. Fort Sumner where William Bonney was shot and buried has been an empty ruin for years now. Who knows what Mr Hough hoped to find there, but I was there when he had Garrett pacing out the yardage between what was left of the foundations to clarify the detail of his story.

At any rate, Mr Hough eventually wrote a classic of the Western genre, which is to be commended for its restraint, eschewing the sensationalist excesses of his peers in favour of a plain narrative enlightened by sober meditation on the causes and consequences of our glorious criminal past. For the most part, my country continues to suffer from a deplorable addiction to whatever seems new or controversial. Both Mr. Wilde and Miss Bernhardt recognised and exploited that weakness. Wilde missed no opportunity to seem contentious and they say he had writers hired to denounce in advance his various tours, for the notoriety and thereby increased ticket sales he would get. Miss Bernhardt promoted a play in New York in which she played Judas and the main protagonists of the gospel were seduced in turn by Magdalene. I think it was banned for a time before it actually closed due to being very bad. I suppose that we consider whatever is new to be most naturally American, on account of forever considering ourselves a young country. Mr. Wilde himself remarked that youth is our oldest tradition, and has been going on for over three hundred years.

Age must give way to youth, but first I might venture one final anecdote that could help explain something of what I've kept locked away over the years, and what kept me going on, in those years when they called me the Cattle Queen.

My businesses were successful and growing. The world beyond White Oaks took on a new expansiveness. Our own community began to look forward to the new century. Fashions started to change. Women wanted to dress in clothes that didn't hold them prisoner. Some ladies occasionally dared to venture out in those heavy pants with rivets for which Mr Levi-Strauss held the patent. Our Spanish speakers called them vacqueros after the cowboys, who first wore them. Supposedly they were good for work, though I never found them comfortable for riding myself.

Anyway, it was a prosperous time and we were assured that we were living in a Gilded Age, which came to an end abruptly in the Great Panic of 1893 when wheat prices fell through the floor and we discovered what an economic depression was. Out of work families don't buy much beef, so my own business suffered. For the railways it was more serious. Suddenly they discovered they had more track than was needed and still they were in the process of building more, while competition between them meant they couldn't make a profit. Towns bigger than White Oaks dried up and died as we continued our own steady decline. For four years America had soup kitchens in the cities and near a third of the population of places like New York were without work. Newspapers told us it was a bank crisis in Argentina that had hit confidence, or the exchange rules for silver. Others blamed the financial establishment they called a conspiracy of International Jewry. The plain fact is we took on too much - it's our way to take up anything that is a success and drive it on past all reason, paying with money borrowed on the strength of future revenue that might never come, until suddenly we all come to our senses together and begin to panic. Even today we'll buy a good story about the future in preference to whatever we need right now.

A man named Baum wrote a successful fairy story about how it all went down - with wicked witches in the East and the West (where the money and power people lived) and the poor North and South suffering at their hands. The Emerald City of the greenback dollar was where the wizard kept everyone confused with his confidence tricks, just like the bankers. Supposedly, the wizard's picture in the book looked a lot like John D. Rockefeller. In the story, the common farmers are finally saved by water, which kills the witch by ending drought and sending the forecloser on his way. For us, I can say the water was a long time coming. Some of my neighbours were not so lucky as I while we waited on it.

Of course, like everyone who made their living from what the land could yield, I had a visit from the bank in that year of 1894. The letter they sent was very polite and informed me that one of their functionaries would like to pay a purely routine call to Three Rivers if I could be so kind as to show him around. I had a loan of around five thousand dollars at that time for my working capital, so I guessed I had a pretty good idea what kind of functionary they were sending - the bank had never shown any interest in my property before other than to know I had collateral.

Their man was delivered to the ranch by a driver with a pony and trap. I supposed that bankers were unaccustomed to riding horses. The passenger alighted and asked the driver to wait for him. He was much occupied with brushing imagined dust from his business suit, as if he feared contact with the common earth might leave some permanent mark. At the same time his eyes were darting everywhere with the furtiveness of an assessor who wants to be taken for a social caller. I don't know if he even recognised me at first, or perhaps he thought I would have forgotten him, but of course I knew it was Mr. Duesenberg as soon as his carriage pulled up in front of the porch.

My ex-neighbour from Kansas seemed a little flustered when I greeted him like an old friend.

"Mr. Duesenberg, it's been such a long time. I never did find out what work you did in those long hours at the office. I should have realised you'd be in the banking business. Come inside. Coffee is in the pot."

Mr. Duesenberg did not drink coffee. He claimed it was overly harsh for his palate. He intimated that he would prefer an infusion with a small twist of lemon, if it be not too much stewed. If I had no mint tea or similar he would be perfectly content with water. We repaired to my study. I had already confirmed to my satisfaction that Mr Duesenberg was not much changed by the years, in appearance or manner.

"You will recall from our previous acquaintance that I am not one for small talk, Mrs. Barber," he confidently began. "I like to come straight to business. You'll be very aware that you are indebted to the bank in the sum of, let me see, five thousand three hundred and seventy two dollars and some trifling cents, as at close of business on Friday."

"Due to be repaid in three months time, a few weeks after we ship this year's herd to the stockyards, with interest due monthly in the meantime, which I am paying in accordance with our written agreement," I nodded.

He frowned. "The fact is, Mrs. Barber, it has come to the attention of the bank that prices in your particular commodity market have been falling for some time. It's likely you will not realise the profit on your stock that you expected. You may not even cover your costs."

"I'm grateful that your employer takes such an interest in my business. I am painfully aware of market prices, I can assure you."

"Our concern is, Mrs. Barber, to be absolutely frank, when the time comes you may not be able to pay back the five thousand three hundred and seventy two dollars on the allotted day."

I took a sip of my coffee, served in decent china but still strong and black as I'd grown accustomed to. "I see. And I expect that would be quite serious. Tell me, what happens if I can't pay?"

"I believe in facing facts, Mrs. Barber. I have to say if that should occur, and no-one at the bank wants to think this will happen, but we'd need to look to our collateral. You did sign a legal charge against the ranch to secure the debt."

"Hmm, so you'd look to take over the ranch for the trifling sum of five thousand. It's worth a lot more than that I think."

Mr Duesenberg became quite animated at this. "Oh no, Mrs. Barber, you misunderstand me. The bank wouldn't take over the ranch. It would be sold and you'd receive the balance after the debt to the bank was settled, less our costs of arranging the sale of course."

"I see, but Mr. Duesenberg, it is not a good time to sell, with beef prices in the condition we've just been discussing. And I believe I read somewhere that when the banks foreclose, they'll sell the security for a fraction of its worth just so long as they can get what's owed to them back quickly."

"Those stories are greatly exaggerated, I assure you. Of course, the bank has a duty to its stockholders to get in assets as they are due."

"And you have friends who can't wait to buy cheap as much land as you can get your hands on," I interrupted him.

He seemed shocked and even hurt, but Mr. Duesenberg wasn't easily put off his duty. "There might be some means of addressing this problem in a mutually beneficial way," he suggested. "For example, if you were able to make a substantial early repayment now, perhaps from savings, as a sign of goodwill, we might say, then we could talk about rescheduling the reduced debt, give you a few more months perhaps."

"That sounds uncommonly generous," I admitted, "but if I pay the money back early, the bank won't get its interest on the loan for those months. I mean, I suppose your stockholders expect you to earn a return on their capital."

Mr. Duesenberg informed me that in the changed condition of the current market, the bank had a strong preference for gathering in as much capital as possible, even if that meant forgoing interest.

"Now you have me really worried," I answered him. "I thought you were telling me you were concerned I might not have the means to settle my debts, but now it sounds like it's the bank that is short of cash. Think of all those investors who have their savings with you. Don't you think they should be told?"

No, no, he insisted, it wasn't like that at all. The poor man was becoming quite flustered. I put my empty cup back on its saucer and the saucer back on the occasional table by my chair. I stood up.

"I want to show you something," I told him. "Come with me."

I led him to the small room in the back of the ranch house where I kept the safe. "It's an old model," I told him. I explained that I'd once been in the banking business myself, and this was what I had to show for it. The door still operated smoothly. I opened it fully and pointed to the wrapped bundles of clean notes inside.

"That's ten thousand dollars," I informed him. "It's a number that has a certain significance for me, but anyway more than enough for you to advise the bank not to concern itself on my account."

Mr. Duesenberg seemed thrown into confusion. "But why would you borrow from the bank if you have this."

"Yours is working capital, sir. This is what I keep for a rainy day, so that I should not end up beholden to the likes of your employer if my affairs should suffer a temporary setback."

I could see that my ex-neighbours view of the proper order of things had been overthrown. "But you can't keep a sum like that in your home," he protested. "It isn't safe."

"Hardly anyone knows of it but you and I," I assured him. "I presume I may rely on your own discretion."

"It should be deposited in the bank, for security reasons," Duesenberg insisted. "We can take it this afternoon. Or you may entrust it to myself. I'll give you a full written receipt of course."

"No thank you," I informed him. "You've just advised me the bank is trying to scratch together as much as it can in case there should be a run on its funds. I rather think this money is safer exactly where it is."

It was my small victory and the extent of my revenge for all I had suffered - that I'd endured and prospered. I'm afraid that I asked Mr. Duesenberg to leave my property immediately, in rather harsh terms. The poor man was only doing his job, but then a lot of other men like him who were only doing their jobs put some of our local ranchers and other enterprises out of business in those black months. Who was to blame? The Murphys and Dolans were gone and in their place were faceless men who convinced themselves they were acting for the public good.

When I remembered the efforts Alexander McSween made to bring law to the territory and what those efforts cost , I sometimes concluded that both he and I were fools. When the writ of law came, it took away rights, such as voting, that I'd enjoyed in our previous state of savagery. As we became civilised, the place of women became an issue, where before there'd been rough equality.

Women were better off when the ranch was new and all was partnership - the rancher depended on a wife who could work as hard as he did, and strong children to help. Later if the venture was successful, that same man would wish his wife domesticated, since it was a measure of his success that the missus did not have to work. Then the poor woman would become completely baffled by the pointless complexities of fashion and manners that were the only business of her new life, and the couple would sit by the fireside at night with nothing to say to one another since the management of their enterprise was now regarded as an exclusive male preserve.

    It appeared the law was quick to impose prohibitions, but useless in regard to improving humanity. When it came to matters such as the right of that traditional Saxon husband to administer correction to his spouse with a horse whip, the appellate court declined to intervene in dealings between man and wife. I read in detail that case report that had so offended McSween, and I started to read other cases too. Finally, it seemed to me that rule of law in which my late husband placed his hope turned out to be concerned more with property than justice.

    I read of a case recently that has excited the lawyers. It seems the learned senior judges have ruled that we must have regard to other citizens who might reasonably be affected by our actions and not negligently damage their interest or their person by our action or omission. They're calling this 'the neighbour principle'.

I'm sure that my ex-husband the late Mr. Barber would have been greatly enthused by the resulting increase in business that lawyers anticipate in the way of persons seeking compensation. However, it strikes me that my uncivilised fellow citizens of Lincoln who were without benefit of modern jurisprudence yet knew very well the duty owed to a neighbour, without requiring instruction of the Supreme Court in the matter.

And I remember still Major Murphy's assertion of his undelegated personal right to choose what he found good. Murphy was a scoundrel, but I have always found the appeal of his philosophy troubling. When John Chisum came to our territory, he relied on courage and the steadiness of his own hand and brain. Garrett brought order to the territory, but the law that he represented was contained in his own person, not some abstract theory. The lawyers had their way in White Oaks and the town was near consumed by their rapacity. When I consider Mr. Duesenberg, and the thousands of other diligent, conscientious officials who do their duty without taking responsibility for where it might lead, I struggle to consider that what we have now is progress in human terms, though I have no doubt that this is very wrong of me.

We must be ruled, it seems, if our wilder excesses are to be restrained. It is only a shame that our rulers invariably turn out to have feet of clay - for the most part tricky and self-interested. Perhaps It is not them we should fear most, for the world has always been thus. The few who ascend the greasy pole of politics and help themselves to the spoils will always be with us, like death and taxes. It is the many who have relinquished their undelegated personal right, who pretend not to distinguish between right and wrong, and who will follow slavishly the dictates of the few and connive in their deceptions if they only promise a life of easy comfort - these many who are like to become ourselves; this is who we should most fear.

For my own person, there's nothing more to be feared. I've outlived my friends and those I might choose to call my enemies. I shall be buried in White Oaks before too long, at the Cedarvale Cemetery, assuming that there is still someone living in the town by then to dig the hole.

White Oaks might die before I do. The seam of gold that Baxter found petered out finally, as my own silver mine was worked out many years earlier. With no gold and no railroad to draw a population, those that could began to drift away to places that offered better prospects. Once the miners left, prostitution became immoral, since the ranchers all had wives. We'd never minded the working girls before, so long as they were clean, in fact I dread to think what walking through White Oaks at nighttime in its great days would have been like for a woman if the bawdy houses had not existed. When they left, it was another industry lost, and the Starr Opera House shut down soon after. The persons of reckless character who'd lived among us were long departed, either faded away quietly or having got themselves shot in some other place.

Patrick Floyd Garrett, whose frequent presence in our town could be counted on to maintain order among the unruly elements when he was an officer of the law, and even when he was not, died February 29, 1908 at El Paso. He'd been personally appointed by President Roosevelt as Customs Officer and even returned to law enforcement after the failure of his irrigation business. Mr. Garrett had some good ideas for business and he was the first man after John Tunstall to see the need for a proper system of watering the land to multiply its yield. Unfortunately he was never fortunate in his ventures, or to be accurate I should say that he'd a restless nature that caused him to entrust the actual management of his ventures to other men, with bad results. Invariably he'd be thrown back on law enforcement as the one trade he could always count on. Garrett was never a success as a Customs man, unlike Mr Roosevelt's other friend Sheriff Seth Bullock of Deadwood. But then Bullock relied on his quick wits and occasionally his fists to maintain order, whereas Garrett made his name with a pistol.

Garrett made many enemies but in the end he was waylaid and assassinated whilst riding the trail with a false friend, ostensibly over a feud concerning a herd of goats that a tenant introduced on his estate (all cattlemen hate the creatures, since they consume the goodness of any soil). In regard to the slaying, confessions were soon obtained, but there were enough fools willing to face jail or the rope for the sake of being remembered as Garrett's nemesis that the true killer was never discovered. A custom made coffin was needed for the tallest man of the county. He was married to Juanita Gutierrez, and after she died to her sister Apolinaria. They had many healthy children, though he was a man who kept his oath better as a lawman than as a husband.

Nowadays White Oaks is just a few hundred souls rattling around a town built for thousands, like an old couple in a big house after the children are grown and gone. It will be a ghost town soon and I feel like one of the ghosts already.

What else can I say? I had a life - some people might consider it an exceptional one. I never counted on having a big congregation for my valediction as any measure of the value of my living. In any case most of the people I cared for have gone on long before. Some of my neighbours still have certainty of heaven, as far as I can tell. I don't share either that or poor Billy's conviction that hell was real and waiting for him. The faith that McSween put in civilisation and Tunstall in progress now seem to me outmoded delusions that have run their course. Tunstall's material interest is completely ascendant, as he predicted, but I see no New Jerusalem arising from its triumph - people are happy or miserable much the same as they always were and there's a nasty brutalism that seeps in where we mistake commerce for life.

My Alexander left no enduring legacy, any more than Murphy got his statue or a street named for him. The conflict in which he perished was remembered not as he would have liked, as a crusade for honest values, but merely the most bloody in a series of petty feuds which passed into infamy more for the desperate characters who participated as gunmen and cut-throats than for any issue of principal between the parties. Our bank was supposed to develop the town and kindle the spirit of enterprise. We might have had a city by now, but that dream died with McSween. For a long time now, I've tended my own garden and left dreaming to others. If I had any kind of revenge, it was only the success of my own Three Rivers Ranch and the satisfaction of a full life lived as best I could manage.

I did what I could to administer John Tunstall's estate properly, even if I couldn't prevent Dolan getting hold of his ranch. Some of the men who killed Tunstall were sent from this life by the Regulators. Others fell natural prey to their own way of life before they could be brought to justice. I was saddened to hear Tunstall's father was duped by some rogues that got across the ocean and were rewarded for the false claim they'd despatched his killers, for it showed that despite his civility to me, the old man was never reconciled to the loss of his son and had his judgement clouded by grief. Tunstall senior couldn't let the matter be. Eventually the Federal government paid a compensation through the British Embassy to dispose of the business once and for all, but I don't suppose that made any difference to the family either. However, I can not imagine the spirit of J.H. Tunstall roaming New Mexico in quest of vengeance, like the ghost of Hamlet's father. If any vestige of his consciousness persists among us, I suspect it will be more interested to observe the technological wonders of our modern age.

As for my other ghosts - Alexander, I'm sorry. I've neglected your memory these long years. To me, you were the noblest man alive. I tried to be a dutiful wife, though I could not deny my own strong will. I loved you truly even if love could not blind me to your weakness. It cut my heart to think of you broken by the world in your last hours. My consolation was that at the very end you recovered your true spirit and became again the man I knew. But I must be honest, our love was of its time. We were like children, knowing little of each other and next to nothing about the world, and unlike you I had to go on. Now if I try to picture how you and I might have grown old together, my imagination is clouded. There's too much distance between us, not of time but of life. If there was such a thing as a hereafter where we might meet, I fear that we might not recognise one another in that place.

Instead it's to you, my dear almost-beloved J. that I must turn finally. Even long gone, it's with you that my spirit communes almost daily - there's nothing we can't talk about now. You know what I'm going to say and I'm confident of your reply and so we're in harmony. And if these scribbled words contain any explanation for the woman I've been, it's to you that it's directed.

END

Made in the USA
Charleston, SC
06 March 2017